Author Note

Thank you for picking up *The Knight's Maiden in Disguise*. This is the first novel in my new series, The King's Knights. The series begins when King Edward III has only recently taken control of the country from his mother, Isabella, and her lover, Mortimer. Intent on shoring up his control across the kingdom, he forms a band of loyal knights. These four very different men swear an oath of loyalty to the king. They are as tight as brothers and dedicated to their common cause.

William is the kind of hero I love. The youngest of the King's Knights, he's an elite warrior, trained in combat. Despite his physical strength, he is a kind and caring man who thinks about the safety of those unable to protect themselves. Having witnessed his parents' heartbreak due to love, he has sworn never to feel intense emotion for anyone, but he hadn't reckoned on meeting Avva.

When I created the character of Avva, I felt so sorry for her. The only person who's ever loved her, her twin brother, has died and she's been left alone in a world full of danger. Avva soon showed me that she doesn't like to be pitied. She is someone who doesn't take problems lying down. When pushed into a corner, she comes back fighting and she will do anything to protect her way of life. William's arrival in her world turns everything upside down, and when a treasonous plot is revealed, she needs to decide if she will risk her safety for the man she is coming to love.

I hope you enjoy reading *The Knight's Maiden in Disguise* as much as I loved writing it.

ELLA MATTHEWS

—

The Knight's Maiden in Disguise

HARLEQUIN®
HISTORICAL™

PLEASE RECYCLE

THIS PRODUCT IS RECYCLABLE

Recycling programs
for this product may
not exist in your area.

ISBN-13: 978-1-335-40742-9

The Knight's Maiden in Disguise

Copyright © 2021 by Ella Matthews

This edition published by arrangement with Harlequin Books S.A.

For questions and comments about the quality of this book, please contact us at CustomerService@Harlequin.com.

Harlequin Enterprises ULC
22 Adelaide St. West, 40th Floor
Toronto, Ontario M5H 4E3, Canada
www.Harlequin.com

Printed in U.S.A.

Ella Matthews lives and works in beautiful South Wales, UK. When not thinking about handsome heroes, she can be found walking along the coast with her husband and their two children (probably still thinking about heroes, but at least pretending to be interested in everyone else).

Books by Ella Matthews

Harlequin Historical

The King's Knights

The Knight's Maiden in Disguise

The House of Leofric

The Warrior Knight and the Widow
Under the Warrior's Protection
The Warrior's Innocent Captive

Visit the Author Profile page
at Harlequin.com.

To Jan and Cyril

Chapter One

Caerden, South Wales—1331

William leaned back in his saddle, bringing Eirwen to a stop. His squire pulled up alongside him, taking the rest as an opportunity to pull a water skin from his saddle-bag and drink deeply.

'There is something wrong about this town,' murmured William.

'Aye,' agreed James. 'There are hardly any women about for a start.'

William's gaze scanned the centre of the small town. Very few folk were about and those that were seemed to be scurrying away from them like ants from a disturbed nest.

'Yes, I've noticed the lack of women, too, but it's more than that.' He took another look around. The space was virtually abandoned now. 'The place is missing something else.' It was an impression that had been building in him since they'd entered the vast lands of the Caerden region earlier that morning. 'There is no joy among the people at all.' He hadn't seen a single person laugh or smile, not one.

'Aye, well, if there aren't any women...' James grinned and took another slug of water.

William laughed. 'I suppose that could account for it, but...' He twisted in his saddle, the hairs on the back of his neck standing on end when he realised the streets were empty behind them, too. 'It's very...' His voice trailed off—he didn't have a name for the disturbing feeling building within him.

'You don't think you're reading too much into things?'

'I could be.' Lord knew, he was tense enough about this mission, without throwing a mystery into the pot as well.

'You've got a lot riding on this assignment, haven't you, Sir William? You'll lose your opportunity to live in luxury if we get this wrong.'

Normally, William enjoyed his squire's light-hearted jokes, but the young man's quips about William's future were starting to wear a little thin. William had made no secret to his fellow King's Knights and their squires that he had petitioned the King, requesting an arranged marriage to a wealthy heiress. He had made it very clear that it wasn't for his own personal gain but to save his family's barony, and all those who depended on it, from ruin. Far from living in luxury, the wealth would give him some much-needed breathing space, especially when it came to providing dowries for his younger sisters.

In turn, Edward III had made it clear that, if William succeeded on his mission, he would grant that petition. It should be an easy task. All William and James had to do was inform Baron Caerden that the King would visit him in ten days and ensure that the safety and accom-

modation were up to standard for a royal visit. There was
nothing to it and yet William had the sense that something was very wrong with this place. It was difficult to
know if he should trust his normally reliable instincts.
As James said, many, *many* times, William had a lot riding on the success of this mission.

William was beginning to wish he hadn't mentioned
his petition to anyone other than the King himself. The
jokes and insinuations had been relentless for weeks now,
not even stopping when he'd explained why he needed to
marry into money. He knew his friends meant well, but
the outcome of the petition mattered to William more
than anything he'd ever done before and he couldn't afford for this mission to go anything other than perfectly.
The light-hearted mockery was adding to his tension.

'The townsfolk are very thin,' he said to James, deciding to ignore the jibe sent his way. 'And their clothes…'
He'd seen better dressed beggars than some of the townsfolk here.

'It could have been a harsh winter, everyone knows
how the weather is different in Wales to the rest of the
civilised world. It's very wet as I recall. Perhaps it's not
the best climate for growing food.'

'I have visited other Welsh towns. The people do not
look like this.' William shook his head. It was no use
guessing what was wrong. He would have to investigate.
It was just as well as investigating problems was what he
enjoyed. 'Keep your eye out for anything else unusual.'

'Aye, Sir William. You can depend on me.' Despite
James's tomfoolery, William would trust his squire with
his life.

'Good.' William kicked Eirwen into motion. It was
time to head to the castle and meet the Baron who ruled
over this strange place.

* * *

William cantered into the castle's courtyard, Eirwen's hooves ringing sharply on the cobbled ground,
James following close behind. He tugged on the stallion's reins, bringing him to a sharp stop just inside the
gateway. Surprised they'd been able to get so far without being stopped by a guard, he gazed around the cluttered space, seeking out an authoritative figure to help
them on their way.

But as he watched, castle inhabitants melted away, disappearing into shadows cast by the high walls. A young
boy knocked over a pail of water, the bucket clattering
loudly to the floor. An elderly alewife rushed to help him,
keeping her broad back turned to William all the while.

'There are women here after all,' he murmured to
James.

'I think you might be right.' James was serious for
once, alarming William, who was not used to that tone
from his usually jovial squire. 'There is something eerie
about this place. Why won't they look at us? It's very de-
liberate. It's like the town all over again. It's eerie.' The
young man shuddered. 'And where are all the guards?'

William frowned, shifting in his saddle. The leather
creaked beneath him. He'd ridden hard today and he
wanted nothing more than refreshment and to let Eirwen rest a while before he planned his next move. He
turned back to James.

'I want you to do something for me.'

James groaned. 'From the look on your face, I'm going
to guess that this will not be pleasant.'

William smiled. 'Not unpleasant as such, just not as
relaxing as you'd probably hoped.'

James's shoulders sagged. 'You mean there will be no soft bed and a willing woman for me tonight.'

William laughed. 'Not tonight, I'm afraid. I'd like you to find a place to make an encampment outside the town. I want you to observe the goings-on. See if you can spot where these missing soldiers are. The chances are, they're out on a local training mission, but I don't think we can be over-cautious. Not when we're planning for the King's visit. The castle must be secure at all costs. We will meet after sunrise tomorrow morning to discuss anything we have found out.'

'Just as I feared, an unpleasant task.' James cast a look at the castle's façade. 'Or else it could be a blessing in disguise. This does not look the most hospitable of places and the people seem distinctly unfriendly.'

William had to agree. The castle gave off a distinct air of neglect, as if it hadn't been attended to properly in some time. Not only that, not one person had given them any sign of a greeting, friendly or otherwise.

''Til the morrow, then,' said James, whirling his horse around and disappearing back out of the gate before William had a chance to say goodbye.

To William's left came a faint whinny. Eirwen tossed his head and snorted in response.

William stroked a reassuring hand along the horse's neck. 'It seems we've found where you need to go at least.'

He swung his long legs down from the saddle and gathered up Eirwen's reins, still half expecting a guard to stop him in his tracks. Nobody did.

From the state of the disordered courtyard, William didn't hold up much hope for the stables, but he needed somewhere to store Eirwen while he went about his assignment and Eirwen had seen worse things than mouldy fodder. He would survive a few days in less than ideal conditions.

The stables appeared to be to the left of the castle entrance. The wooden slats of the stables' outside were hanging loose and needed replacing rather than banging back into place. William wondered briefly if he and James could improve the appearance of the courtyard in the ten days they had available to them, but decided it was doubtful. If the outside of the castle was anything to go by, then he would certainly have plenty to do inside. The King would expect nothing less than luxurious accommodation. William swallowed. If he couldn't provide such a thing, would the King count it against him? Whatever happened, increasing the presence of guards had to be a priority over comfort. If the King was caught in a castle without adequate protection in place, the results could be fatal.

Everything he'd been planning for years was hanging on him making sure that this whole mission went perfectly. William could not afford to fail. He sighed. It didn't look as if he would be getting much rest in the days to come.

He paused at the stable entrance, blinking a few times as his eyes adjusted to the gloom. The sweet smell of fresh straw hit him as he stepped inside. As his eyes accustomed to the change in light, he could make out the clean-swept floor and tools lined neatly against the wall. Where the courtyard was littered with clumps of rotting hay, the interior of the stables appeared to be as ordered as a military garrison. There were not as many horses as he would expect either—perhaps wherever the guards were, they were on horseback.

In the far corner, William could just make out the shadow of a stable lad mucking out one of the stalls.

'Hello,' he called out.

The lad froze, his arms outstretched, a sweeping brush clutched tightly in his hands.

William paused for a beat and then cleared his throat when it was obvious the lad wasn't going to move. 'I'm sorry, I didn't mean to startle you. I'm visiting Baron Caerden and Eirwen needs a rub down and some feed.'

The lad slowly leaned his brush against the wall and turned. It was impossible to make out any features in the darkness, but from the man's slender figure William guessed he was a young adult, maybe nineteen or twenty. He heard a gentle inhale of breath and then, 'Of course, sir. Your mount will be safe with me, sir.'

The youth's voice was soft and gentle, a good cadence for difficult horses. William waited for him to step forward to take Eirwen's reins, but the lad stayed back, keeping to the shadows.

William shrugged. He had other things to worry about than the stable master's strange behaviour. It was fitting with the other inhabitants of this strange place. As long as the lad did his job, William would be happy. 'I'll be staying for a few days.'

There was no response to this. The lad appeared to be rooted to the spot, unable to move towards William and his horse. The lad might be a bit strange, but the stables were in such a good condition and the horses remaining looked healthy—at least Eirwen would be in competent hands. Some people were better at dealing with animals than humans and, if the state of the other castle dwellers was anything to go by, this young man wasn't anything unusual anyway.

'I'll leave Eirwen here.'

'Yes, sir.' Still the stable master didn't move.

William nodded and ran his hand down Eirwen's neck, patting him briefly before turning to leave.

The full force of the sun's glare hit him in the face as he stepped back into the courtyard. It was going to be a warm day. He tugged at the clasp of his cloak. He'd worn it against the chill of the spring morning, but it was quickly becoming suffocating. He pulled it off and glanced down. He wore his armour strapped to his body and the metal glinted in the sunlight. He debated removing some of it, but decided it wouldn't hurt for him to keep his weapons with him. If his instincts about this place were correct, then it was possible he would need them at some point—besides, it never seemed to hurt for people to see the complexity of the weapons strapped to him. It made them take him seriously.

He turned, intending to store his cloak in the saddle-bag he'd left strapped to Eirwen. But one step into the stables had him staggering to a stop.

The man had stepped away from his position by the wall and was standing in a patch of sunlight thrown by the open door. He was gazing up towards Eirwen. Dark hair curled softly at the base of a long and slender neck. For a moment the world tilted, as William beheld the illusion of the most beautiful woman he had ever seen. His heart began to pound in a painful rhythm. He must have made some sort of sound because the young man turned towards him. Blue eyes, the shade of a summer's sky, met William's. The breath left William's lungs so quickly he reached over and grabbed a pillar, the rough wood biting into his hand, tethering him to the ground.

The lad's eyes flashed with an emotion William

couldn't read, his lips parting softly. William was overwhelmed with the urge to cross the space between them and crush the soft mouth beneath his own.

William's grip on his cloak tightened as his body hardened.

'Who are you?' William swallowed. His voice sounded strange, strangled almost.

'I…' The young man cleared his throat and straightened. 'I'm Aven Carpenter, sir. Most people call me Ave.'

Aven, a man's name. Of course this wasn't a woman standing before him. Women didn't work in stables, especially beautiful ones. They'd be snapped up into marriage as soon as a hint of their beauty emerged.

He stepped backwards, swallowing hard. He'd heard of men being attracted to other men, but it had never happened to him before. He'd never had such a strong, instant attraction to a woman either. His liaisons were full of laughter, an afternoon's pleasure at most. There had never been this raging fire burning through him. It took all his years of disciplined training not to step back into the stables and pull Aven's body flush against his, to bury his fingers in Aven's soft hair and taste those soft lips.

He shook his head. He was a logical man—almost to a fault, some of his friends would say. William was never distracted and he certainly could not afford to be right now. He needed to remember just how much depended on his actions over the next few days.

He inhaled deeply, regaining control over his body. He nodded pointlessly at Aven, almost tripping over his feet as he forced himself away from the stable door. Never had he experienced desire like this, so completely overwhelming that he could almost forget everything for the touch of skin against skin.

'Eirwen loves oats,' he croaked.

Aven was gazing at him, a look of puzzlement in his eyes. Heat flooded William's face. He was acting the fool. This mission was already meddling with his sanity and he was only a few days in.

Without another word he turned on his heel, still clutching his cloak, and strode back into the sunlight.

Avva sagged into Eirwen's steadying bulk. What on God's earth had just happened to her? That man... He must be a noble from the cut of his clothes, most likely a knight, too, from the many weapons he wore. But he was nothing like Caerden's normal visitors who were rude and brusque and treated her, and the rest of the castle inhabitants, like dirt.

He was the most beautiful man she'd ever seen. His broad shoulders had nearly filled the stable door and those eyes... They were a deep, rich brown and the moment they had fixed on her, her whole body had leapt into awareness. It was as if there was some invisible force pulling her towards him and she'd had to force herself not to cross the stable floor to go to him. *That* had certainly never happened to her before.

It was as if his penetrating gaze had seen her, the real her, and not the man she was pretending to be. Almost as if he...desired her, but not in the coarse brutal way other noblemen made their interest in women known, by taking what they wanted and damn the consequences. It was as if he had been tongue-tied by her presence, but that surely couldn't be the case. She was passing herself as a man and no one had questioned that from the very first moment she'd done it, just over a year ago now. She could not be enticing, else she would have had attention before. And yet, in that short, fleeting moment his sear-ing gaze made her feel as if she was so. When he'd looked at her through those dark, brown eyes of his, she'd been pinned to the spot, her heart hammering in her throat as if she'd run rings around the castle grounds.

She shook her head. It was no good thinking about someone like him. His clothes had marked him out as nobility and nothing good had ever come from one of them. She was living proof of that. She was the result of a nobleman taking a liking to her mother, only to discard her when he grew bored of her.

She only had to close her eyes for a moment and hun-dreds of other images came to mind, scenes of drunken debauchery and random cruelty from men of his ilk. Not directed at her—she'd had her brothers to hide her, but she'd seen the aftermath of noblemen visiting Caerden at the invitation of the Baron. She'd seen the women who'd not hidden quickly enough and known that whatever had happened to them during the visit had scarred them in a way that would never heal. Now the townsfolk knew to hide, to make sure their women were not around, to disguise them as hideous or to try to send them away as soon as they came of age. It was a dangerous game with life-altering consequences if you failed. Her decision to live as a man had given her a degree of safety, until now.

Like most women in town, she was ready to flee if things became difficult. She would have to watch and see exactly what this newcomer would do because the last thing she wanted was trouble.

The whole town lived on a knife edge expecting, at any moment, more blows to fall from Caerden and his vicious cohorts. They would want to know about Wil-liam and his motives for being here. They would ask her questions, knowing she would have dealt with his horse. There was not much she could tell them.

He'd seemed polite, but just because one of them was well mannered, it didn't mean he wouldn't turn out just the same as every other nobleman the town had the misfortune to encounter. She certainly wouldn't tell anyone of her visceral reaction to his dark gaze.

She turned to Eirwen. Now this stallion was a very handsome specimen, a deep chestnut colour, which matched his rider's eyes. No. She mustn't think like that. She *never* thought like that. She couldn't allow herself to.

Ever since her twin brother, Aven, known to his friends as Ave, had died of an infection fifteen months ago, she'd been living as a man. In a town like this it was safer to assume a male identity than live as an unprotected woman. She and her brother had looked enough alike for her to get away with it and it was not as if anyone in the castle spared her a second glance. Everyone kept their heads down and got on with their own business. It was easier to protect yourself that way.

'You look like your master takes good care of you,' she said to Eirwen as she rubbed his long nose. 'But I've never known a trustworthy lord or knight through these doors. He might well have a handsome face, but I'm afraid it's not enough to tempt me into anything foolish.'

Eirwen snorted and Avva took this as his agreement.

The horse nudged her hand. 'Sorry, boy. You're hungry, I bet. Let's get that saddle off you.'

Avva untied the saddlebags and made to carry them towards the door. As she did so, she caught the scent of the man, a deep woodsy smell, and her heart began to pound. She dropped the bag to the floor, shocked by the strange reaction. What on earth was happening to her? She pushed the bag to the edge of the stable with the tip of her foot and busied herself with seeing to Eirwen's needs.

When Eirwen's master next came for him, she would make sure she wasn't around. She didn't need any further complications in her life.

Chapter Two

William strode into the keep as if the hounds of hell were on his heels, desperate to get away from that all-encompassing desire. He paused just inside the entrance and inhaled deeply, willing his body back under his control. The attraction for the stable master had been strong and unexpected but that didn't mean he had to act on it. He was a knight and not just any knight, he was one of the King's elite guards, a relatively new band of five brothers-in-arms brought together to defend Edward III's interests. They'd been christened the King's Knights and he had never been so proud to belong to such a group of men.

His training to become part of the brotherhood had been rigorous, even brutal, and gathering his wits because he'd been attracted to a man should not be so difficult.

He clenched, then released, his fists. He was known among his fellow knights as the one who was always logical and calm. He'd made a decision, early in life, to follow a plan and, much to his friends' amusement, he'd stuck to it. To be so thrown by one individual was as foolish as it was unusual.

He took a deep breath and straightened, looking around him as he did so. The entrance to the keep was strangely deserted. Only one guard, lounging against a wall, his eyes almost closed as he dozed in the warm, morning air. The thin thread holding on to William's temper frayed further.

'The Baron,' he barked.

The guard sprang to attention at the sound of his voice, blinking slowly. 'I…'

A growl slipped through William's lips and the guard paled. There was something seriously wrong with the running of this castle. Where there should be a legion of guards, stopping unannounced visitors, there was only this one imbecile, whose gawping mouth reminded William of a landed fish.

'Where is he?'

This complete lack of security also did not bode well for the success of William's mission.

'He's not here,' mumbled the guard eventually.

'Not here?' Perhaps that explained the general lack of security, although a good leader would surely double the safeguarding during his absence from home.

'No.'

William frowned. 'Where is he?' There were no reports that Caerden was away from home.

The guard shrugged. 'Don't know.'

Where was this man's deference? It wasn't William's job to insist the guard spoke to him with the respect due his station, but the lack of courtesy had him grinding his teeth. 'Who's in charge in your liege's absence?'

'Master Thomas is the Baron's steward. He's in the Great Hall.'

Finally, some definite information, even if it came without the word 'sir'. William stalked towards the Great Hall, unsurprised when the guard didn't try to stop him.

There were not many people inside the hall. A few groups were scattered around the place, but it was easy to identify the steward. At the far end of the room, a large man sprawled on an ornate chair, his wide girth in direct contrast to the almost emaciated townsfolk William had seen on his journey towards the castle. The man was focused on a woman standing to his left, the look on his face leaving William in no doubt as to the direction of his thoughts.

William strode down the length of the room, coming to a stop before the portly man. 'Master Thomas.' The steward didn't look up at William's salutation. William resisted the urge to pull Thomas to his feet and demand he show proper respect and then, while he was at it, march Thomas down to the settlement that depended on Caerden for its livelihood. William wanted the steward to explain to him why the villeins, who moved as if the weight of the world was resting on their shoulders, were so desperately thin while he was so corpulent. He also wanted to know why the crowds had melted away at the arrival of a stranger.

Instead he stepped closer to the man and deepened his voice. 'Master Thomas. I am Sir William from the Devereux family and a member of the King's Knights. I am here on the business of King Edward III and, in the absence of Baron Caerden, I require a word with you.'

The effect of his words on Thomas was astounding. The steward jerked back as if he had been punched, the colour draining from his face. He turned to look at William, his eyes bulging in his florid face.

'We need to speak privately,' said William, his voice as hard as steel.

Thomas's gaze swept over William's body, no doubt taking in his size and his many weapons and obviously coming to the conclusion that William had not been making a request.

The steward struggled to his feet. 'Of course, Sir William, it is a pleasure to meet you. Welcome to Caerden. We'll be more comfortable talking in my liege's private rooms.' He gestured to a door to the left of the Great Hall. William nodded, but remained where he was. He wasn't about to let Thomas walk behind him—his instincts were screaming at him that Thomas was not to be trusted. Although William knew Thomas wouldn't be able to take him in a fair fight, William wasn't immune to a knife in the back.

Thomas finally seemed to realise William was waiting for him to begin and started shuffling in the direction of the exit as various hangers-on moved silently out of their way.

'I'm sorry Baron Caerden is not here to welcome you himself,' wheezed Thomas as they passed through the door. 'He's been called to Caernarfon, a castle north of here as I'm sure you know. They've been experiencing some troubles with raiders and Caerden's gone to offer them our support, along with some of our finest men.' He paused to heave in a deep breath. 'I'm sure he will be disappointed to have missed you, being as he is such a loyal subject of King Edward.'

William scrubbed a hand over his emerging beard, the skin itching beneath the stubble. He didn't believe

Thomas's words for a moment, but he couldn't fathom out why the steward would lie to him about Caerden's whereabouts. If a castle to the north was experiencing problems with raiders, it would be more logical to increase the guard here, not deplete it. It made no sense at all. Unease shifted in William's stomach. If Caerden wasn't here and he wasn't defending a castle in the north, what was he doing? It couldn't be good, if his steward was lying to cover up his actions.

The listless townspeople suggested that Caerden was not a man who valued chivalry and fairness. These were the qualities the young King valued above all others. Could this be an indication that Caerden was not loyal to the King or was William's mind running away with him again, seeing problems where there weren't any?

Caerden's private suite was lined with luxurious hangings and soft rugs. A fire burned in the grate, despite the room being empty of occupants, a monumental waste of resources.

Thomas sat, but William preferred to remain standing. He moved over to the window and looked out over the courtyard, his gaze immediately seeking out the stable even while his brain urged him not to. He spied Eirwen, who had been moved into the sun, his burdens removed from his back and a bag of feed within easy reach.

William's breath caught in his throat as Ave stepped out of the stables, carrying a grooming kit in one hand. Ave tilted his head towards the sun for a moment. The gesture caused his hair to fall backwards, revealing the pale skin of his long, slender neck, and William's throat went dry. Despite the distance between them, William could imagine running his thumb from the dip at the base of Ave's throat up until he reached the soft lips.

He tore his gaze away, his heart pounding erratically.

His friend, mentor and fellow King's Knight, Theo Genville, had personally recommended him for this mission to the King's Knights leader, Benedictus. William couldn't let Theo down by becoming distracted by the stable master, not when the safety of the King depended on him. That way, only disaster lay.

He stepped away from the window, firmly keeping his back to it. 'I'm here to inform you that King Edward III will be visiting this castle in ten days' time.'

Whatever colour Thomas had regained drained right back out of his face, his gaze darting to the fireplace and back. He wetted his lips. 'To what do we owe this honour?'

'You may have heard that the King is making a tour of his kingdom. He is keen to meet all the Barons loyal to him. He wants to thank them for their backing of his defeat of the traitor, Mortimer, and his supporters. Recently, he realised he had left Caerden out of his tour and is keen to make amends for his oversight, but of course it does not give us much time to prepare for the King's arrival.'

This wasn't the whole truth, but it was fairly close to it. King Edward was only in the first year of his reign without his mother, Isabella, and her lover acting as regents. He wanted to shore up control of the kingdom and bring peace and order to the country after a tumultuous few years. Edward also wanted to ensure that everyone, from the peasants through to the lords, knew that he demanded their complete loyalty. He would not tolerate dissension or even the slightest hint that anyone wanted Isabella back in charge.

William's respect and allegiance for His Majesty was infinite and he had sworn to serve, and even die, for the young King, although he was going to make damn sure that didn't happen. Up until now nothing had ever distracted him and so the way his body was reacting to Ave was especially irksome. Even now, at this critical time, he wasn't focused entirely on Thomas—part of him was still struggling to keep his thoughts away from the stable master. He had never before had a problem focusing.

'My role,' continued William, fighting with himself to keep his gaze away from the window, 'is to ensure Castle Caerden is ready for the King's visit.'

'I see,' said Thomas weakly.

'In the Baron's absence I will have to work with you on the security. We need to ensure this castle is able to withstand surprise attacks.' It was an unlikely event, but William needed to excite some sort of reaction from Thomas. 'I trust you have suitable chambers for the King to use during his stay.'

Thomas's mouth hung open, a dark pit in his rotund face.

William lost the battle with himself. His gaze swung towards the window, unerringly fixing on Ave, who was running a brush along Eirwen's flank.

He turned back to Thomas, who was watching him closely, no longer gaping at him.

'Has something caught your attention, Sir William?'

There was something about Thomas's voice which had the hairs on the back of William's neck standing to attention.

He met Thomas's gaze. He would show no weakness in front of this man. 'I'm merely concerned about the lack of security—even a small attack would meet with little or no resistance.'

Thomas looked away. 'As I said…'

'Yes, you did, but unfortunately the paltry provision displayed here is not going to be sufficient to guard the King after his arrival.'

'The head of our guards, Barwen Montford, is also away with the Baron. He will be in a much better position than I am to talk you through our security arrangements.'

'And when will he return?'

'I am expecting him any day now.'

'And Caerden?'

'I… The Baron does not like to be away from home for long. I am sure he will be back soon, too.' Thomas's gaze flicked to the left, an almost sure sign he was lying about something, although William couldn't fathom what it could be. 'Will the King be bringing many of his own guards?'

William stilled. The look in Thomas's eyes was strange. He looked almost excited now. William felt as if he was only experiencing half of this conversation—something else was at play, but what? 'Of course the King will be bringing his own guards, of which there are many.' It wasn't his imagination, Thomas's shoulders *did* sag at that statement, which was odd. No King would travel without an extensive guard—to do otherwise would be suicide.

William stepped away from the window. Thomas was his sole focus now, all thoughts of Ave pushed to one side as he began to take Thomas to task.

The afternoon went by incrementally slowly. William was sure that he had aged nearly a hundred years by the time it ended. Thomas threw up obstacles at every turn and, although he professed how much of an honour it was to have a visit from the King, his gaze was shifty whenever he said it. William wished he'd kept James with him now. To have a second opinion on Thomas's behaviour could have given him an advantage. Now, he wasn't sure if he felt uneasy because so much was riding on this mission being a success or whether there was something going on that was so potentially worrying that the King's life could be in danger.

By the time the sun was setting, William had had enough. Thomas offered him a bed for the night, but the thought of spending any more time with the man had William almost running for the castle gate. He would find a bed in the town or sleep in the woods. Anything was preferable than another moment with Thomas and the sycophants William had received the dubious pleasure of being introduced to during the course of the long afternoon.

Stepping outside, he took a deep breath of the warm, spring evening air, the soft breeze clearing away the cloying atmosphere of the castle. His head pounded. Thomas had said all the right things, but his words hadn't matched the cagey expression in his eyes.

Then there was the matter of the missing Baron and his guards. A baron didn't leave his castle unprotected and yet Baron Caerden had done just that. The security he'd left behind was laughable and would never repel even the weakest of attacks. Caerden must be very secure in his position and that, in itself, was something for William to ponder.

Trying to approach inhabitants of the castle who weren't in charge or part of the defence of the place was proving impossible. Every attempt he made to get close to someone Thomas hadn't introduced him to was thwarted.

The servants here melted into the shadows, their expressions blank and uninviting.

The whole place reeked of something noxious, something so foul it made William's stomach turn.

He could almost hear James laughing at him, telling William he was losing his mind at the thought of his potentially rich bride being taken away from him. But William believed it was more than that. The whole day had been unsettling and he wanted nothing more than a long drink of ale and a hearty stew to settle his insides.

Walking through the jumble of the courtyard, he forced himself to keep his gaze away from the stables, focusing instead on the wide gateway. It wasn't until he was standing under the archway, checking his belt for coins, that he realised someone was walking closely behind him.

He turned slightly to check the level of threat. His heart jumped into his throat, as he noticed it was Ave, his dark head bent as if studying the floor intently in front of him, seemingly deep in thought. William decided not to interrupt him, he had nothing of importance to say and he didn't want to make an idiot of himself again. He turned back around and continued on his way, promising himself he would not look again.

He managed to make it out through the walled gate before he finally gave in to temptation. Before he could stop himself, he turned and blurted out, 'Good evening, Master Carpenter.'

Ave stopped, a delicate pink flush stealing over his pale skin. William was struck once again at how feminine the lad looked, almost as if he wasn't a man at all. Yet why would anyone pretend otherwise? 'Good evening, Sir William.'

Ave spoke so softly William could barely hear him. William slowed, waiting for Ave to catch up with him, even as his mind urged him to run. An attraction this strong could only end in disaster. Although, perhaps talking to Ave would help give William an insight into the irregular behaviour of the town and castle.

Or perhaps William was deluding himself. Despite all promises to himself, he wanted to spend time with Ave. He wanted to try to understand the overwhelming power Ave had over him, to discover why, for the first time in his life, he was drawn to a man. If they spent a little time together, the overwhelming pull towards Ave might go as quickly as it had arisen. And if it didn't... well, he'd worry about that when it happened.

'Perhaps you could help me, Master Carpenter. I'm looking for a good place to bed down for the night.'

There was a long pause. William began to think Ave wouldn't answer. 'There's a tavern in the town, Sir William. Dai Bach will have room for you there.'

They walked a few more steps in silence. William swallowed. 'Perhaps you would allow me to buy you an ale this evening.'

Ave stopped dead in his tracks. 'Why?'

William kept going, he didn't want to scare Ave off by being too intense. 'To thank you for taking care of Eirwen.'

'It's my role in the castle. I'm the stable master. I take care of all the horses,' stated Ave flatly.

William shrugged. He wouldn't force Ave to spend time with him, if the young man really didn't want to, even with this new desire coursing through him. He wasn't a brute. 'I'm new in town, Master Carpenter. I don't know anyone. I'd like a bit of company, someone to introduce me to the people of Caerden, that's all.'

Ave resumed walking. 'The townsfolk don't take kindly to newcomers.'

He concentrated on keeping his breathing even and not asking why the townsfolk were suspicious of anyone new to their ranks, even though the answer could hold the key to everything. He would ask later, even though he doubted Ave would answer honestly. A few ales might loosen Ave's tongue and he'd be able to find out more about this strange town.

Finding out about the town and the way it worked was paramount to finding out whether it was safe for the King to continue with his plan to visit the place. It was more important than his initial mission and overrode everything. Or at least it should. For some reason it didn't appear to be nullifying his attraction to Ave. He'd always been able to tamp down on desire before. He had certainly never allowed it to rule his actions before today.

'People are always wary of me at first, but they have nothing to worry about. I am a straightforward man. If I am treated right, I will respond in kind.'

Ave didn't respond to that statement and they walked the rest of their way in silence.

The streets of Caerden were still eerily silent, despite the warmth of the spring evening. William was used to towns which thronged with people going about their business until the sun went down completely. The silence caused the hairs on the back of his neck to stand on end. His hand moved to the hilt of his sword, but he dropped it when he caught Ave watching his movements.

'Is it always this quiet?' he asked as they rounded a

bend and a rickety old building, which could only be the local tavern, came into view.

Ave shrugged. 'Not always. It could be that news has reached the town that a stranger has arrived. The town does have a tiny population, though. When we're not working, we're resting.'

Not that small, thought William as they approached the tavern. He'd certainly been in smaller, far busier places. Places where the inhabitants didn't run from strangers. From outside of the building he could hear the babble of lots of voices all talking at once, so there were at least some people in the town.

Ave's hand brushed his as he pulled open the door. William's heart began to race at the slight contact and he pressed a fist to his chest. That really needed to stop happening. Until proven otherwise, Ave must be treated like everyone else in this place, as someone who was hiding something. If that secret turned out to be something that impacted on the safety of the King, then Ave would prove to be guilty of treason just like everyone else here. William couldn't allow this unexpected attraction to make him drop his guard.

The general murmur of voices which filled the tavern dropped to an almost deathly silence as soon as the patrons caught sight of him walking behind Ave. This behaviour William was used to—people were naturally wary of outsiders, especially ones carrying the amount of weapons that were currently strapped to his body. It didn't exactly mark him out as friendly.

The conversation didn't resume, even as he and Ave had made their way towards the tavern owner, and *that* was unusual. Even the owner, normally the friendliest person towards a stranger in any town, if only because they were anticipating the money they would make from him, was holding himself stiffly behind a counter and was resolutely not looking at William.

For the first time irritation began to build behind William's breastbone. He wasn't the enemy here, he'd done nothing to cause suspicion and yet he was being treated as if he'd arrived and threatened to murder the town's young folk.

Ave stepped up and rested his arm against the countertop and William's irritation melted away. He couldn't tear his eyes away from Ave's wrist, slender and delicate-looking, more feminine than male. He wanted to encircle it with his fingers, to feel the soft-looking skin against his rough palm. He nearly jumped when Ave spoke, only managing to hold himself still because of his years of training. 'Sir William is looking for a place to stay.' She nodded towards him.

The tavern owner swallowed and swung his head in William's direction, his gaze fixed somewhere just above William's head.

'We have room and board here, Sir William.'

William forced himself to remain calm, his words measured and polite. 'Thank you. I'd like to stay for at least a week, possibly longer. For now, I'd like two tankards of your finest ale.' He passed a coin across, more definitely than the beer was worth, and watched as it quickly disappeared out of sight. Whatever problem the landlord had with him, it didn't stop him taking his money.

Ave and William took their ale to an empty corner of the taproom. The conversation in the room gradually resumed, but it was quiet and there was no sound of laughter among the other patrons. William took the seat so that his back was to the wall, facing the room, leaving Ave to face him. At first William was only vaguely aware of the muted background noise. He was only conscious of Ave, of the way they were so close together despite the small table between them and of a subtle fragrance, a mixture of straw and something else he couldn't name. Even in the darkened room, he was close enough to see the smooth skin of Ave's cheeks. Ave didn't look young enough not to have started even the smallest of beards, but there was not even the slightest fuzziness along his jaw. Was it just possible that Ave was indeed a woman and not a man, or was it wishful thinking on his part, because why on earth would anyone do that? William was pondering the conundrum when he realised that there was a slow but steady exodus from the tavern.

He placed his tankard on the wooden table in front of him. 'What is going on here, Ave?'

Ave wetted his lips. William clenched his fist to prevent him from reaching out and tracing the path Ave's tongue had taken with his fingertips.

'What do you mean?' Ave's eyes were wide, a sure sign of guilt.

'My arrival appears to have emptied the place.'

Ave's shoulders sagged, which was interesting in itself. What did the lad think William had been about to ask? Ave twisted round in his seat and took in the nearly empty room. 'I told you, we don't welcome strangers.'

'So I can see. But what I don't understand is why. It's quite normal to be wary of newcomers. I don't much like surprises myself, but this level of animosity is unusual. Perhaps I smell.' He lifted up an arm and sniffed himself, ridiculously pleased to see the gesture bring a smile to Ave's eyes.

'You don't smell.'

'Well, that's a relief. But I doubt I'm going to be the landlord's favourite customer, seeing I've emptied the bar of all his patrons.'

Ave's smile faded. 'That coin you gave him is probably more money than he's seen in months. I don't think he'll mind too much.'

'And yet he wasn't pleased to see me either, which is unjustified because I haven't done anything unusual... yet.'

Ave took a long sip of ale. 'I think it's the *yet* we're all worrying about. There's been trouble round here.'

He'd sensed as much, but he still couldn't get a firm idea on what exactly that trouble might be. That the castle wasn't supportive of the town's inhabitants was clear enough, but there was something more than that, of that William was becoming increasingly sure.

'Trouble of what kind?'

Ave lifted a shoulder in a shrug, still clutching his tankard. 'Fighting, hunting, that sort of thing.'

That wasn't unusual in itself. Fighting was a way of life in most towns and didn't warrant the level of panic his presence appeared to be creating. William decided to try a different tack. 'The people of Caerden don't need to worry about me. I am not here to cause problems.'

Ave continued to take a long swallow of his drink. 'Why are you here, then?'

The purpose of William's mission wasn't a secret as such, but he wasn't about to reveal the King's imminent visit until he understood the undercurrent of this town. 'I'm the King's messenger,' he said, not untruthfully. 'I have business with Baron Caerden, but he appears to be absent at the moment. Do you know where he is?'

Ave shrugged again. 'He left a few weeks ago.'

'Did he take a lot of guards with him?'

Ave leaned back in his chair, William hated the way he was aware of every movement Ave made. This evening was a bad idea. He wasn't discovering anything and spending time with Ave was only making this strange obsession worse. Ave licked some ale off his top lip and William had to clench his jaw to stop himself from groaning.

Ave rested a hand on the arm of his chair. 'Baron Caerden has an inflated view of his own importance. He always takes a lot of guards with him whenever he travels. Why do you ask?'

'Was it more than normal this time?'

Ave tilted his head to one side, exposing the long, smooth neck William seemed to have developed some kind of fascination with. William momentarily forgot what they were talking about as images of running his lips along the creamy skin swamped him. He'd never had an interest in necks before, but there was something about Ave's which was making him lose his mind. 'I'm sorry, what was that?' he asked, realising he hadn't heard Ave's answer and shaking his head to rid himself of the images of what couldn't be.

Ave frowned at him, probably wondering why he was so distracted. William was acting more like a randy young lad than a fully trained knight. In fact, William hadn't been like this when he had been a young man. He'd approached his women in the same methodical way he approached everything, much to the amusement of Theo, who'd thought he needed to relax in his technique. Forming a plan for everything was what he did, his interactions with women were no different—until now. He needed to concentrate.

Ave licked his lips and William's thoughts scattered again. 'I was saying that, yes, Baron Caerden has taken more men with him than normal. He's taken all his best horses, too.'

William cleared his throat. 'Steward Thomas said a castle to the north of here was experiencing trouble with raiders.'

Ave tried to take another sip of his ale and glanced into the tankard, his eyes widening with surprise as if he hadn't realised he'd drunk the entire cup. He put the empty vessel down. 'I don't know anything about raiders, but then the Baron is unlikely to confide in me. My only role is to look after the horses.'

'Of course. Let me get you another.' William didn't know why he was prolonging the agony of this evening. He only knew that he didn't want his time with Ave to end just yet. And not just because of the attraction; William had yet to find out anything significant.

Without waiting for Ave to agree, William stood and quickly ordered two more tankards. He handed the landlord another large coin as the man finally met his gaze. 'I've made up a room for you, Sir William.'

'Thank you.' William glanced across the tavern at Ave. Ave's shoulders were more relaxed now, after the ale. Surely they weren't broad enough to be a man's? He did know some slender men, but... Here was yet another mystery for him to solve. Was Ave a man or not? He could ask outright, but he doubted he would be told the truth.

'The landlord seems to like me a bit better now,' he said, placing the tankard down in front of Ave.

'Dai Bach is unlikely to turn anyone away, especially if they're flashing coins like you are.' Once again there was a hint of a smile in Ave's eyes. And once again, that lit something inside him, something he hadn't known was missing.

He took a slug of his ale. 'It doesn't hurt to have a landlord onside. They normally know everything.'

Ave laughed and William's heart raced at the musical sound. 'Get Dai Bach talking and you'll never get away. I can't say you'll learn anything useful, though.'

William tapped the edge of his tankard. 'Will he tell me about you?'

Ave's smile dropped. 'There's nothing to tell. I work at the stables, that's all there is to my life.'

'Do your parents live here?'

Ave took a deep drink of his ale and stared at the wall behind William's head. William thought he wasn't going to answer, but then he said, 'My parents are both dead. How about you?'

'Both of mine are still alive and are no doubt in the midst of doing something ridiculously foolish and prohibitively expensive. Whatever scheme it is, it will no doubt result in me trying to unravel it when I next visit. Sometimes, it is as if I am their parent rather than the other way around.'

Ave's lips twitched. 'How so?'

William rubbed his forehead. There was nothing wrong with telling Ave the truth about his family. It didn't impact his mission in any way. 'My father is as madly in love with my mother as the day he met her. He indulges her every whim.' He sighed. 'It's not that her whims are particularly overblown, but they often seem to be costly. They are also far too kind-hearted. They are taken advantage of by nearly everybody.'

Ave grinned. 'That's sweet.'

William grimaced. 'A lot of people seem to think so.' William glanced down at his own tankard. He'd only taken a few sips, but he appeared to be telling Ave things he never normally shared with anyone else. Perhaps the ale was stronger than he was used to.

'But if they aren't hurting anyone, what is the problem?'

'The problem is their spending depletes the barony's resources. I have much younger siblings, all girls.' William didn't mention the children who hadn't lived. The pain those deaths had caused his soft-hearted parents and the lengths his father had gone to, to try to cheer his mother up. William never wanted to experience that level of emotion—with deep love came deep pain. He pushed the thought aside. He'd had a long time to think about this and it was irrelevant at this point.

'Those sisters of mine are going to grow up wild. I'm going to need substantial dowries to get them off my hands.' Hell knew, his parents wouldn't be able to provide them. At the current rate, William was on course to inherit a barony that was so far past the brink of ruin it would be impossible to pull back unless, of course, he married into a wealthy family, hence the petition to the King for an heiress.

'It must be nice to have parents who like each other,' said Ave, breaking into his thoughts.

'I take it yours didn't.'

Ave smiled sadly and William moved his hands to under the table to prevent himself from reaching out and offering comfort.

'Do you have any brothers and sisters?' He shouldn't be asking these questions. He should be concentrating on Baron Caerden and the mysterious disappearance of the missing guards, but he couldn't stop himself from finding out more about Ave. He could no longer lie to himself that this line of questioning was about the mission either. This was all about Ave and the mysterious hold the lad had over him. He wanted to know everything about him.

'I have two younger brothers remaining.'

'Remaining?'

'Like most people, I have siblings who did not live very long after birth.' Ave inhaled deeply. 'I also had a twin…sister, Avva, who died about a year ago.'

'I'm sorry to hear that. It must be difficult to get over a loss like that.'

This time he didn't stop himself reaching out and covering Ave's slender hand with his. He squeezed gently and was rewarded by the soft stroke of a thumb across his wrist. The small movement caused a wave of sensation to race up his arm. He moved his hand away before he could be tempted to hold on for longer.

'It was difficult. It still is, but my younger brothers rely on me.'

'Do they live with you?'

Another sad smile crossed Ave's lips. 'No. I sleep above the stables and there's only room for one person up there. I've managed to find them room and board at the smithy's. They're working as apprentices, but I still have to pay for their upkeep.'

William nodded and listened as Ave spoke about his younger brothers. They obviously meant a lot to Ave, whose eyes shone as he spoke about the two boys.

* * *

By the time William handed Ave his third drink Ave's shoulders had relaxed and his blue eyes were less guarded. William had even managed to coax another couple of smiles from the lad with tales of his eccentric parents. When Ave lifted his tankard and missed his mouth William suspected that drinking ale wasn't something he did often.

William wasn't going to buy him a fourth one otherwise tomorrow would not be pleasant for Ave. As it was Ave kept slipping from English into Welsh. William had to fight to keep the smile from his face when Ave frowned because his sentence came out so muddled, even he couldn't understand it. But then Ave said something that had William sitting bolt upright.

'Pan fy mrawd wedi marw...'

William lost the rest of the Ave's sentence. It had been a while since he had learned Welsh. It was a complicated language, nothing like English or French, but he was fluent, something he'd not mentioned to Ave. Could he have misunderstood or had Ave just talked about his twin *brother* dying? Earlier Ave had mentioned a twin sister and getting the sex wrong wasn't a mistake Ave was likely to make, even with the complexities of mutations in the Welsh language.

'I'm sorry. What did you just say?' The answer meant a great deal to William. It might mean that his instincts that Ave was a woman were correct after all.

Ave blinked owlishly at him. 'Did I speak Welsh again?'

William nodded.

'Sorry. I was talking about when my sister died.'

If William hadn't been focusing all his attention on

Ave, he wouldn't have noticed the tiny hesitation before the word sister.

'Ah, yes. You mentioned *he* had an infection.' William held his breath, waiting to be contradicted.

Ave nodded. 'Yes, it was so sudden. He had a wound that got infected. He...' Ave shook his head. 'She was gone within a few days.' Ave peered into his tankard, William couldn't see, but he would bet there were no more than a few dregs left. His own tankard was almost untouched. 'I'd better go.' Ave stood, wobbling a little. William reached out and grabbed hold of Ave's tiny waist, his suspicions solidifying by the moment. 'I'm fine,' said Ave.

William couldn't help but smile, despite the doubts swirling through him. Ave was going to have a sore head tomorrow, but for now the owlish blinking was adorable.

'Thank you for keeping me company, Ave.'

Ave glanced down at William's hand, the hand which William still hadn't taken away. 'You can let go now. I won't fall.'

William released his grip and stood. 'I'll be seeing you tomorrow.'

Ave only nodded, before turning and stumbling out of the tavern.

William waited until he had given Ave enough time to start on his journey before getting up to follow. Yes, it was underhand to go after him without his knowledge, especially as they had spent a friendly evening getting to know one another, but William wanted to know what was going on and he had a suspicion Ave was not going to tell him. He needed to see for himself because he was now nearly completely sure that Ave was, in fact, a woman.

Chapter Three

Avva stumbled along a rutted path, careful to stay in the shadows and away from the main castle thoroughfare. There weren't many people out on the road tonight, William's arrival had put paid to that—the men would be busy hiding their women or else making sure they themselves were as inconspicuous as possible. Nobody wanted to get caught up in Caerden's games. For the townsfolk these games were at best painful or, at worst, fatal.

She'd meant to visit her younger brothers this evening as it had been a couple of days since she'd seen them, but the sun had long since set and she wasn't as steady on her feet as she'd like. They'd also wonder why she was turning up so late. She'd have to give a reason and she didn't want to lie to them. She couldn't tell them how she had spent her evening either.

They'd probably find out soon anyway, the town was notorious for gossip, and the fact that the stable master had spent time with a man such as William would shock the whole community. Her heart twisted. Had she made herself even more vulnerable? Her whole purpose in life was getting through each day without drawing any attention to herself. Tonight, she might as well have run through the town naked, shouting her real name. Yet somehow Sir William had managed to get under her defences in a very short time, talking to her as if they were old friends. How was that even possible?

Strangers were regarded with deep suspicion by the Caerden townsfolk. Noblemen, in particular, were known to be completely untrustworthy, something she knew from painful experiences. If she told David and Dylan how she had spent her evening laughing and talking with such a man, her brothers would question why she had put herself at such a risk. She was questioning it herself.

It was as if Sir William had held some sort of compulsion over her. She'd been unable to leave, no matter how many times her head had told her to stand and walk out of the tavern. Instead, she'd listened to him talk, the warmth of his voice flowing through her like honey.

She shook her head. She was being foolish. The evening air was beginning to clear her head, but she still wished she had not imbibed so much ale. She'd barely eaten all day and it was the beer that was having such a strange impact on her thoughts. It had nothing to do with the knight, whose company she had reluctantly enjoyed.

Thank goodness William... No, she mustn't think of him like that, he was not her friend, nor would he ever be. Thank goodness *Sir* William didn't speak Welsh. She'd tripped herself up several times, referring to herself as female when speaking in Welsh and to her dead twin brother. She was a fool. She shuddered when she imagined Caerden's reaction if he found out she had been talking to a knight who was very interested in the goings-on in the town and the castle. If she was lucky, he would kill her outright. If not, then she faced the dungeon. Her legs weakened at the thought. She *must* be more careful from now on. There could be no more ale or long, convoluted conversations with Sir William, no matter how good his attention made her feel.

She was not only a fool but also a drunken one.

For a whole year it had been easy to assume the identity of Aven, her twin brother. Aven and she had been almost inseparable, he'd been her closest companion for so long, sometimes he'd been her only one. For her, becoming Aven after his death hadn't just been a good disguise, it had also made his passing easier, as if he were still around to laugh and talk with.

David and Dylan understood the need to keep her sex hidden. This town was dangerous for unprotected women and, even though they were young, they'd seen enough of the goings on in the town to know what could happen to her. Without a father or a husband to keep her safe, Avva was an obvious target. Even women with such males in their lives had fallen victim to the more sinister forces in Caerden.

Assuming Aven's identity had given her the same level of protection as a man. Granted, being male could still lead to all sorts of other problems under Caerden's regime, but it ruled out the worst of them. It also gave her the job she loved and funds to support her brothers' apprenticeships.

Avva was the only family her brothers had left. They needed her and, she hoped, they loved her enough to keep her true identity a secret. They never referred to her as a woman any more and sometimes she wondered whether they had forgotten it was Aven who had died and not her. Sometimes that was the way it felt to her, too.

Nobody, other than her brothers, looked closely at her.

She had no friends, nobody that she spoke to much at the castle either. Everybody kept their heads down and worked hard, not wanting to draw unnecessary attention to their business. Avva was content that way. If nobody looked at her, then nobody would notice she wasn't developing a beard or that her voice hadn't dropped yet. She probably had a year left of living as if she were Aven, two at the most. She would be twenty-one then and the fact that she didn't have a beard would be apparent. But that was all the time she needed. By then Dylan and David would hopefully have completed their apprenticeships. They would have less need of her. She could move to another township and begin living as a woman again. She didn't think about the future much. Life was about getting safely from one day to the next.

She stumbled over a root, before righting herself. She had definitely had more ale than advisable. An evening with William Devereux was not safe. She should have taken him to the inn and left him as soon as he'd secured a room with Dai Bach. She still could not understand why she hadn't done that. There was something about the way his gaze caught and held hers which felt as if he was seeing straight to her heart, as if he knew her soul and he liked what he saw. As if he wanted to be her friend. She'd never had one before, not outside her family. If the situation was different, if he wasn't a knight, then maybe they could have been. But it wasn't to be and there was no reason for her to feel so sad about the fact. He would be gone soon and she would never see him again.

This evening, drinking ale with William, was the longest she'd spent with someone outside her family for a very long time, if ever. She and Aven had been close. They'd had to be. They had no one else. Their mother had been ashamed by their very existence. Their step-father had alternated between disgust and indifference. Their younger brothers had idolised them, but had been too young to provide much in the way of friendship. She knew they loved her, but they were also her responsibility.

She'd tried to tell herself she was drinking ale with him to find out what a knight was doing in Caerden. If there was trouble afoot, then it would be to her advantage to find out about it before it hit the town. That way she could plan how to keep her brothers safe. If Caerden was planning another one of his famous hunting parties, she would do everything in her power to make sure her brothers were not involved. It was how she had lost Aven after all.

She'd told herself that spending time with William could prepare her for any eventuality, but she knew that she was lying to herself.

William's eyes, which were so penetrating, were also a deep, rich brown. Throughout the evening she'd found herself almost mesmerised by them, often unable to pull her own gaze away. She'd wanted to lean against his broad chest and to feel his strong arms around her, as if he could take away all her responsibilities and keep her safe. These strange and unusual desires went against everything she held dear.

He was a nobleman, an elite one at that. He represented everything that she despised: nobility, authority and wealth. His eyes should mean nothing to her. She should be immune to such physical beauty. Baron Caerden was not an ugly man, yet his soul was diseased, as were all of those who surrounded him.

Besides, her evening with William had been a failure.

She hadn't learned anything about his reasons for being in town and had nearly given herself away on several occasions. Her heart contracted painfully as she remembered what she had said to him in Welsh. She would do well to steer clear of William from now on.

She heaved a sigh of relief as the castle gates came into view. The journey from the town to the castle seemed far longer than normal with the ale making her movements drag.

The castle grounds were all but deserted. The guards, who should have been on duty, were no doubt taking advantage of the Baron's absence and were not around. She was rarely stopped anyway; they were used to her coming and going.

She couldn't decide if the guards did it to irritate her or whether they were dim enough not to recognise her every single time. Probably it was the former. Men, she had come to realise at an early age, liked to assert whatever little power they had. Her stepfather had certainly been one of those. He'd lorded himself over her mother, despite the fact he was only a merchant and a fairly lowly one at that.

A small voice inside her head reminded her that William hadn't seemed that way.

This evening he had been nothing but courteous and attentive, displaying all the manners of a true knight. She squashed that errant thought ruthlessly down. She hardly knew the man—he would surely show that unattractive trait soon enough.

The night air was warm and the thought of climbing up to her tiny loft was very unappealing.

She spied a barrel of water she'd collected earlier. She was glad she'd done so; it would save her from hauling it up in the morning when she was bound to have a woolly head.

Right now, shimmering in the moonlight, water had never looked so inviting. She skimmed the surface with her fingers and then splashed some on her face, the cool droplets so refreshing against her heated skin. She tugged off her cloak and dropped it to the floor. She loosened her tunic and quickly pulled it off.

She was in dangerous territory now. She wasn't an overly curvy woman—hard work and not much food helped with that. Her tunic, tightly bound, did a good job of hiding what assets she had, but if anyone was looking closely now they might be able to spot she was not the man she was pretending to be.

She glanced around, but the courtyard was still and quiet.

Not wanting to fully expose herself to the night air, she splashed some water on to her hands and dipped her fingers under the edge of her neckline. It wasn't as satisfying as a proper wash but it was enjoyable nonetheless.

Feeling cooler and refreshed, she picked up her cloak and tunic and made her way into the stables.

She didn't look back.

If she had, she might have seen a figure peel itself away from the shadows and head back down towards the tavern.

Chapter Four

Dawn was still a little way off as William stepped into the forest on the edge of the Caerden settlement. He hadn't gone five paces before a faint coughing drew his attention. To his left James was leaning against the trunk of a large tree, his arms crossed over his chest.

'Can't you hear that, Sir William? That's the sound of an owl. It's still night.'

William grinned at James's grumbling. 'You do seem to want to spend an awful lot of time sleeping, James. Are you sure you even want to be a knight? Not sleeping is part of what makes a warrior great. Perhaps you would be better suited as a lazy nobleman, whose every whim is indulged.'

'If that will keep me from sleeping on a forest floor, then that would suit me.'

William laughed and moved to the small campfire James had made for himself. Despite the man's words he could see that James had been awake a while. His bags were packed and his horse saddled: good.

'What are your observations?' he asked, crouching

down and stretching his fingers out to the glowing embers.

'Aside from the fact that the townsfolk are seriously underfed and lacking in decent clothing and housing, there is something deeply suspicious going on.'

William nodded. 'I agree, but tell me what have you observed which makes you think this?'

'There are messengers coming and going frequently. While this isn't suspicious on its own, what with the Baron being away, the messengers are not coming to the front gate, but going around the side of the castle.'

'That is unusual but not a crime. Go on.'

'I bribed a merchant.'

William rolled his eyes. He did not trust merchants to be truthful in their dealings, especially when money was involved. 'What did he have to say?'

'That Caerden has put it about that he has taken his soldiers for a training exercise by the coast—'

'I was told they are in Caernarfon,' William interrupted.

'Well, they are not at either place. The merchant says they are camped to the east of here, just outside Chepstow.'

There was a beat of silence as the men stared at each other. William's blood ran cold. 'Are you sure?'

'It's you who says to never trust a merchant, but I could detect no signs of the man lying.'

'Chepstow was the King's next destination.'

'Until he decided to come here?'

'Exactly.'

There was another beat of silence as William's whole mission changed in an instant. He stood and began to pace around the fire. Caerden's men outside Chepstow could surely only mean one thing: an ambush.

He came to a stop in front of James. 'You know that I cannot afford for this mission to go wrong.'

'I know, neither can I.' For once, James didn't laugh at him.

William nodded. James's elevation to knighthood stood on the line. Between the two of them, they had to find a solution.

'You will ride to Chepstow.' James nodded at William's command. 'If Caerden's men are stationed there, you will head straight to meet with the King's Knights. They should still be camped near Warminster. Inform them of our concerns. If there is no sign of them, you will head straight back here. If you are not back within two days from now, I will assume the worst and rendezvous at Chepstow on day four.'

'Aye, Sir William.'

'If we assume that there is an ambush planned, then my arrival here and my announcement that the King is due to come here instead of Chepstow may have changed their plans. It is possible Caerden will return here with his soldiers instead. If that appears to be the case, I still want you to go to the King's Knights, but send word to me before you leave. I don't care if you have to bribe a whole score of merchants. I will work on the proviso Thomas has already sent a message about our arrival to Baron Caerden and I will prepare for the worst.'

'Aye, Sir William.'

'You will leave now.'

James merely nodded and reached for his mount's reins. For all his jibes and mockery, James was exceptionally good at following commands.

They began to walk back out of the forest.

'Who was the lad you were walking with last night?'

William's whole body jolted at the mention of Ave. He frowned—that had never happened to him before. 'That was Ave, the stable master. I was trying to get some information out of him.'

'Did you manage?'

'Not really.' Unless you counted the soft curves he'd seen in the moonlight. The fact that Ave was a woman pretending to be a man was yet another mystery he hoped to understand.

'I told you, you should use bribes.' There was a hint of laughter in James's voice, but William's mind was already elsewhere. What would it be like to touch the soft skin behind Ave's ear? Would she tremble or push him away? Why was she hiding her beautiful self, when she should be showing the world her loveliness? Good God, had he just thought the word, loveliness? What on earth was wrong with him and why was he thinking of this right now? The King's life was on the line, as was William's own future. A woman's earlobes should be the last thing on his mind. Ave should be the last thing on his mind, aside from being a valuable insider he could use to help uncover the truth.

'Are you all right, Sir William?' William turned to look at James. His squire was frowning at him. 'You seem a little…' James waved a hand in the general direction of William's face '…distracted. I know I have joked with you about your choice of a wealthy bride, but I am taking this mission seriously. You do not need to worry about me.'

'I know you will, James.' He didn't add, *It is not you I am worrying about.*

James nodded, apparently satisfied with William's response. He vaulted up onto his horse. 'Until we meet again.'

William nodded. 'Godspeed.'

He stood, watching James race away from him until he turned a bend in the road and disappeared out of sight.

The sun was rising now and in the distance he heard a cockerel cry. He turned and gazed up at the castle. It dominated the skyline. What secrets lay within? There was only one way to find out.

Chapter Five

Avva stood on the edge of the training yard, her arms resting on the ringed fence. A couple of young pages were riding, a lacklustre trainer watching their moves. Avva wished she could show the boys how to control their mounts. If she could get across to them the joy of riding, then perhaps they wouldn't treat her horses with such indifference.

She closed her eyes and turned her head. A cool breeze soothed the slight headache she'd woken up with this morning. She was still reeling from her actions last night. Now that she wasn't addled with too much ale she couldn't imagine what had possessed her to be so foolish as to spend an evening talking with a complete stranger. A noble one at that! The very sort of person she normally avoided at all costs. And to think she had drunk so much ale at the same time. Her blood ran cold as she tried to remember everything she had said. Last night she'd been sure she hadn't given the game away, but in the fresh light of the morning she wasn't so sure.

She had been caught up in the depths of his charming smile and the interest he'd shown in her. He'd asked her questions and she'd answered, the words pouring from her. His attention had warmed a part of her she'd thought frozen. And…and it would do no good to think of him any more. Hopefully she'd said nothing ill-advised or, at least, nothing that would draw attention to her and her brothers.

She would just have to forget about William. If the thought of his long fingers running along the back of her hand popped into her head, she would push it to one side.

She opened her eyes and turned her attention back to the riders. She winced as one of the boys jerked too hard on his reins—she longed to yell at him to pay more attention, his sloppiness was hurting her animals. She held her breath, but fortunately for the young man the pony he was riding was a placid, old mare, who merely tossed her head in annoyance at the rough handling.

'That lad's going to have to greatly improve his riding skills if he's going to make a competent knight.'

Avva closed her eyes again, half hoping the deep voice she'd heard was in her imagination. But of course it was William who spoke and who was standing behind her. He'd been in her thoughts ever since she'd awoken that morning, it was inevitable that he had appeared just as she'd resolved not to think of him any more.

She didn't want to turn around and look at him. She knew she would be ensnared by those eyes once again and, in the midday sun, she was sure he would be able to read the strange feelings she was experiencing in her expression.

'He's got a few years to go until he finishes his training,' she said instead, watching as the boy in question fumbled a turn.

William snorted. 'By now, he should have mastered

the basics. He's not going to be much more than a foot soldier at this rate.'

She didn't comment. If she didn't engage him, perhaps he would go away again.

Instead, he moved forward and copied her stance, leaning and resting his arms next to hers on the wooden fence. Even as she told herself not to, she glanced down at his arms next to hers. He'd pushed up his sleeves, revealing the muscled length of his forearms beneath. Avva tried to keep her eyes on the riders, but her gaze kept returning to William's exposed skin and the corded muscles that bunched beneath.

Neither of them spoke.

Moments passed. Everything faded into the background—the riders, the cool breeze and even her headache disappeared. She became aware only of his breathing, the steady rise and fall of his chest in the periphery of her vision. The sound became her world.

Many heartbeats passed. Neither of them moved.

And then the strange spell was broken. The pages' lesson came to a halt and the sullen boys began to move their horses towards her.

She half expected William to go when the riders dismounted, but without speaking, he took the bridle of one of the horses and walked back with her towards the stables. There was something strangely compelling about this man. She knew that if she spent much more time with him she would fill the silence with her secrets. Maybe that was his plan.

'You can tie her up there.' She nodded to a post near the stable entrance.

He shot her a smile, but completely ignored her remark. He led the mare into the stable and proceeded to remove her saddle.

Avva stood stock-still. She'd never seen a knight act like this—those that visited Caerden were lazy and privileged and barely even spared her a glance when they deposited their horses in her care. It was almost as if William wanted to help ease her burdens, but that couldn't be right.

Although she'd like to believe that he was helping her because he was a good man, experience told her that most people only went out of their way when there was something in it for them. The problem was, Avva couldn't see what she could offer William.

Following him into the stable, she watched as he worked in methodical silence, seemingly unaware that she was staring at him. After a while she turned to her own gelding and began to strip him of his saddle.

'Thomas has been showing me around the castle.' Avva looked up. William had finished and was leading his horse into a stall. 'It is not in a good condition. Do you know why that is?'

Ah, here it was. Her heart thudded painfully. Deep down, she'd known Sir William wasn't interested in her really, but to have confirmation was more painful than she'd anticipated. Sir William was after information and he thought Avva could provide it. But unless he was after knowledge about the running of the stable, Avva couldn't help him. She did not get involved in the goings-on at the castle, not even wanting to know any of the gossip that fuelled most people's interest. Even if she did know anything, no matter how small, she would not impart any of her insights to a stranger.

'I'm afraid I know nothing about Baron Caerden's

spending habits. You would do well to speak to some-one else.'

She held out a grooming brush to him, wondering if he'd take it now that she was of no help to him.

He smiled slowly at her, as if he knew exactly what she was thinking. He reached out and took the brush, his fingers brushing against her hand as he did so. Just like last night, his touch sent a strange tingle across her skin and she snatched her hand back, pressing it against her stomach. His smile deepened. She frowned and turned her back on him. She wasn't sure, but she thought she heard his soft laughter before his footsteps headed into the stall and the sound of the brush passing over the pony's hair reached her.

'I'd like to see the underbelly of the castle,' he said, after more moments had passed in silence. 'Would you show me?'

Her stomach twisted. Spending more time with William was dangerous, not just to her safety but also her equilibrium.

'I…' What reason could she give not to help him? 'I…'

She was saved from having to think of a reason by the sound of heavy hoofbeats approaching the stable. Her heart fell—there was only one person who rode quite like that. She quickly led her pony into a stall and closed the door, standing to attention just outside. She knew how much the rider expected his every need attended to.

Sure enough, Barwen Montford, the Baron's consta-ble, chief of the guards and one of the most feared men in Caerden, rode in. He didn't stop to see whether any-one was in his way, before bringing his horse to a stop in the centre of the stable. In Barwen Montford's world only he existed.

He swung his leg over and jumped down, handing Avva the reins without comment.

Sweat coated his horse's neck and the stallion panted wildly. Barwen paid no attention to his horse's distress, only stopping to remove his sword from the side of the animal. 'Bring my saddlebags to my quarters. Don't dally.'

She nodded in response. She'd made the mistake of answering back once. The faint scar she carried on the base of her throat reminded her never to do it again.

Barwen cuffed her over the back of her head with the back of his hand anyway, the casual slap making her teeth hurt. As Barwen made to walk out of the barn, William's arm shot out from over the top of the stall door. His large hand wrapped around Barwen's upper arm, bringing the man to a sharp stop.

Barwen froze, as did Avva. She wanted to say something in warning to Sir William, but her words stuck in her throat.

Barwen had probably not been stopped in his tracks for years, if ever. As far back as Avva could remember Barwen had been mean and avoided by anyone not in his inner circle. Even Steward Thomas feared him and he was one of Caerden's most trusted men.

Barwen tried to twist away from William's iron grip. All Barwen succeeded in doing was putting himself in an uncomfortable position.

Even as her heart raced, Avva had to suppress a smile. Barwen, half turned towards the door and with an expression of shock on his face, suddenly looked ridiculous rather than fearsome.

'Do you have any idea who I am?' Barwen growled, his neck turning purple.

'I know that you are not the King of England and that is the only man I answer to.' William's voice was calm and measured, but the muscles in his arm flexed as he kept a tight grip.

'Take your hand off me, you insolent cur. Or I shall remove it from your body.'

William only smiled at the threat. Avva wanted to warn him that Barwen was completely serious, he would remove William's arm without a second thought, but her tongue stayed rooted to the roof of her mouth. It didn't matter if Barwen found out Sir William was one of the King's Knights, he would still carry out his threat. Barwen was clever and manipulative, but he also had a disturbed mind and Avva had seen him do some truly terrible things, without even blinking with remorse.

'You can try.' William smiled, but this was not the warm gesture he'd shown to Avva. It was a truly terrifying grimace of teeth and for the first time Avva saw William not just as a nobleman, but as a fierce warrior, a man who was more than a match for Barwen. Her heart skipped a beat at the thought. 'But you won't succeed in your attempt. I know you're not Caerden and you are not his steward, so who are you?'

Barwen's jaw went slack. No one had ever spoken to him like this, no one had shown such a lack of concern at his threats. It was gloriously terrifying. Avva didn't know where to look. Half of her was thrilled at the way William was speaking to Barwen, the other half was petrified. Fearful at what this confrontation might mean for William's safety, but also for her own. Barwen would not appreciate Avva witnessing his humiliation. It could mean bad things for her in the future.

Barwen's eyes were tiny slits in his face, his face a mottled red. 'More importantly, who are you?'

William's arm flexed and Barwen's scowl deepened.

'I am Sir William, a member of the King's Knights. I am here on His Majesty King Edward III's behalf. Now perhaps you will answer my question. Who are you?'

Barwen puffed out his chest. 'I am Barwen Montford, constable to Baron Caerden.' He clearly thought his name and rank would impress William, but the knight's expression remained blank and Avva couldn't tell if it meant something to him or not.

Even Avva wasn't sure of Barwen's exact role. Oh, she knew he was officially the head of the Baron's guards, but his role seemed to be more than that. He appeared to be everywhere. He, Caerden and Thomas appeared to be the unbreakable threesome and it wasn't clear who was the worst out of the group. Barwen was the most terrifying, but she avoided them all for good measure.

'Well, Montford, I am sure we will meet again. In future, don't hit anyone who hasn't done something to deserve it.'

Barwen's eyes cut to Avva and she shrank back against his horse, trying to hide herself in the shadows.

'Montford.' Barwen turned his gaze back to William. 'Take care that you listen to me.'

William released his hold, shoving Barwen away from him. Barwen snarled, but seemed to think better of carrying on the confrontation. After one last glare at Avva, he turned and strode towards the stable door without a backwards glance.

'What were you thinking, Sir William?' hissed Avva when she was sure Barwen had left.

William turned his attention back to her. 'He hit you

across the back of the head. Did you expect me to stand around and not do anything?'

That stopped Avva in her tracks. No one had ever looked out for her before—not even Aven had stood up to Barwen on her behalf. But that wasn't the point. 'I can fight my own battles when I need to. Now all you've done is draw attention to me.'

William frowned. 'He will take heed of my warning or face the consequences.'

'And when you leave?'

William let out a long exhale. 'I will make sure he will not bother you after I have left.'

'How?'

Avva wanted to shake him. How could he stand there so calmly, stating so confidently that he would protect her when he had no way of ensuring that?

'You don't need to worry. I will take care of it.' He let himself out of the stall. 'I need to return to Thomas. We have more things to discuss. I will return tomorrow morning for you to show me around the castle.'

'I... I...'

William grinned at her. Before she could regain her power of speech, William strode out into the courtyard.

Chapter Six

Avva awoke to the sound of the cockerel. She jerked up and scrambled to her feet, narrowly avoiding hitting her head on the roof of the loft. She'd overslept. It had been so hard to get to sleep last night. Every time she'd closed her eyes, she'd seen Barwen's glare directed straight at her. Fortunately, whatever business he was attending to within the castle had kept him from meting out any punishments for her witnessing his humiliation yesterday. But that hadn't stopped her from worrying about it all night. She'd seen first-hand the havoc he could wreak. She had to hope William would stay away from her today and that Barwen would forget all about her.

She scrambled down from the loft, muttering apologies to the horses in her care as she went. Bluebell, a high-maintenance mare, was particularly angry at being kept waiting for longer than normal for her morning feed. She placated the horse by giving her oats, but it was still some time before Avva got to Eirwen.

'You're a well-mannered beast, aren't you?' she said, rubbing the stallion's nose. 'Your owner's obviously taught you how to behave.'

'I can't claim any credit for his behaviour. He came to me this way.'

Avva screamed and clutched her chest. She hadn't heard William approach, but, turning, she saw he was standing behind her, an amused twinkle in his eyes.

Irrational anger surged within her and she couldn't stop her voice coming out curtly. 'How long have you been there?'

'Not long.' William's lips twitched, as if suppressing laughter. 'Only enough time to hear you chatting to the horses.'

William grinned and Avva felt heat flood her cheeks. How embarrassing to be caught talking to the animals as if they were humans. She did it frequently, but she always made sure she was alone first. She didn't want anyone to accuse her of madness. William's smile was kind, though, and the muscles in her shoulders relaxed slightly.

She turned back to Eirwen and checked on his feed.

'Eirwen's comfortable,' she said, hoping that this reassurance would be enough to send William on his way. She was not going to show him around the castle—the danger it could possibly cause her by drawing attention to her was unfathomable. Besides, she'd had quite enough of his interfering ways already. If Barwen thought she was in league with him in any way... She shuddered—spending time being punished by Barwen made the dungeons seem almost palatable.

'I can see he's well, thank you for your care,' said William, but he still didn't leave.

When she turned back to him, he'd moved closer. Even in the dim light of the stable he was near enough that she could see faint stubble against his jaw and the firm outline of his lips. She stepped back, desperate to get away from him and from the strange flickering sensation in the base of her stomach. Her back met the wall of the stable, preventing her from moving very far.

'I hope you are still able to help me this morning.' William's gaze flicked to her lips and then back up again.

Avva's mind went completely blank, her thoughts scattering away from her as her lips tingled. She ran her tongue over them. William's pupils darkened and he shifted towards her.

She jerked her head back and he froze.

Could William possibly be thinking of kissing her? But, no. He thought she was a man. Unless... She knew some men preferred men. Was it possible William felt that way? Was that why he was always seeking her company? If William pulled her into his arms, expecting one thing and feeling another, what would he do? And, more importantly, who would he tell?

William cleared his throat and subtly stepped back. 'I need to take a look around the castle and I was hoping you would be my guide.'

'Er... Thomas.' Heat flooded her face at her response. He'd flustered her so much she could only manage a one-word answer.

William's lips quirked and her face became hotter still.

'Steward Thomas will only show me what he wants me to see. I would like to see the underside of the castle.'

This was the absolute last thing that she wanted. His presence disconcerted her, making her forget herself. She scrabbled around for a reason to say no. 'The horses. They need taking care of.'

William glanced around the nearly pristine stable. 'I'll help you. What needs doing first?'

Avva tilted her head to one side—she'd imagined that

yesterday's help had been a one-off. Not only had she told him she couldn't help him, she'd also been cross when he'd stepped in to protect her. She kept coming back to the fact that knights and noblemen did not help out those beneath them in society. She knew they were all about chivalry, but that was rarely put into practice as far as Avva could see. At least not until she'd met William.

There was no doubt the strong-looking knight had done his fair share of hard work. His firm build didn't come by handing heavy duties over to his underlings. Then again the man hadn't met Bluebell yet. Hopefully her highly strung antics would put him off.

'Bluebell needs mucking out.' She nodded to the stable at the end of the room. The mare was prancing restlessly, snorting every now and again.

William smiled but didn't comment, merely pushing up his sleeves and picking up a shovel. 'I'll get started then.'

Avva watched open-mouthed as William strode to the stall. He leaned over the door and Bluebell, the traitor, came to his outstretched hand. Avva couldn't hear what he whispered to the horse, but she was reluctantly impressed as the mare calmed almost immediately.

She moved away, carrying out her own chores, trying to ignore what William was doing in his section of the room. She'd hoped he was like the other noblemen she'd come across, that he'd baulk at the first sign of hard work and leave her alone. But William worked in concentrated silence and her normal chores were finished quickly.

'Is that to your satisfaction, Ave?'

Avva glanced into Bluebell's stall—he'd done the job well. Everything was clean and he'd even put fresh feed out for the mare. She couldn't complain and it *would* allow her some extra time, but spending time with William was not wise. 'You'd make a good stable boy.'

William laughed, his eyes lighting up with delight, and she couldn't help but smile in response. A strange tingling sensation started up in the pit of her stomach. She pressed her hand against it. This new sensation was happening with alarming frequency in William's presence.

'Should the King dispense with my services at least I will have something else I can do.'

And just like that she was reminded why she couldn't trust his disarming smile. A member of the ruling classes could never be depended on.

'What have I said to put that frown on your face?' William stepped closer towards her and gently stroked the skin of her forehead with his thumb. The tingling in her stomach shot out to all parts of her body and she jerked backwards. 'Sorry. I didn't mean to frighten you.' The look in his eyes was hard to read, but she knew, without doubt, that he'd had no intention of hurting her. She was not going to tell him why she'd reared away from his touch.

'I'm not afraid.' At least, she wasn't afraid of him. He hadn't threatened her or made her uncomfortable with his actions. It was her reaction to him that terrified her. She had never experienced anything like this and it was so wrong, not least because he believed her to be a man. Somehow her deception had never felt like a lie before. She was disguising herself as a man to keep herself safe and the deception didn't hurt anyone. There was something about William that made her want to shed her disguise and declare herself a woman.

'Would you help me now?'

She still didn't want to—spending more time with William was dangerous in more ways than one—but now that he'd helped her, she couldn't claim she didn't have time.

'There's no need to be afraid. I believe Barwen and Thomas are locked in discussions. They will not see us together.'

She looked up at him. How was it that he was able to read her like that? No one else ever had. Her gaze roamed over his face—there were faint lines around his eyes suggesting that he laughed a lot. The hard cruelty she saw in Caerden's visage was missing from him. He really was a beautiful man. She felt her resolve waver. It wouldn't take her long to show him around the castle and with Caerden away no one would be paying much attention to her. If she walked briskly, they could be done quickly and Barwen and Thomas would be none the wiser.

'Fine.' She nodded and strode out into the courtyard without waiting to see if he was following.

'Thank you for being so gracious about it,' he murmured when he caught up with her. She could hear the laughter in his voice and she pressed her lips together to stop herself smiling in response.

She gave him a brief tour of the courtyard, not stopping to take him into the alehouse. The alewives were all elderly women. The villagers made sure that the young ones stayed far out of the sight of Baron Caerden and any of his cronies, but even so the women wouldn't thank her for bringing a strange man into their space. They knew, as well as anyone, to steer clear of newcomers.

'The carpenter,' she said, nodding towards John, who was carving a piece of wood outside his workshop. He didn't look up at them as they passed, although Avva was sure he was aware of their presence.

'Why are people so unfriendly?' asked William as they rounded a corner and more castle inhabitants scurried out of sight.

'Why do you think they are unfriendly?'

William laughed without humour. 'When I arrived yesterday, no one would look at me. I emptied the alehouse with my presence and you're the only one who will speak to me. And I get the impression you would prefer to rot in hell than spend another moment in my company.'

Avva coughed. 'It's not that... I mean, I...'

'You don't have to pretend to like me. I have a thick skin.' His tone didn't quite match his words. Could it be that the hulking, great knight did want her to like him?

He slanted his gaze down at her and heat rushed over Avva's skin. She hadn't meant to make her distrust so obvious. So far, he seemed like a decent man and she knew that, despite herself, she did like him. 'It's not personal,' she said inadequately.

'I know that. It can't be because you, and everyone else who lives and works here, don't know me. My fellow knights would say avoiding me was a perfectly reasonable action after you've come to know me.' Somehow Avva doubted that. There was something appealing about him that made her want to spend more time in his company, even though she knew it was a bad idea. 'I can't show people they're wrong to be wary about me if I don't know what I'm fighting against.'

He made a reasonable point, but Avva was still wary. 'How do I know I can trust you?'

'You don't, I suppose, but I swear to you that I will

never purposely harm you, or any of the other innocent occupants of this castle. My intentions are honourable.'

Avva pushed her hair out of her eyes. She hadn't missed the stress William had put on the word *innocent*, so he was intending harm to those who weren't. Did she really count as innocent or was she tainted by association?

There were only a handful of people who had ever known the truth of Avva's birth and four of them were dead. Unfortunately, it was the one who was left who could do the most damage.

The current Baron Caerden knew the truth. He knew that they were half-siblings, although, of course, he thought she was his half-brother. He knew that their despicable father, the late Baron Caerden, had taken her mother as a lover and discarded her without thought when she became pregnant with twins. She needed to keep reminding herself what noblemen would do to those they considered their unequals. It would help her to remember why depending on William was not a good idea.

'Whatever you are thinking, Ave, please know that you can trust me.' William's brown eyes were soft and gentle. What she wouldn't give to lean on a man like him, to know that someone brave and strong was on her side for once.

She could tell him some of the truth about Caerden, or at least a version of it. He didn't need to know about her parentage—the knowledge would make no difference to his visit. He was a newcomer and so far hadn't exhibited any of the normal noble behaviour. He'd even made an enemy of Barwen, so perhaps it was only fair to warn him what might be in store for him. 'Strangers often spell trouble for anyone in the town who isn't part of Baron Caerden's inner circle. There is a lot of violence here, more I think than in other parts of the country. Although, of course, I don't know that for a fact, having never lived anywhere else.'

'In what ways is it violent?'

She stopped and turned to him. 'Please, I don't want to go into detail. It's safe to say it isn't good. Barwen is at the centre of it—it was not wise to make him your enemy.'

His gaze searched her face for a long moment. Whatever he saw in her expression caused him to nod briskly. 'Fine, I understand. Shall we get on with the tour?'

She turned away from him and stepped into the coolness of the castle. 'This is the route to the kitchens.' She took him to the large room, the busiest, and hottest, in the castle. Even though Caerden wasn't in residence, a large meal was being prepared. Avva's stomach rumbled as she caught the smell of roasting meat, reminding her that she hadn't yet eaten today. She didn't want to take anything now in case it slowed them down. She would have to return later. The cooks were used to her coming and going. Among the chaos, no one spared her or William a second glance.

William paused at the entrance to the room and took his time looking around. Avva didn't know what he was taking in, but his sharp gaze seemed to linger in certain areas and pass over others. Finally, he gave a nod and turned away. Avva couldn't fathom what he could have gleaned from the experience.

She continued through the castle, William following silently behind. Sometimes he would stop and look around, but it was never clear what exactly held his interest. She told herself not to be disappointed by the lack of conversation, but she found she missed the deep timbre of his voice and the way it often held a thread of laughter.

Her guided tour was coming to an end. She wouldn't have to see him again apart from their dealings over Eirwen. This was a good thing, she reminded herself as her heart dropped.

'This is—'

His hand on her arm had her coming to an abrupt stop. 'What—'

William put his finger to his lips. She frowned, but before she could question him further he pulled her into an alcove behind a large arras.

Heavy footsteps sounded further down the corridor and the unmistakable tones of Barwen Montford reached Avva. She stepped closer to William, trying to hide herself behind his bulk. As if sensing her distress, William slipped an arm around her shoulder and pulled her close. The temptation to lay her head on his broad chest was overwhelming but she held herself slightly apart from him, not wanting to succumb to the desire for contact.

'Why didn't you keep the knight where we can see him, Thomas? Where did you say he was staying?'

'At the Boar's Head.'

William's arm tightened around her.

The footsteps came closer.

'This visit changes our plans.' Barwen's voice sent a shiver down Avva's spine. He was gleeful about something and she knew from experience that was never good. William's other arm came around her, his fingers slipping into the hair at the base of her neck.

'Can it really be that simple?' Thomas sounded equally pleased.

'We need to keep that knight away from us while we

get things in place but, yes, if you can perform that task then I think it really is that easy.'

The two men laughed and moved away. William's arms were bands of steel around her. Up close she could see his pulse beating in his neck. She wanted to rest her fingertips against it, to feel it move under his skin.

William let out a long breath. She thought he would release his hold, but he didn't. He appeared to be staring at the back of the arras, but she rather thought his mind was elsewhere.

'Sir William,' she whispered.

'Hmm.'

'Should we move?'

'We should.'

But still he didn't let go.

She didn't pull away.

She had never been held so tightly before. If she'd been asked, she'd have said this close contact wasn't something she needed, but she'd have been wrong. She was enveloped in his strength, protected, for the moment, from the world outside.

Her own hands hung down by her side. Without conscious thought, she lifted a palm and pressed it to William's stomach. Underneath the cloth of his shirt, she could feel hard ridges of his muscles. She sighed softly.

He tilted his head to gaze down at her. She waited for him to say something, anything, but he remained silent. The look in his eyes gradually changed, the hardness leaving them to be replaced by something else, something she didn't recognise but which made her heart race and her breath hitch.

Her lips tingled oddly, she bit her bottom lip. He made a noise between a groan and a grunt and then slowly he lowered his head. Their breath mingled as his chest began to rise and fall as quickly as hers.

His mouth brushed hers in the gentlest of touches and everything inside her stilled. He lifted his head slightly, his gaze meeting hers for a fleeting moment before he lowered his head again. His lips moved over hers, their warmth sending strange shivers through her body. Without conscious thought her mouth began to move, too, mirroring his movements.

His other hand stole into her hair, his strong fingers sliding deliciously against her scalp. A strange sound filled the small space and it took a moment for her to realise it was coming from her. The noise seemed to stir something within him and his mouth became more insistent, his tongue teasing the edge of her lips.

Her arms slid around his waist and her hands splayed at the base of his spine, his muscles moving under her fingertips.

All her worries faded away in a wave of sensation. Nothing had ever felt so good. She wanted to stay here for ever, doing just this.

But it seemed William was not as lost to the feeling as she was.

He lifted his head and looked down at her. She swallowed, unable to think of anything to say.

'Thank you for the tour, Ave. I think I've seen enough for today.'

And with that he dropped his arms, swept the arras to one side and stepped out into the corridor beyond.

The material of the tapestry quickly fell back into place, leaving Avva cocooned, alone, in the small alcove. Her lips were still tingling from William's touch. She reached up and ran her fingertips over them, the scent of him still clinging to her skin. She closed her eyes tightly. What had she just done?

Chapter Seven

William hurried out of the castle, his heart pounding as his thoughts swirled.

The overheard conversation confirmed that Barwen and Thomas were planning something, something which involved getting William out of the way, which probably only meant one thing. William's fears were confirmed—the King was in danger. William's whole life had been building towards this moment. All his training, the fealty he'd sworn to his brothers-in-arms and his liege, it was all worthless if he didn't act now.

And yet…

And yet, that wasn't at the forefront of his mind. Every time he tried to bring it to the front his thoughts scattered off in an entirely different direction.

That kiss, the one that should never have happened. The one he had been imagining ever since he'd met Ave two days ago. The one which he had sworn would never happen and the one which he had taken as soon as the opportunity had presented itself. It had rocked him to the core.

He'd kissed women before. In his youth he'd have said

he was something of an expert at it, but never had he experienced the bone-weakening desire he'd felt when Ave's hand had brushed his stomach. All thought of potential plots against the King had vanished from his mind like puffs of smoke.

He'd been fighting his desire for Ave from the moment they'd first met.

Hell, he'd never wanted someone so badly. His dreams had been plagued with images of her limbs wrapped around him, of his name on her lips.

While his mind had tried to concentrate on the puzzle of this town, his body had betrayed him, leaving him hot and heavy from wanting her.

Before he'd seen her delicate curves in the moonlight, he hadn't even been sure she was female, but after he had, well, his thoughts had become even more dominated by her. He wanted to know why she was pretending to be a man. He hated to think that someone as lovely as she could be caught up in whatever strangeness was gripping this town. Yet why disguise who she really was?

Was Ave even her name? Dear God, how could he have kissed a woman while not even knowing who she really was? He'd never be able to share this with Theo. Theo would think that he had lost his mind. He had certainly lost his famous reasoning. It was shameful just how the part of him he'd always thought of as intrinsic to his very being, his logic, could be wiped out by one glance from Ave. Just to see her peeking up at him from beneath her long eyelashes and he'd been lost.

Never again would he ridicule his father so much. No wonder the man lost his mind when his wife was around him. In that moment, William would have given Ave anything she asked for, even the Devereux barony if that was what she'd desired. This was why desire was so dangerous. It caused men to lose their heads.

He'd seen this so often with his parents. Their life was chaotic. They never planned. They could have spared themselves the pain of losing their children in infancy if they'd been able to restrain their desires long enough. And, although William now had sisters his parents adored, he couldn't imagine going through the painful losses his parents had endured.

It was better not to love at all than to suffer all that anguish. The desire he felt for Ave could not be allowed to grow into anything more.

He would not do that to a woman.

That's why his plan to marry a wealthy heiress was a pragmatic solution in more ways than one. He would not marry for love and would therefore always be in control of his emotions and he would have the means to restore the Devereux barony to its former glory.

It made sense in every way.

His attraction to Ave did not.

Yet, he did not seem to be able to stop himself from seeking her out. He could argue that it was essential to the mission to keep the one person who would talk to him on his side. But that would be a lie. He might dissemble the truth to others, but never to himself.

He wanted Ave desperately.

Even the day before, when he should have gone straight to Thomas, his feet had carried him to the training ring as soon as he'd spotted Ave watching some pages practise their lamentable riding skills.

He'd abandoned all his plans and all his reasoning and walked straight towards her. His head had urged him to turn around, but it was as if his body were being pulled by invisible rope, straight towards her.

Even when he'd spoken to her once, he could still have turned away. He could have gone about his business without her, but some insanity had prompted him to offer his help in caring for her animals. Today, he'd been the same. Instead of walking around the castle and assessing the situation by himself, he'd insisted she come with him, even when she clearly didn't want to.

He was a fool. And now, he had made matters worse.

That kiss, which was imprinted on his soul, should never have taken place.

This whole morning had been a disaster, since the moment he had stepped into the castle grounds.

It was essential that he knew the castle inside and out. If James was too late to stop the King coming here, then Edward might well be walking into an ambush. The purpose of this morning was to check for hidden passages or secret stores of weapons, yet he had only taken in around half of what he'd seen.

He'd been too aware of Ave, hovering on the periphery of his vision, to see anything out of the ordinary in the mundane everyday detail of castle life.

Nothing, that was, until he'd heard heavy footsteps coming towards him and Ave.

Without stopping to second-guess his decision, he'd pulled Ave behind the large tapestry and waited.

The words he'd heard had confirmed his fears. The Baron and his men were planning something dark and dangerous, something that required William being kept out of the way.

The only plot that would make sense was one that was against the King.

Suspecting that, he should have followed Barwen and Thomas. If they were happy to talk about their plan in the corridor, they might have continued in their conversation. He might have learned details that would help him and his other knights later. He'd let himself, and his fellow knights, down and all because all thought of the King had been driven out of his mind. All it had taken was the simple act of Ave brushing her hand against his stomach.

Everything, his mission, his training and his mounting responsibilities, had disappeared in that instant. His only thought had been to make her belong to him in every way possible.

He leaned against the castle wall and groaned as he remembered how his body had taken over in that moment, his mouth seeking hers with unerring precision. If she hadn't responded he would have stepped back. He would have apologised and moved on, but she'd met his passion with a force of her own. Everything had swept away and his world had become the spot where their bodies connected, her delicate curves fitting against his chest.

And how had he ended the most sublime moment of his life? Like a fool, that's how. He'd thanked Ave for showing him around the castle and left. No apology, no explanation. It would serve him right if she hit him next time she saw him—it was no less than he deserved.

As he'd run his fingers along the length of her smooth jaw, the desire to touch her soft skin all over had swamped him and he'd known then he had to stop, because if he succumbed to that hunger all would have been lost.

There were so many reasons why she could never truly belong to him and so he had no right to take it further. He banged his head back against the stone wall. He should have apologised and offered her some sort of explanation, not just walked off. He was an idiot in every sense.

The fact that he had so nearly lost control while on a mission terrified him. Thank goodness Theo was not here to see him; he would be ashamed of the way William was acting right now.

William inhaled deeply. He could swear to himself that he wouldn't make the same mistake again, but he knew that would be a pointless endeavour. He would only fail again when he next encountered Ave. The best thing he could do right now was to concentrate on the reason he was here in the first place: the safety of the King.

Pulling himself upright, he marched back towards the entrance to the castle. He needed some answers from Thomas and Barwen and, in the mood he was in right now, he wouldn't object to using force to get them.

The Great Hall was smoky and crowded. Thomas lounged in the ornate chair on the dais, but there was no sign of Barwen.

'Ah, there you are.' Thomas pushed himself into standing and came towards William, smiling widely. 'I was expecting you earlier. Baron Caerden has sent word that he is sorry he was not here to welcome you, but he will return in a day or two. In the meantime, I am to make sure that everything is made ready for the King's visit. We are to spare no expense.'

William frowned. 'What?'

Thomas's smile faltered at William's tone, but he pressed on. 'Baron Caerden wanted to come straight away, but he has very pressing business in the north and we thought you would understand, given your calling in life.'

'In the north? My calling?'

'Yes, oh, I see your confusion. I mean of course to the north of here, not to the north of England. Caernarfon, I think I told you, requires the Baron's help and he is the most attentive of neighbours, anything to help a fellow baron. As I said, Caerden has given me leave to make any arrangements with you on his behalf. And by calling, I meant the fact that you are a chivalrous knight, bound to protect the peace.' Thomas laughed, a high-pitched noise, which grated on William's skin.

If William hadn't overheard Thomas and Barwen's conversation only a short while ago, he might have believed this show of hospitality—it *was* a great honour to receive a visit from the King. Now that William knew what he did, he was hard-pressed to see how this civility was going to ensure that they kept William away from the castle. Unless Thomas's plan was to agree to everything William suggested, in order to get him to leave quickly.

'Perhaps I could see where the King will stay during his visit,' he said.

'Of course,' said Thomas, his full smile firmly back in place. 'The rooms will need some further preparation but I think you will find their size adequate for a royal visit.'

William nodded. He followed Thomas out of the Great Hall, the man's new civility making him loquacious, William tried to concentrate as Thomas rambled on, but it was difficult to listen to the man's surprisingly shrill voice. It would appear that William was going to get a full history of the castle today, along with a description of where each wall hanging had come from and their cost. William kept silent, hoping to give Thomas room to slip up, but the man continued with his boring monologue.

'And this is the chamber I have marked out for His Majesty.'

The room was indeed sizeable, running as it did above the length of the Great Hall. William strode to the centre of the chamber and turned slowly around in a circle, taking in all the features. An ornate fireplace sat in the centre of the outside wall, but aside from the size and the possible warmth the fire might throw out, it was not a suitable place for the King to spend even a moment of his time, let alone a prolonged visit.

'Some work will need to be done in here in order to get it ready for His Majesty,' William said, not even hiding the disdain in his voice.

'Of course. I will set Caerden's finest men on it today. The chamber will be ready in no time.'

William sincerely doubted that.

Thomas continued to rattle on about the room while William walked the length of it. He prodded a rug and a waft of damp hit him. This room would not be ready in time for the King's visit—it would not be ready in a *year*. William very much doubted Caerden had any intention of doing up this room, but time would tell. William would need to return here without Thomas and to explore every stone. In the unlikely event that Edward made it into this room, William would need to be confident that there was a quick way out and where any potential traps could be hidden.

He made his way over to the long window at the end of the room. It was a substantial piece of glass and must have cost the Baron quite a sum. 'What is this room normally used for?'

'It was the late Baron's room, but since his father's passing the current Baron Caerden has preferred his old chambers.'

William would have to investigate why. Caerden's

chambers would have to be something special to not use the potential of this room. It was strange to let a large space like this go to waste.

William rubbed a pane of glass and looked out at the view. Below him, the courtyard bustled with life—without anyone in authority to watch over them the inhabitants were smiling and the whole picture was more relaxed than he'd seen it before.

William's body tightened as he spied Ave stepping out of the stables and his gaze instantly locked on her. Behind him, Thomas continued spouting nonsense, but William lost all concentration as he watched Ave scurry across the courtyard towards the carpenter's workshop. The carpenter looked up at her approach and smiled. William's fists clenched as Ave reached out and ran her fingers over some of the woodwork, the carpenter nodding, clearly pleased at whatever she was saying to him. Did the carpenter know that Ave was a woman? From the way they were speaking, they were obviously friends.

William forced himself to uncurl his hands and step away from the window. Jealousy was not an emotion he was entitled to have.

The afternoon dragged on. Thomas seemed intent on showing him every item of furniture the chamber had to offer, not seeming to mind when William pointed out that none of it was fit for the King.

'We will make sure it's all buffed and polished before he steps through our gatehouse, don't you worry.'

Twice, William tried to leave and both times Thomas found a seemingly spurious reason for him to stay. There was some tapestry William just had to see. William kept a hand close to his sword's hilt, half expecting a trap around a corner, but nothing out of the ordinary happened.

By the time William extricated himself from Thomas's cloying presence he had to roll his shoulders to loosen the muscles, which had tightened in his neck over the course of the afternoon.

He inhaled deeply as he stepped into the courtyard. There was a cooler breeze this evening, as if winter had not relinquished its hold on spring quite yet. A few guards were milling by the gate, more than when he'd arrived two days ago but still nothing like the provision needed to defend a place such as this. They barely looked up from their game of dice as he walked past and out of the castle grounds.

He wondered if James had reached Theo yet, but he sincerely doubted it. He scratched his chin. The stubble was beginning to itch now and he could do with a close shave. Heat spread across his face when he realised his desire for a close shave was pure vanity. He'd survived a month or so without one before. He'd been told he looked better without a beard and he wanted to look good for Ave. He was absurd.

He shook his head to clear his mind. Perhaps he shouldn't wait for James's return message. He could just leave.

He ignored the strange pang in his chest that materialised at the thought of leaving Ave. He'd only known her for a few days, but already he knew it would hurt to be away from her, knowing he might never see her again. It was for the best, she unsettled him, bringing out a reckless side he'd kept buried so deep within him he hadn't even known it existed. That side of him was buried for a reason and he had no desire to bring that aspect of his personality to the fore. Getting away from Ave would bring him back to himself and he needed that.

No, he had done all he could here. He would leave on the morrow and return only with the support of the rest of the King's Knights. Together they could investigate just quite what was wrong with this castle and its strange inhabitants and quell any potential uprising before it got started.

He rounded a bend and came to a stop. Slightly up ahead of him on the dusty track, he could see Ave walking, her head bowed as if she was walking into a strong wind. He grimaced. His actions behind the arras were probably responsible for the look of defeat.

Part of him argued that he should catch up with her and apologise. He'd treated her badly, when she'd only ever been courteous to him. The other part of him screamed that speaking to her for any reason was a really bad idea.

His body appeared to make the decision for him. Without conscious thought he realised he was walking faster, almost running, in a bid to get to her quickly.

'Ave,' he called out when he was only a few footsteps away.

Her shoulders tensed at the sound of his voice and he cursed. He'd made her wary of him and that was the last thing he'd wanted to do. Aside from his ridiculous desire for her, she was his only ally in this strange town.

'Ave, please wait for me.'

She slowed and stopped then, but didn't turn to face him.

'I'm sorry about earlier,' he said, as he drew alongside her. 'I shouldn't have…done what I did.'

To his utter mortification he felt heat sweep across

his face. It had been years since he'd blushed in front of someone, not since he'd been a young man and Theo had continually beaten him at sword practice. It had taken him months to work out a successful counter-attack and the mockery he'd received from his fellow pages had been relentless. This was worse than that.

She still didn't look at him.

He tried again. 'It was uncalled for. I shouldn't have taken advantage of you.'

She nodded, mumbling something under her breath.

'Can I buy you something to eat as way of an apology?' *What?* He'd just made the resolution not to spend time with Ave from now on.

'I've eaten,' she said quietly.

'Right.' He doubted she had. The kitchens hadn't produced the evening meal before he'd left, but he wasn't going to press the issue. She obviously didn't want to spend any further time with him. He would walk on now and leave her alone. Any moment now he would do just that, any moment now. But his feet weren't obeying his internal commands. He remained rooted to the spot, next to her. She didn't appear to want to move either.

'Ave, I…'

'Somebody's coming.'

'What?'

'I can hear footsteps, from more than one person, heading in this direction. They sound as if they are in a hurry. We should get off the path.'

She tugged on his sleeve and pulled him off the rough track, into the scrub bushes that lined it.

Now that he was no longer looking at her, he, too, could hear the sound of people approaching from the direction of the castle. The heavy footsteps appeared to be in a hurry.

Men rounded the corner in a cloud of dust and ground to a complete halt when they caught sight of Ave and William at the edge of the path.

William's hand moved to his sword. 'Stay behind me.'

Ave didn't argue, moving into position, her body tensed. 'What do you think they want with us?'

'They want nothing with you. You should run.'

He was surprised when she stayed behind him. 'I'm serious, Ave. You should leave now. I doubt they are even aware you are here.' At least, he hoped not. If the men were here to cause trouble, then they wouldn't want Ave to witness anything. She was in as much danger as he was and that was his fault for not leaving her alone.

The lead runner moved towards William quickly, the others followed. Without comment the man nearest William swung his sword through the air. It was a clumsy move and William was able to dodge it easily. The leader stepped back, an unpleasant sneer across his face.

Ave still didn't run. Fear flooded his veins. Not for him—he'd fought worse and was trained to die—but if a blade as much as touched Ave, it would cause him great agony. He tugged his dagger out of its sheath and handed it to her. She didn't comment as her fingers closed over the handle, her gaze fixed on the men in front of them. A surge of admiration rushed through him, quickly followed by fear. If anything happened to her, he would never forgive himself.

The five men fanned out.

The oldest one grinned and William rolled his eyes—this bravado he was used to. Men who thought they were going to win before they started the fight didn't usually fare so well.

Ave moved out from behind him and stepped to his left.

'You need to go.' He said it firmly, hoping, rather than expecting, she would take heed.

'I'm not going to leave you.'

He turned to her. She was gripping the dagger so tightly William could see the white of her knuckles. Her gaze was fixed on the men in front of him, her expression determined.

'Ave…'

He didn't finish his sentence before the first man took another swipe at him.

It was a slow move and easy to deflect.

Ave held steady next to him.

Five wasn't too many. He'd had worse odds and survived, but he'd never fought alongside someone he desperately wanted to protect before. Ave's presence complicated matters considerably.

The first man came at him again.

His sword swipe was harder this time, but just as easy to deflect. This was a man with confidence but little skill.

No one had spoken, but there was no need. The intention of the men before him was very clear. They were not here to warn him off. They were here to kill him. And he'd unwittingly led them to Ave. That very fact had sealed their fate. He could not let them live. If he did, Ave would be a target for having witnessed this attack for ever.

This was a fight to the death.

Another swipe had him ducking, but he got lucky and

caught his assailant in a deadly blow. The man's eyes widened before he hit the floor.

Next to him Ave screamed.

He gripped her arm. 'Ave, you must run. These men are serious.'

She shook her head. He had no time to argue with her further. The four remaining men converged on him, anger for their fallen comrade making their moves wild.

Ave rushed forward and took a swipe at the weakest assailant. It was a good tactical move. It took the fourth man's attention away from William, leaving him with only three men to fight. Three men was easy, he could do that in his sleep. Ave just had to keep the weaker one distracted long enough for him to finish off these men.

He went in for the attack. His world became a blur of swords and the clash of metal against metal. And then there were only two men left in front of him.

Ave cried out and William turned.

She was holding her own, but he could see that she was starting to tire. Sweat coated her brow. She stumbled and fell to her knee, picking herself up only just in time.

He couldn't leave her to face this man alone.

He moved towards her, but as he did so his assailant struck a blow to the back of his knees, bringing him to the ground with a grunt. He raised his arm to ward off a strike to the head and he felt metal graze his skin.

Ave screamed again. She reached out and blocked another blow. The dagger was flung from her hands, leaving her defenceless. He surged up, anger propelling him forward. His third assailant fell to the ground, mortally injured.

'Behind me,' he yelled to Ave.

This time she obeyed instantly.

Neither of the two men left were skilled fighters, but he'd given them an advantage. Now they knew William was trying to protect Ave, they began to use that against him.

'Get the lad,' yelled the stronger of the two.

William swung out his arm to protect Ave and was rewarded with a jarring blow to his shoulder. He grunted and staggered to the left, leaving his side unprotected. A short, sharp kick to the ribs followed. He heard something crack and a burning pain spread through his chest.

He needed to end this.

He began to move faster, his sword a blur in front of him.

On his periphery, he could see Ave searching through the scrub, obviously looking for the dagger. He wanted to yell at her to get up. She was leaving her back wide open for attack, but he couldn't get his words out—every breath was painful.

One of his assailants spotted her and grinned. Moving away from William, he raised his sword. William dodged to the left, blocking a blow that would surely have killed her. His foot slipped and he fell to the ground. Pain lanced through him as he jarred whatever had snapped in his ribs.

His assailant kicked him and the air whooshed out of his lungs.

He staggered to his feet and began to fight again. His assailants moved around him, trying to take swipes at Ave. With no weapon to defend herself she was completely vulnerable. Panic began to claw up William's throat. He hadn't lost a fight in years, but he'd never been defending someone he so passionately wanted to not only live, but leave here without so much of a mark on her perfect skin.

He managed to get a good blow on the stronger of the two. The man dropped back for a moment, cursing.

William saw his opportunity, but before he could follow it up the weaker one rallied and charged him. Blows were raining freely now. He could not say who was winning, only that he was keeping Ave safe from getting hurt.

His ribs screamed in agony, but he was not going to go down and leave her defenceless.

And then there was only one of them left.

He felt, rather than saw, Ave slip from behind him. His concentration was fully on his remaining opponent. He hoped, rather than believed, that she was running far away from this scene.

The man was fresher than William—he'd only had to fight against one man instead of five—but William had managed to get in some significant blows and so they were evenly matched with William having the advantage of rigorous training and skill.

Beside him he heard the unmistakable sound of metal being dragged across the ground.

'Stop.' Surprisingly his opponent took notice of Ave's command.

Ave was holding out one of the fallen men's swords. William had a moment to experience a surge of pride at her bravery, despite her shaking arm, before blinding fear set in.

Instead of continuing his fight with William, his opponent surged towards Ave. Ave held the man off as he rained down blows with his sword, but he was advancing on her quickly. She would not be able to hold him off for long.

William ran forward, but he was too late. The man had knocked Ave's sword to the ground and was holding his weapon to her throat.

'Don't move,' he growled.

William froze. He had no doubt the man would slit Ave's throat whatever happened, but he needed to plan his counter-attack to stop Ave getting hurt in the process.

He didn't look at Ave, he didn't think he could continue if he saw the terror on her face.

'It seems we are at an impasse,' he said.

Their assailant grunted. William guessed the man hadn't thought through his own plan. If he killed Ave, then William would kill him anyway. That didn't mean William could dally—with every heartbeat Ave was in danger of getting hurt.

Without giving himself time to think, William threw himself at the remaining man. He succeeded in getting him away from Ave as the two of them hurtled to the ground.

The landing caused the pain in his chest to radiate outwards, but William had no time to dwell on it as his assailant's fist connected with his jaw. He tasted blood.

Fists flew. William knew he was winning, his assailant getting tired, his punches were weakening.

'William!' Ave's scream had William looking up just in time for him to see one of the men he'd thought dead dragging himself towards them on unsteady but determined feet. The man raised his arm and punched William squarely across the face.

He must have blacked out because he came round to find himself airborne. Rough hands held him at the

shoulders and legs. He grabbed a knife he had strapped
to his leg and, twisting, managed to hit the man who
held his ankles. The man went down with a grunt, but
the other one held on tight. William twisted and turned,
but the bash to his head had lessened his strength and he
didn't appear to be able to break free. William realised
what the man's intention was moments before he landed
in the stream. Icy, cold water rushed over him, waking
him from his stupor.

His assailant waded into the river and grabbed on to
William's tunic, pulling him under the water. William
reached up and grabbed hold of the man, pulling him
down with him.

It was difficult to see in the murky depths. The man
thrashed in William's grip, struggling to get free, but
William held on. His only thought was that he had to win
this. He managed to break through the surface, gasping
in a sustaining breath before his assailant pulled him
back down.

Gradually his assailant's struggles slowed and finally
stopped. William held on for a little longer, just to be
sure.

He was so tired now. He could barely move. He tried
to kick his legs to bring himself to the surface, but his
body refused to respond to his commands, the armour
and weapons he wore with pride dragging him down towards the bottom of the river.

He had one, final feeling of relief that Ave was safe
before darkness set in.

Chapter Eight

Avva's lungs burned as fear coated her every breath. 'Where is he? Where is he?' she muttered as her feet slipped on the uneven terrain of the river's bank.

How could this have happened?

She'd been so caught up in trying to understand what William was saying about their kiss, not able to tell from the few words he'd said whether he regretted kissing her or not, that she hadn't really appreciated the threat they were under until it was too late. She'd stupidly been wondering whether William would kiss her again when she'd heard the running men—it had taken her several moments to realise that the men meant harm.

Even now, with the men's bodies scattered across the pathway and their blood soaking into the dirt, she almost couldn't believe all that had passed.

She stumbled over the root of a tree and dropped to her knees. Tears burned the back of her eyes as she pushed herself back up to her feet. If she didn't find William quickly, he could drown. She couldn't allow that to happen. Not when it was her fault he was in the water.

There hadn't been a moment when she had believed

William would lose against his assailants. He had swooped and whirled and easily overpowered them. If only that final one hadn't woken—neither she nor William had been watching the fallen men. She'd assumed they were all dead. William had seemed disorientated after the blow to the head, but even then he'd kept fighting, not giving up even as he was dragged towards the river.

Now he'd disappeared beneath the murky water. She'd seen him surface once, but he hadn't reappeared in an eternity. Neither had his assailant.

She raced along the riverbank, praying she would spot him before the sun set completely and the light disappeared.

A glint caught her eye and she paused. She squinted— yes, the glint was coming from one of William's weapons.

She clambered down the edge of the bank and waded into shallows, gasping as icy water splashed against the skin of her legs. Something solid bumped against her. Looking down, she realised it was William's body. He was eerily still. She reached down and grabbed hold of the front of his tunic.

She was strong, working in the stables required that, but William was a dead weight.

She heaved and stumbled backwards, half falling into the edge of the water. She pulled again, managing to get William's face out of the water while the rest of him stayed submerged in the shallows.

She rolled him to his side and thumped him soundly on the back. 'Come on. Wake up!'

Nothing.

She pummelled his back, screaming at him.

His shoulders heaved and then his whole body spasmed. He began coughing violently.

Avva staggered upright, splashing through the shallows until she reached the bank. She stumbled on to the grass and sank to her knees. William was alive and awake. She'd done the best she could. She should leave. That was the sensible option. She was already entangled in trouble, but with those men dead, they couldn't identify her as the person who had been with William.

William rolled on to his back, still coughing, his face just above the water level,

Avva's feet refused to move, even as her mind roared at her to stand up and leave. He looked so vulnerable, despite his solid bulk.

William's coughing gradually subsided, but he didn't pull himself out of the river. Avva could see the rise and fall of his chest and so she knew he was still alive.

She made her way back down to his side. His eyes were closed and he was an unhealthy shade of white. 'Are you able to get up?'

His eyes opened into little slits. 'Ave.'

'Yes. It's me.' She crouched down next to him, alarmed by the weakness of his voice. 'Can you stand? We need to get you out of the water.'

'I…' He appeared to lapse back into unconsciousness.

Avva rolled him slightly and hooked one arm under his shoulder. Using all her strength, she managed to lift him slightly, enough to get her other arm under him as well. She couldn't pull herself up to standing but, crouching low and bracing her legs against a boulder, she was able to drag him out of the water and up on to the bank.

She touched his forehead and he moaned. His skin was icy cold and, now that the water wasn't washing it away, she could see a deep cut across his forehead, blood pouring from it ominously.

He stirred again, his eyes half opening to look at her.

'I'm going to get help,' she said.

His arm shot out and grabbed her, his grip strong despite his weakened state. 'No.'

'No?'

'You can't tell anyone.'

'But I can't...'

'You'll have to,' he rasped.

'I...' She should have run. She should have left him to fend for himself as he'd told her to. If she carried on helping him, she was a conspirator in whatever was going on and that would definitely bring trouble into her life. Yet, if she hadn't been there he wouldn't have been distracted, he probably wouldn't be lying by the stream half-dead if it wasn't for her. Besides, he had promised to protect her against Barwen—the least she could do was help him when he was in need.

'Please.' William's grasp on her arm loosened and she could tell he was about to lose consciousness again.

'Fine, I won't get help, but we need to move you from here.'

He moistened his lips, but whatever he'd been about to say was lost and he went under again.

Darkness had fallen while they'd been down at the riverbank. Avva pulled her cloak tightly around her. Dragging William from the river had made her hot, but the water from her dip into the river had soaked through most of her clothes and she was shivering violently now.

'What should I do?' she muttered. She wished Aven was still alive so she could go to him for help. He'd always been the braver of the two of them and would have thought of a solution which kept everyone safe, but she was floundering. She had no friends, no one to turn to for aid, wouldn't involve her younger brothers in this. She was going to have to use her own wits.

'Ave.' She looked down at him—she could just make out the whites of his eyes. 'The fallen men. They need to go…river.'

His eyes fluttered shut again and she stood. He wanted her to dispose of the bodies, possibly the worst thing she had ever had to do in her life. 'Please, God,' she muttered under her breath. 'Let this be over.'

She scurried back up the riverbank and saw the bodies where they'd dropped.

Her breathing came in rapid pants as she rolled them into the river, trying not to think about what she was doing as each body hit the water with a splash, disappearing beneath the murky depths.

She checked on William. He was still unconscious, but he was breathing, and so she began to walk briskly back to the castle. Running would look suspicious, but no one ever questioned her coming and going into the castle grounds. It was well known that her younger brothers worked at the smithy's and that she visited them often.

The guards didn't look up from their game of dice as she walked back through the gates, but even so her heart was racing by the time she reached the stables. She climbed up to the loft and grabbed her blanket. It wasn't thick, but it would have to do for covering William.

Pebble, a fat, contented pony, allowed himself to be led out of his stall. Her hands were shaking as she attached a cart to him and led him out into the courtyard.

She tucked her hands into her sleeves to hide the tremble she was sure was obvious and began to make her way to the gatehouse.

She kept her head down as she approached the guards.

'What you up to, Ave?' Avva's heart sank. She was so rarely stopped at the gates, she hadn't thought it would happen tonight.

Avva looked up, glad that it was Gawain who'd addressed her. He was one of the friendlier guards and quite often chatted to her when he collected a horse from the stables.

'Collecting some supplies for John,' she said, amazed that her voice came out steady and assured.

'You're good to that old carpenter.' Gawain smiled.

'Aye. Let's hope he remembers that when I've something that needs fixing.'

Gawain grinned and Avva carried on walking through the gates and out into the open.

John would cover for her, Avva was sure of that. She was pretty sure John knew she was a woman, but he'd never said anything and he treated her like one of his other grandchildren. She hated to put him in the position that he'd have to lie for her, but she hadn't had enough time to come up with a better idea.

She leapt up to the front of the cart and encouraged Pebble into a brisk trot until they'd turned the bend in the road. She hoped William was awake because it was going to be difficult to find him in the darkness.

She looped Pebble's reins over a tree stump, although he was so placid she was fairly sure he would stay put regardless.

'William,' she called softly as she clambered back down the embankment.

There was no response.

'Don't do this to me, William. Where are you?'

She heard a slight moan a little to her left and began to tread carefully in that direction. Eventually her foot hit something solid. She reached down and found William's chest—it rose and fell beneath her hand.

She traced a path up his body until she was touching the skin of his face. He was as cold as death. She patted his cheek gently. 'William, I need you to wake up.'

'Aye.' His breath whispered over the skin of her hand. 'You came back.'

'I did, but it's not going to do you any good unless you can make your way up the river bank. You're too heavy for me to carry.'

William groaned, but she felt him shifting. She dropped her hand as he made it on to his front. In the light of the crescent moon she could just make out his shape as he tried to pull himself to his feet. He only made it on to his knees before he fell into a heap.

'Here, let me help.' She slipped an arm under him and his solid weight settled against her.

Together, they managed to get him to his feet. She didn't think he could manage to walk unaided and so she kept an arm underneath him as they staggered up to the top of the bank, his breathing rasping in her ear.

'You're going to have to go in the cart.'

She felt him nod against her hair. It took several attempts to get him in it and, even then, the cart was far too small for a man of his size.

She arranged the blanket around him. 'Where shall I take you?'

'Not…the tavern.' He was shivering in earnest now, his whole body shaking.

'I don't know what to do.' She spoke quietly.

'I'm… I'm…sorry.'

It was that apology that made her mind up. If he'd demanded something from her, she might have taken him to the tavern and considered her duty done, no matter how lovely his brown eyes were or how delicious his kisses. That apology had touched something within her. The humility she'd heard in his voice was so unusual for one of his rank. It had reminded her more of her brother Aven and she knew she couldn't leave William now.

'I'm going to have to take you on a little ride.' She didn't know if he'd heard her or not, there was no response to her statement.

She swung herself up onto the front of the cart again and clicked Pebble back into a brisk trot. She'd have to head to the town to make her story believable and then she would return to the castle. It was risky, but no one would consider her to be harbouring someone in her cart. She was the unassuming, hardworking and polite stable master. No one would suspect her of any wrongdoing.

She pulled up outside the smithy's and was relieved to find Dylan, her youngest brother alone inside, hammering some molten metal into shape.

'Ave,' he called, pulling off his gloves. 'I was hoping I'd see you tonight. Why didn't you come yesterday or the day before?'

'I had something I needed to take care of.'

'I heard you've been spending time with a stranger in the tavern. The word is he's quite a handsome stranger, too.' A smile was playing around Dylan's mouth, a knowing glint in his eyes. Perhaps her brothers hadn't forgotten she was a woman after all.

'I had to. He's a knight working directly for the King. I couldn't say no to spending the evening with him.'

All humour left Dylan's gaze. 'What did he want with you?'

Unbidden images of the kiss earlier that day sprang to mind, but she shook her head. 'Background information, I suppose. I don't know. He didn't get any details from me. Listen, I can't stay. I was wondering whether you had a spare blanket or something. I'll pay you, of course.'

Dylan's lips tightened. 'You don't have to pay me. You give David and me enough. Is everything all right?'

'Yes, everything's fine. I'm in a bit of a hurry, do you think you could…?'

Dylan frowned, but didn't say anything as he disappeared off to his sleeping quarters.

'Are you in trouble?' he asked as he handed Avva the spare blanket.

'No. All is well with me.' That wasn't technically a lie. It wasn't her lying unconscious in the back of the cart. Dylan would help her if she asked, but the less her remaining family knew the better. 'Thank you very much for this.'

'It's nothing,' said Dylan with a shrug.

She nodded. 'Bye, then. I'll come and call on you again soon.' How she wished he was still young enough to pull into her arms. She remembered the soft tickle of his hair under her chin as she'd held him close and told him stories. Now he was bigger than she and wouldn't appreciate the gesture. He was almost grown now, it wouldn't be long before he and David didn't need her any more. She didn't know what she would do then. Unbidden, images of her and William sitting in front of a fire sprang to mind. She shook her head—that could never be. Not even if the impossible happened and they fell in love. They were from two very different worlds and neither one could fit. She would do well to remember that.

Back by the cart, she tucked the new blanket into a corner, careful to avoid touching William. He'd need something dry to cover him later, so that he didn't catch a chill. She reached out and put a hand on his chest. He was still breathing—she just had to hope he carried on doing that. Life would be a lot harder if she had to get rid of another dead body.

She set Pebble in motion, her heart galloping wildly in her chest, now, for the most daring part of her plan.

She let Pebble walk the rest of the way. Although he was a strong pony, it was too much to ask him to trot uphill with his heavy cargo. Unfortunately, the slower pace gave her more time to think about what she was doing.

It was unlikely she would be checked going back into the castle, but that didn't stop her imagining what would happen to her if she was. 'I'll just say I found him by the side of the road,' she muttered to herself. 'As far as I'm aware he's a guest of Thomas and there's nothing unusual. I can say I thought he was drunk. That's not odd behaviour for one of Thomas's visitors.'

Despite her plan, her knees shook as she neared the heavy, iron gates. The noise of the wheels passing over the entrance seemed far louder than usual and she had to force her breathing to remain even as the first of the guards came into sight.

But her fears were unfounded. Gawain was nowhere to be seen and the other guards were as uninterested in her as normal. She was able to get Pebble and the cart into the stable without any fuss or abnormal attention.

She got down from the cart and leaned against Pebble's sturdy body, relief weakening her knees. She took a few, deep steadying breaths before moving around to the back of the cart. William was lying as she had left him, alarmingly resembling a large sack of potatoes.

She reached over and touched his leg. 'William, are you awake?'

'Yes.'

'You're going to have to help me get you out of the cart and up the ladder.'

There was a long silence and no movement.

'William?'

'You've brought me to the stables?'

'Yes.'

'In the castle grounds?'

'Yes,' she said irritably. 'It's not as if I have various places to hide wounded knights. It's not something I go around doing often.'

She heard the faint croak of a laugh. 'I'm not going to be able to manage by myself.'

'I'm not going to be able to get in there and help you out,' she countered. 'You're huge.'

There was a resounding silence to her statement. She thought he must have lost consciousness again, but eventually she heard the slats of the cart creak as William began to move. It seemed to take half a lifetime, but eventually his legs appeared over the edge of the back, followed by the rest of his body. He grunted with pain as he pulled himself upright, but at least he was standing.

'Here, let me help.' She slid her arm underneath his again and helped him across to the bottom of the ladder. 'You're going to have to climb up by yourself. Can you manage?'

Avva looked around the stable to see if there was

anything she could use to help haul him up. There was nothing.

'I can manage,' he said.

He grasped hold of the side of the ladder and put his foot on the bottom rung. He wobbled and Avva went to steady him.

He waved her off. 'I can do it. It's only a short climb.'

Avva didn't know how he achieved it, but William began to mount the wooden steps. It took him a while, but eventually his legs disappeared out of sight as he pulled himself over the top.

She grabbed the dry blanket and climbed up after him.

The loft above the stables was a small place. She had space to store her few possessions and room to sleep, but that was it. With William filling up the space with his broad shoulders and long legs, the place was miniscule. In the darkness she could just make out the shape of him as he lay down on his side.

'You're going to have to take your wet clothes off.'

He grunted. 'I'll be fine.'

'You won't, you'll catch a chill and die and I'll be left with your dead body decomposing on my bedroll.'

'I'm sorry if my dying would cause a great inconvenience for you.'

'I'm sure it would be worse for you.'

She heard him grunt again, but this time she could make out a thread of amusement in the sound.

'I'll go and light a candle while you get undressed.' She made to move out of the loft and stopped. 'Do you…?' She cleared her throat. 'Do you need me to help?'

She held her breath as she waited for his answer, unsure whether she wanted to help him or not. The thought of touching his bare skin was not as unpleasant as it should have been.

'I'm fine,' he grunted.

She nodded. It was a good thing he had turned her down. Although that didn't explain why her heart was fluttering so wildly as she descended the ladder. If William had said yes to her offer of help, it would have been a completely innocent gesture. It would have been the same as when she'd cared for Aven in the last few days of his life and he'd needed help with all his basic needs. She'd seen him undressed and was familiar with the male body. William might be more powerfully built than most, but the thought of him without clothes was surely nothing to disturb her peace of mind. Yet she realised her hands were shaking as she made her way across the almost empty courtyard, *probably from the shock of the whole evening*, she assured herself and nothing at all to do with William's undressed body.

Fortunately, John was nowhere to be seen because he was sure to guess that something unusual was occurring from the jittery way she took a candle from the stock he kept at the back of his workroom. She lit it from John's fire and made her way back to the stables, careful to avoid hot wax dripping on her hands.

She didn't normally bother with candlelight during the spring and summer months. She knew her way around in the dark and the danger of falling asleep with a flame was too risky. But there was little chance of sleep tonight. Not with a hulking great warrior in her space, a warrior who had kissed her so thoroughly she could still feel the imprint of his mouth. A warrior, who might die from his wounds or exposure to the icy water and, in death, would leave her with more problems than she had right now.

She carefully carried the candle to the top of the ladder and settled it on the floor near the entrance to the loft.

In the flickering light she could make out the imposing shape of William. He had manoeuvred himself to the edge of the room, as far away from the hay she used for a bed as was possible in the small space. He'd removed his outer layers, but kept his undergarments on. She could see from the way the fabric clung to his skin that he was still soaked. He was lying on his back, an arm thrown over his eyes.

'Stubborn man,' she muttered.

She thought she saw his lips curve slightly.

She reached out and touched his shoulder, her hand coming away wet. 'You must be freezing.'

'The cold is not as bad as the pain,' he said roughly. 'And even that's manageable. I'll be out of your way shortly.'

Avva snorted. 'I don't think so. You can barely stand. I'm going to help you out of the rest of your clothes and then you are going to rest. We'll talk about what we'll do next, in the morning.'

She crawled forward until she reached his side. 'You're going to have to help me.'

With only a few grunts of pain but with no further protests, they managed to divest him of the rest of his clothes. She caught glimpses of toned flesh, but she tried to keep her eyes averted from his skin. She didn't want to be tempted into touching him. He was breathing heavily by the time they'd finished and he didn't protest when she pushed him towards the hay and pulled the blanket over him.

She thought he was asleep until he murmured, 'Where will you sleep?'

'Don't worry yourself.' She had no intention of sleeping. During Aven's final days she had stayed awake throughout the nights, keeping an eye on him and making him comfortable. Missing sleep wasn't pleasant, but she knew she would survive. She didn't want to close her eyes and wake up to find him dead.

He opened his eyes slightly. 'When I pictured myself in your bed, it wasn't like this.'

Avva gasped.

'Sorry… I shouldn't have said that.'

Avva opened and closed her mouth, completely at a loss as to how to respond. No one had ever said anything like that to her before. She'd never even thought it was possible for someone to desire her. She was so long and broad shouldered. But then he didn't desire the real her, did he? He thought she was a man and there was no way she was going to let him know otherwise.

'No, you shouldn't have said such a thing,' she said eventually.

William lapsed into silence again. Avva hoped he had fallen asleep. She didn't like the way her body wanted him to finish that conversation. She wanted to know exactly how he had pictured himself in her bed and what he thought they would be doing. These were dangerous, treacherous thoughts that could lead her into exactly the same position as her poor mother, saddled with unwanted children and forced into accepting a loveless marriage. She laughed softly—of course William still believed her to be a man. He wouldn't be expecting any babies to result from a union between them. How shocked he would be!

She crossed her legs and leaned back against the loft's wall. Below her the horses moved in the stalls. Normally, she loved the sound of their hooves among the hay; it reminded her that she was not alone. Tonight, it made her realise just how tenuous her position was. If someone from the castle came to the stables with a need to travel urgently, William might easily be discovered.

Ice dripped through her veins at the thought. There was no innocent reason for having the injured knight in her quarters, no way could she explain his presence.

'May I ask you something?'

Avva jumped at the sound of William's voice rasping through the silence. She'd been so wrapped up in her worries, she'd been convinced he was asleep.

'You may.'

'How is it that no one notices you're a woman?'

Avva's heart constricted painfully. 'What?'

William groaned. 'Do you have any water? I'm very thirsty.'

Avva handed him a water skin, her heart pounding. 'That's not what you said.'

She heard him take a long sip of water. 'I know it wasn't, just as I know you don't need me to repeat my words.'

'How did...?'

William shifted slightly, the floorboards creaking under his weight. 'It's obvious.'

'No, it isn't. Nobody's suspected for nearly a year.'

William made a sound between a laugh and a grunt. 'I can believe Thomas and his ilk not noticing, but anyone who looks at you, your curves, that long, creamy neck—trust me, there is nothing manly about you.'

Avva crossed her hands over her chest and stared into the darkness. She'd been mistaken for a man *before* Aven's death. It was absurd to suggest she looked womanly. She might not have a beard, but she was tall and broad shouldered. She was strong and controlled the horses well. She might not look like Dai Bach, who was a walking, hairy mountain, but she could easily pass for a young man. She'd been doing so daily, so how dare William suggest otherwise. 'You're wrong.'

'I'm not.'

'You only know because…because…' Heat flooded her face as she remembered what had passed between them earlier. The way he'd held her tightly against his body as his lips had moved over hers. Perhaps he had worked it out then.

This time there was no mistaking his laugh. 'Aye, I could feel your curves against me earlier. There's no point denying you're a lass, but I knew before that. There is nothing manly about you at all.'

Avva doubled over as if she'd been punched.

'I can see you're offended, but you shouldn't be. You're beautiful.' William had rolled over on to his side and was squinting at her through the darkness. The position didn't look comfortable and a small part of her was glad. 'Perhaps you are right and it is not obvious to everyone else. I've been trained to notice things.' He smiled at her and her heart flipped, despite her anger at some of his words—she'd never been called beautiful before.

She turned away from him. He had no right to come in here with his deductions and his smile that did strange things to her insides. No right at all.

'Have you always lived as a male?'

'No.'

'Tell me, Ave.'

'Tell you what?' She wanted to walk away from this conversation, to ignore everything he was asking her. If he had noticed she was a woman, did everyone know? Her stomach roiled. Did the Baron know she was his half-sister and not half-brother? She shook her head— he couldn't know because he would have done or said something. Anger rolled through her. William was making her doubt herself and she'd never had cause before.

'Who is Aven?'

Avva rested her head on her knees. She should end this conversation and get away from the man who was confusing her so much. She didn't want to tell this story and yet…she hadn't spoken about Aven in so long, the words were bubbling inside her just waiting to escape. 'Aven was my twin brother. He died last year.'

'I'm sorry.' William was looking at her, and, although she couldn't make out his expression, his tone was so kind it made tears come to her eyes. In the days after Aven's death, she'd had no one to talk to. Her younger brothers had been too worried about their own future to really comprehend her grief. After the three of them had come up with the plan for Avva to take over Aven's life, her brothers had treated her as if she truly was a man, with a man's stoicism. There had been no time for crying.

'What was he like?' William asked softly.

Avva didn't want to talk to William—it was better that he didn't know her secrets—but the words just spilled out of her. 'He was always laughing. Our upbringing was grim, but he sheltered me from the worst of it and when we were at our lowest, he would find the humour in our situation. Even when he knew he was dying he would try to make me laugh. I used to pretend to keep him happy.'

'It sounds as if you were lucky to have him in your life. Did he work at the stables?'

She found herself nodding. 'Yes, he started here as

an apprentice, but he worked his way up to stable master very quickly. He was good with horses, but I...' It felt disloyal to say she was better with the animals, but it was true. She had always had a natural affinity with horses. Whenever he'd had a problem, Aven had sneaked Avva in and she'd been able to deal with it. It was why he had progressed through the ranks so quickly, that and the fact that hardly anyone else wanted to work so closely with Caerden and his men.

'It's obvious you have a gift,' said William softly.

Avva felt her cheeks warm at the compliment. She shrugged. 'I love horses. Aven was grateful for the work, but he didn't care for them the way I do.'

'What happened to him?'

'He...there was...' She took a deep shuddery breath. 'The people who run this place are casual about those who work for them.'

'What do you mean?'

Avva toyed with the edge of her tunic. She had gone so far now. There was no need for her to hold back, but the memories were so painful. 'Caerden and Barwen wanted some sport one day.' She swallowed. She was not sure she could make it through this conversation. 'They involved Aven. They...he...' She took a deep breath. 'He got hurt. Not badly, he could have recovered, but an infection took hold in one of his cuts. I don't think he had eaten much, I think he was giving his rations to me and our younger brothers. Perhaps, if he hadn't, he would still be with us. I don't know. He died quite quickly, but not quickly enough that he didn't know what was happening to him.'

She buried her face against her knees as memories from that terrible week assailed her. Aven lying on a pallet, his pale skin beaded with sweat, knowing that he was going to die, but pretending he wasn't frightened. It had broken her heart to hear the worry in his voice as he spoke about her future. It had been his idea for her to assume his identity—he had wanted her protected from the evil that ran through this town. Their younger brothers had readily agreed with the plan. It was better for them if they had an older brother looking out for them rather than a sister they had to protect.

'Tell me about the games Caerden and his men play.'

Avva lifted her head. Her eyes had adjusted to the darkness of the stables and she could tell that William was looking directly at her. What had she done? Once again, she'd been drawn in by the man, telling him things she had normally kept hidden. She had nothing left to hide and only William's honour to protect her. She did not want to be pulled any further into this nightmare. She didn't want to explain Caerden and his evil games. She wanted to protect the life she had built up for her and her remaining brothers. Why was she trusting him, when she had no evidence, other than his politeness, that he was any better than any of the other nobility who had let her and her family down in the past?

Avva pushed herself to her feet, the roof of the ceiling stopping her from reaching her full height. 'I'll leave you to get some rest. I'm sure you'll be strong enough to leave in the morning.'

She didn't wait to hear his response. She shuffled over to the edge and, not bothering with the ladder, jumped to the ground, ignoring the pain in her knees as she hit the floor.

Sir William might have better manners than the nobles who frequented Caerden, but she was being foolish confiding her secrets.

The sooner he was gone from her life the better.

Chapter Nine

Everything ached.

William ran his tongue over his lips, but his mouth was so dry it had little effect. His throat burned as if a red-hot poker had been shoved down it. He cracked open his eyes and promptly shut them again as the light seared his vision. He reached out a hand and felt around. He appeared to be lying on a bed of straw, but it was difficult to remember how he had got there.

William remembered the fight and the bone-chilling terror of the men turning their attention on Ave. Ave, who would have been much further down the hill and away from the ambush if William hadn't tried to talk to her. He'd had to get the men away from her. If anything had happened to her, then it would have been his fault. He knew that he had succeeded in that. He also remembered the cold of the river as it rushed over him and the heaviness of the water as it had dragged him down into its depths.

The rest of the evening came to him in flashes of broken memory. Ave's hands beneath his shoulders, dragging him to the bank of the river and the rocking of a cart as it travelled over a rough path jolting his already painful ribs. And the feather-light touch of Ave's fingertips across his brow.

She had taken him to her loft, installing him above the stables. His heart contracted with a strange emotion. She'd put herself in unspeakable danger by helping him and yet she'd done it without him asking. She could have just let him drown. By helping him, she'd put herself in danger.

William rolled on to his side, biting his lips as pain burned through him. He prodded his ribs gently, the pain intensifying under his touch. Some were definitely cracked, but he was hopeful that they weren't broken. He'd be better in a day or two, if he didn't overexert himself. The problem was...he'd received that beating for a reason. Someone wanted him out of the way and that meant he couldn't just lie here and recuperate. There was work to be done.

He pulled himself up into a sitting position, his muscles protesting vigorously. He scrubbed a hand over his eyes, forcing them to open fully. He must have slept through the night as daylight was filtering through from the stable below.

He could hear the faint shuffle of feet moving about in the stalls. He hoped it was Ave and not someone else. He had to assume that it was only her who was on his side in this strange town—everyone else was to be treated as if they were out to kill him.

Ave had helped him so far, but would she be willing to continue to do so? He hadn't given her much motivation to want to carry on.

He dropped his head into his hands and groaned softly as more memories from last night assailed him. He'd asked her so many intrusive questions. The way she had rushed out of the loft told him she hadn't welcomed the turn in conversation.

There was no question that Ave had saved his life. He'd repaid her by mocking her ability to appear as a man. It was true that to him she was the most beautiful woman he'd ever seen, but he hadn't got that across. Instead he'd subjected her to a detailed questioning, raking over her past which had seemed painful to her.

Now, if he wanted to stay in the safety of her loft, he needed to convince her he wasn't a complete ass.

There couldn't be any more kissing either. As much as his body craved it, he had to use his head. He was in dangerous territory and he needed his wits about him to survive. He couldn't allow himself to be distracted. It was exactly this sort of foolish emotion that had led his father and the barony into so much trouble. He was better than that, he had spent his whole life believing it and he wasn't about to be proved wrong at this critical moment.

Kissing Ave was delicious but wrong.

Ave deserved so much better than what he could offer her, which was essentially a passionate but ultimately dissatisfying encounter. She was beautiful and strong-willed, quick-witted and brave. She deserved someone who could take care of her for her whole life, not just a few stolen moments. He couldn't be the man who offered her a marriage based on love—he didn't want a union based on such an intense emotion. Love drove logic out of everyone's minds. He had enough honour not to be the man who offered her nothing but momentary pleasure.

He swallowed—he shouldn't lie to himself, he did want to be the man that gave her physical pleasure, more than he'd ever wanted anything. To touch her skin with his would be… He shook his head, laughing at himself. The movement involved in merely lying next to her would be beyond painful given the current state of his body. He could barely sit up without wanting to howl in pain, let alone engage in any other physical activity.

Not to mention how morally wrong kissing her would be.

After long years of training, he had finally reached an enviable position. He might be the newest recruit to the King's Knights, but he was damned good at what he did—at least he was normally.

As a child, he'd watched helplessly as his parents had squandered the wealth of their barony. Their shared grief over losing their children had caused them to be unwise in their spending. William was so close to being able to restore that wasted wealth, to being able to offer his younger sisters a dowry, that he mustn't throw this opportunity away.

As well as the necessary dowries, William had extensive plans for land management, but before that he needed quick access to wealth. The petition for marriage to a wealthy heiress was a practical decision. He didn't care who it was, he'd seen enough of his parents' foolishness to know love was not for him. He hoped for companionship, he would be a faithful, kind husband, but as long as his wife brought with her the resources to restore the Devereux fortunes, then he would be content.

Ave was a complication he did not need, yet his body did not seem to be listening. He had never craved anyone in the way he wanted Ave. Even now, with his body screaming in pain, part of him still wanted to touch her lips again. Hell, it wasn't part of him, it was most of him, the thought so appealing it banished the racking pain throughout his body and made it tighten with desire. Ave was like the finest wine on the hottest day. Now he'd kissed her once, he knew what he was missing.

But Ave didn't strike him as someone who gave away kisses freely and, with marriage into a wealthy family on his mind, he wasn't in a position to offer her anything other than a few nights of bliss. He wouldn't regret it, but she might and he didn't want to leave her feeling badly about him, especially when she had done so much for him.

Footsteps sounding on the ground below brought him back to the present. He strained to listen as the gentle murmur of voices reached him.

Ave laughed and William's body tightened, even as he felt the sting of jealousy. What was happening to him? Even after the talking-to he'd just given himself, he still longed to be the one to make her smile.

He was a fool who wasn't listening to his own advice. The sooner he could get out of here and away from Ave, the better.

The mumble of voices continued and then came the sound of someone leaving. The ladder creaked and William froze. The thugs who'd attacked him last night had stripped him of his sword and some of his favourite weapons, but he still had his dagger and could inflict damage if necessary. He reached over to his discarded clothes.

Ave's dark hair appeared over the ledge, followed by the rest of her. William scowled as his heart began to pound. What a ridiculous reaction—it seemed his body hadn't listened to his lecture at all.

'There's no need to look so fierce. I'm only here to

bring you some bread and to check you are awake. You have slept for most of the day.'

'Most of the day!' Dear God, he had wasted so much time. It was only seven days until the King was due to arrive at the castle. Hidden up here in the loft, he wouldn't be able to receive any messages from James, even if his squire had sent one. He was in no position to climb down from the loft right now. He was as weak as a kitten.

'You look as if you are about to go on a killing rampage.'

William tried to relax his features, but he obviously wasn't having much success because Ave's gaze was very wary. She pulled herself into the loft and settled as far away from him as possible. Damn it, he was going about this all the wrong way. He needed her on his side if he didn't want to be thrown from the loft before he was ready.

'What's your real name?' What was he doing? Only moments ago he'd berated himself for speaking to her bluntly and now he was barking at her again. 'If you don't mind telling me, that is.' If she hadn't been looking directly at him, he would have banged his head on the wall. He was being such an idiot and he couldn't blame his near death from drowning on his behaviour either.

Without coming any closer, Ave held out a hunk of bread.

'Thank you,' he murmured as he took it from her, his fingers brushing against the back of her hand. The brief touch sent tingles skittering across his skin. He forced himself to act as if nothing was happening to him as he leaned back into his corner of the loft.

That brief display of manners seemed to relax Ave. Instead of returning to the stalls below, she settled down, still as far away from him as possible, but at least she was sitting down and not scurrying away from him.

William tore off a chunk of bread and began to eat. The loaf was hard and flavourless, but he couldn't remember the last time he'd eaten. The dried slab filled a hole he hadn't realised was gaping until he started shoving food in his mouth.

'It's Avva.'

He paused mid-chew and looked across at her. She was watching him intently, her eyes unblinking. He swallowed, the bread forming a lump in his throat.

'Avva,' he repeated.

She nodded and then dipped her head, appearing to concentrate on the hay near her feet.

'That's a pretty name.'

A pink flush stole across her skin. She kept her head down, not looking at him. He tore off another chunk of bread and chewed. What was he doing calling her name pretty? He was more than a fool and an idiot, but he didn't seem to be able to stop himself. His soul wanted hers.

He should keep things impersonal, he could do that. 'Thank you for coming to my rescue yesterday.' She looked back up at him, the delicate flush still evident on her cheeks. 'I'm sure you're regretting it now.'

She smiled at that, the gesture doing odd things to his stomach. Or perhaps it was the bread. Hopefully it was the bread—it was fairly indigestible, after all. Swooping stomachs were the stuff of fair maidens from legends of old, not the behaviour of a hardened knight as he knew himself to be.

'I'll be out of your way as soon as possible.'

She nodded slowly, her eyes wide, and his stomach

dropped. Although he didn't want to involve an innocent in his mission, and a beautiful one at that, he couldn't help but wish she was a little reluctant for him to leave.

'Why did those men attack you?'

He shrugged and then wished he hadn't. It wasn't just his ribs that hurt. There wasn't an area of his body that wasn't screaming in agony after the simple gesture. 'Er…' As answers went it wasn't very articulate. It didn't seem to please her either.

'You must have some idea.' Her eyes were flashing now, irritated with him.

He cleared his throat. 'I suspect there is something here in Caerden that Thomas and his ilk do not want me to see or know.'

Avva snorted. That was interesting. Instead of questioning her, he took another mouthful of bread. This was a technique he'd learned from Theo. People tended to want to fill a silence. For a long moment, William thought Avva wouldn't fall for the strategy, but then he heard her quick inhale. He kept his attention on the loaf, not wanting to spook her as she began to speak.

'I would think there are many things Thomas and his cronies do not want you to see.'

'What about Barwen and Caerden?'

She laughed without humour. 'Caerden is worse than Thomas. Thomas is lazy, but also a bit stupid. Caerden has a cruel intelligence. What he will do to a person…' She shuddered. 'Then there is Barwen. I hope, for your sake, you do not run into him again.'

He continued to chew, but that seemed to be the end of Avva's commentary. She lapsed into silence, staring at her long, slender fingers, which rested on her knees. Over the shuffling of the hooves below, he heard Avva's stomach rumble. She moved her hands to press her stomach. Heat spread over William's face as he realised what the sound meant. 'Is this yours?' He held out the remains of the bread.

She hesitated.

'Why didn't you say something?' His tone sounded sharper than he intended, his embarrassment making him curt. He held the loaf out further, grunting as the effort hurt his battered body.

She waved his hand away. 'You need it more than I do. I ate earlier today.'

'That's not true. Please take it.'

She still didn't come any closer.

'We'll share.' He tore off a chunk and held out a piece to her.

She eyed it, holding herself very still. William forced himself not to move or make any sound. Slowly, she moved towards him, as wary as a sparrow. Her fingers brushed the palm of his hand as she took the bread from him, setting off the strange tingling sensation once more. He swallowed.

She took a tiny bite as she settled back down, this time a lot nearer. He knew he should look away—this close he could see the individual hairs in the thick lashes that framed her eyes. He could remember all the reasons why he should leave her alone, why he should stop thinking about her completely, yet he couldn't tear his gaze away.

The long, creamy skin of her neck was so tantalisingly close. He barely had to move and he'd be able to trace the length of it with his lips. The image was so strong he could almost feel the soft brush of her hair against his forehead. Why? Why was he having such a visceral attraction to a woman who tried to pass herself off as a man? A woman who didn't even like him that much and one who was so beneath his station that even his unconventional parents would baulk at the match. Marriages at his level in society were made for political or financial gain, not for love. Even his parents, who adored each other to the edge of madness, had had their union arranged by their parents after a land dispute.

His father was fond of telling anyone who would listen how he had fallen in love with his bride as soon as he had seen her. He'd been one of the lucky ones, because they'd met at the ceremony to bind them together for ever, having never set eyes on one another before that moment. They could just as easily have loathed one another.

Perhaps this overwhelming desire was what his father had experienced, this need to be with one other person over all other rational thought. It was sobering to realise William was more like his parents than he'd believed. He'd always imagined he was beyond this. Not for him the insanity of falling desperately in lust. But he'd never experienced desire like this, so overwhelming he'd forgotten his training.

He'd been so busy talking to Avva, trying to think about the best way to phrase his apology, when those men had attacked him.

It was the first time, since becoming a knight, that he'd lost a fight. He didn't count bouts between his fellow King's Knights—they were trained to be the best of the best and losing to them wasn't an embarrassment. Getting beaten by a group of barely trained thugs was a humiliation he wouldn't forget in a long time. It was yet more proof that unbridled attraction led to foolishness.

'Where will you go when you leave here?' Avva asked, her soft voice bringing him back to the present.

William clenched his jaw tightly as he heard the words she had uttered. While he was here, battling this unwanted desire, she wanted him gone.

He handed her his last chunk of bread, he was no longer hungry. 'I...'

'Because if you need to stay here a little longer that's...' She stared at the top of the ladder. 'That's fine with me.'

'I thought you wanted me to go.'

Avva nodded, still not meeting his eyes. 'I don't want trouble, but...'

'But?'

'But Aven would have wanted me to help you.'

'Your brother would want you to help a naked stranger, who's currently lying in your bed?'

A huge grin spread across her face and laughter gurgled out of her. He tried to tamp down the ridiculous joy that surged through him at the sound.

'I don't think he'd be thrilled about the naked bit, no.' That beautiful pink colour spread across her cheeks again and it was William's turn to grin. 'But he would want me to help someone who nearly died last night. Even though...' She waved her hand about. 'I'm still...'

William waited, but she didn't seem to be able to find the words to finish her sentence. He decided to help her out.

'I'm sorry I upset you yesterday evening. You saved my life and, afterwards, I didn't treat you with the respect you deserve.' That had her looking up at him, her eyes wide like a startled deer. He swallowed a smile. 'Perhaps we could start again.'

For a moment she only stared at him, mistrust clear in her expression. She nodded slowly. 'All right. Let's start again.' She popped a morsel of bread into her mouth, a slight frown creasing her forehead. She swallowed. 'Will you tell me why you think those men attacked you?'

Damn, this wasn't the route he wanted to go down. He wanted to know about her. He suspected her trying to pass herself off as a man was somehow linked to the unusual goings-on in this strange town. The more he discovered, the less of a hapless idiot he would feel when he reported back to his fellow knights and that was a perfectly valid reason for finding out more about her. But he had to admit to himself, if not to anyone else, that he wanted to know more about her because she intrigued him. And…and, as well as his overwhelming desire, he also liked her. She was kind, curious and brave.

'I'll trade with you,' he said. 'You tell me why you are pretending to be your twin brother and I will tell you why I *think* I was attacked.'

She tilted her head to one side and he waited. He was beginning to recognise this as her way. She wouldn't be rushed into talking. For a man who'd been raised by impulsive parents, it was a restful experience to know that her actions were being thought through. Eventually she nodded. 'I will tell you why I am pretending to be Aven if you swear an oath that you will never reveal my secret.'

'What sort of knight would it make me if I revealed your secret?' He was affronted by her suggestion, even though he understood her reluctance to talk. 'If it will make you feel better… I swear on the Devereux name that I will never tell a soul what you reveal to me now. You also have my word as a member of the King's Knights that I will never impart the knowledge that you have taken your brother's identity.'

She fixed him with her piercing blue gaze. He concentrated on keeping his breathing steady. He would never break his oath, so he was not worried that she would find a lie in his countenance. But he didn't want her to know how her gaze made his heart race and his body tighten. As the moment stretched he curled his fists to stop himself reaching across and tracing the curve of her cheek with his fingertips.

She took a deep breath and let it out slowly seemingly coming to a decision. 'This town...the women... it's not safe.'

The blank, flat look in Avva's eyes made him want to tear the world apart with his bare hands. Instead he said, 'What exactly do you mean?'

There was a faint tremble in Avva's long fingers as she carried on.

'Baron Caerden thinks the women of the town are here for his entertainment and that of any of his noble friends who pay him a visit.' Her tone was soft, almost gentle, but William could hear the fear behind her voice and the edge of his vision blackened. It didn't matter what else was happening in Caerden, William would make sure the Baron faced the full weight of William's vengeance for frightening Avva and putting that look in her eyes.

'Are you referring to the current Baron?' he asked.

Avva nodded. 'And his father, and any guests of either of them.'

When William was finished with the younger Baron, he would dig up his father's bones and crush them into paste and then hunt down the men who had stood alongside them both. He would not stop until the men who had scared Avva were completely destroyed.

'You are angry.'

William looked up at Avva, realising that his fists were clenched tight and that he'd been glaring at them as if they were responsible for the Baron's actions. He hoped he hadn't scared her further with his actions. 'A baron's role is to protect those under him, not to put them in further danger. It…frustrates me that you have been subjected to an ordeal by the very people who should protect you. Will you tell me more?'

Avva tucked her arms under her legs and rested her head on her knees—the gesture was oddly vulnerable. William wanted to pull her into his arms, to comfort her and to reassure her that he would always keep her safe. But he knew he couldn't do that; it was a promise he could not keep and a gesture she might not enjoy.

Avva fiddled with the edge of her tunic. Recognising that this was her way, William didn't press her. She would talk when she was ready.

'It's…' She looked up, staring into the distance. 'If…a woman is lucky…' she let out a bitter laugh '…I don't mean lucky, I mean…' She shrugged. 'My mother was discarded by one of the nobles when she was no longer of interest. He didn't treat her too badly before that.' William frowned. So Avva was an unwanted offspring of a noble. He ran through the images of older barons he knew, but he could think of no one who looked like her. It was yet another mystery about her he would have to solve, but at least it explained one of the reasons she had such a low opinion of nobility.

'Others…' She took a deep breath before continuing. 'When I was a child there was a girl. She was so beautiful. The old Baron was dying and his son had some young noblemen visiting. There were days of feasting. The girl disappeared at some point—her body was found when the men moved on to another castle or hunting ground, I don't know which. Anyway, the girl had been discarded in the forest like a broken cart. It wasn't the first time something like that had happened, but it was the first death.'

William's anger burned along his skin in a white-hot rage.

'Things deteriorated quickly after that. I suppose the young Baron realised there were no repercussions for the death of a villein. The townsfolk quickly learned to hide their women or to make them as unappealing as possible.'

'I've noticed only older women work at the castle.'

'Yes. They are not as attractive to Caerden as the younger ones. Mostly, they are safe.' Avva nodded.

'How do other women hide? Not everyone can disguise themselves as men.'

Avva smiled slightly. 'You saw how it was the other night. When a stranger arrives in town, the women are hidden pretty quickly.'

'That's what the tavern's patrons were doing? They were hiding their women from me?'

Avva smiled sadly. 'There's no need to take it personally. Nobody knows whether you are a good person, or one of them.'

'I would never... I...'

She reached out and lightly covered his hand with hers. 'I believe you.'

It was inevitable that his skin would tingle where she touched it. He held himself still even though he wanted to turn his hand and touch her palm to palm. He feared she would pull away if he moved.

'Why do you believe me?' he asked. 'I've not done

anything to prove I'm trustworthy.' Heat flooded his face. 'Quite the opposite really.'

An answering blush stained her cheeks, her mind obviously going back to the same place as his. That darkened nook, behind the arras, where he'd lost control and tasted her lips.

She leaned back, taking her hand with her, and he wished he'd stayed silent.

'You're not like the other men who stay here.'

He waited, hoping for more, but when she didn't continue he realised he'd been holding his breath. He'd been hoping for some sign that she thought well of him. He was beyond pathetic. Apart from responding to his kiss, she'd not given him any sign that she found him any more attractive than the next man. He certainly wasn't getting the impression from her that she was experiencing an overwhelming desire for him.

'Why do you not leave?' he asked, when it became clear she was not going to say anything else.

She laughed, although the sound was without humour. 'You and your kind may be able to move around freely, but it is difficult for us villeins. Besides...' she tilted her head to one side '...my brothers are in this town. I cannot leave until they are established.'

'Why not? You said they are apprentices. Surely they can manage by themselves now.'

Her eyes flashed. 'I love them. I will not abandon them until I know that they are settled.'

William nodded. There it was again: love. It made people act irrationally. Avva should leave and save herself from living in fear as soon as she had the chance.

'Now it's your turn,' she said.

'Huh?'

'You promised you would share your thoughts with me. You're not going to renege on your promise, are you?' Ah, of course he had and her reminding him proved that her mind was on their conversation and not on him.

'No, I'm...' How much to tell her? She had been honest and open with him, far more so than he'd been anticipating. His attraction to her should not make him careless, but for the moment he was stuck up here, at least until nightfall. She could help him if he told her the details of his suspicions.

'Sir William.' Her tone was sharp—she obviously believed he was backing out of his promise.

'I'm wondering where to begin,' he said placatingly.

'Why are you here?'

'King Edward III is planning a visit. He will be here in seven days. It is my duty to ensure everything is ready for him.'

Her eyes widened. 'King Edward. Coming here. Why?'

That was an easy one to answer. 'He is touring the country, making sure his people know him.'

She shook her head. 'That cannot be the whole reason. His father was concerned only with the bloodshed of Welshmen in the pursuit of his own power.'

From the tilt of her jaw, William suspected Edward II's Welsh campaign had not endeared Avva to the Royal Family. That was going to pose a problem when he asked for her help. From the little he'd gleaned from her she would do the right thing, even if it went against her feelings. She'd rescued him from the river, after all, when the sensible thing would have been to let him drown.

'Well?' she challenged. 'What do you have to say about that?'

He had quite a lot to say about it really. Edward II hadn't been his favourite person—there were mistakes he'd made that had cost William personally—but he was loyal to his son, Edward III, and he believed, with everything he held dear, that the young King would unify Britain and make it a strong, wealthy country. But that was not what Avva wanted to hear.

He couldn't quite blame her either. Her experience of nobility was not how it was meant to be. Those who were stronger took care of those beneath them. It was what honour and chivalry dictated. He knew that was what Edward III believed in, otherwise William wouldn't have dedicated his life to serving him. Seeing the glint in Avva's eyes made him realise he would not be able to convince her of that quickly and time was already running away from him. He would have to use shock and awe to convince her to help him.

'I think Baron Caerden is plotting against the King.'

She inhaled sharply, her whole body jerking away from him. 'No! He would not be so addle-brained as to commit treason.' She started to shake her head. 'He is a lazy, indolent man. His only interests are feasting, hunting and bedding women. He would not stir himself to... No, you're wrong.'

He didn't want to do this to her. He didn't want to disrupt the safe life she had built for herself. But time was pressing and he needed her on his side. 'Then why was I attacked?'

She opened and closed her mouth a few times, closely resembling a landed pike. Even impersonating a fish, she really was exceptionally lovely. She was obviously befuddled and clearly angry with him, but, even so, he still wanted to press his mouth to hers, to forget about everything as he explored her body. Unfortunately for him there were many reasons why this could not happen. Not least because his body still hurt like hell and any movement was causing him extreme discomfort. Even if she welcomed his touch, reaching out to her would cause him pain.

'I think I have accidentally stumbled on something, something bigger than you and me.'

Avva was still shaking her head. 'Just because the Baron wants you out of the way, it doesn't mean he is plotting against the King. There could be many other reasons behind the attack on you.'

'Like what?'

'Like...'

'Five men beat me almost senseless and threw me in the river to die. They didn't take my coins or the clasp of my cloak, even though they are worth something. They were not motivated by wealth. Do you think Thomas or Caerden or this Barwen person arranged an attack on me because he took offence at me staying in the town rather than at the castle?'

She frowned. 'Don't be ridiculous.'

'Then what do you think was behind the attack? Because it looks suspiciously like Barwen and Thomas have something they wanted to keep hidden. Remember what they were talking about when we were...when we overheard them.'

'I don't... I don't have time for this. I have duties to attend to.'

She began to shuffle to the edge of the loft. He was losing her and he couldn't let that happen. She was his only link to outside this stable.

'I need your help, Avva. At the very least I need you

to try to retrieve my sword. I lost it while fighting those men, but the chances are quite high that it's still in the undergrowth near where I went into the river. If I could…'

She paused. 'I am giving you help. You are staying here while you recover. I'm feeding you and keeping you safe. There is nothing else I can do for you.'

'I appreciate the help you have given me so far. It has put you in danger and I regret that deeply.' He was still losing her, her eyes kept darting to the edge of the loft. He needed something powerful, something that would shock her into acting for him. 'It is not just me who needs your aid. It is the King of England.'

He could see immediately that he had said the wrong thing. The softening he'd seen in her countenance hardened, her shoulders straightened and her look became firm.

'And therein lies the problem.' Her voice was firm now, there was no wavering in her speech. She had made up her mind and it was not in his favour. 'Edward III is the English King and I am a Welsh woman.'

She didn't give him time to respond before she swung her legs over the edge of the loft and dropped to the ground, effectively ending their conversation.

Chapter Ten

Avva concentrated fully on the rhythmic sweeping of her brush as she cleaned out the stalls. Every time her mind strayed to the man in the loft, she forced it in another direction. Sir William had fallen asleep not long after their conversation yesterday afternoon. She had checked on him during the night, climbing up to the loft now and then to make sure he was still breathing.

When she was sure he was sleeping deeply and would not rouse, she slipped from the stables and went to hunt for his sword, even though she'd not promised to do so. The sight of him sleeping peacefully had tugged on her heart. Covered in bruises, with his body soft in sleep, he had seemed more vulnerable than the hardened warrior she was used to. Asking for his sword was not an unreasonable request and it would allow him to defend himself better, if the need arose.

She'd found it along with a few other of his weapons scattered around—getting them into the castle grounds had been harder. Eventually, she had settled for collecting some hay and stored the heavy weapons among the feed until it could be collected later.

Tiredness dragged at her movements, but she could not rest until William was gone.

She had decided to keep Sir William safe until he was well enough to walk away by himself. It was what Aven would have done and what was right, but she wanted no part in his mission. Becoming embroiled in a treasonous plot, even if it was on the right side of the law, was not something she could risk becoming involved in, especially in her precarious position.

Besides, it would do no good for her to spend any more time with William.

Her brother's blanket had done little to hide the man's broad shoulders and muscled forearms. He might have been able to converse easily with her while naked save for a slight covering of woollen material, but it had taken all her resolve not to let her eyes stray below his neckline.

The urge to run her hands over the bare skin of his torso was so overwhelming she'd had to clasp her hands together under her knees to stop herself from reaching over and touching him.

She might be naive where men were concerned, but she knew enough to know that these wild cravings did not end well. She and Aven had been the product of their noble father's unbridled lust. There had been no love in the union and when his passion had been sated, she and her twin brother were the unwanted by-blows. She would not wish that burden on any child of her own.

If she was ever able to break away from her male disguise, then she wanted a marriage based on mutual love or, at the very least, mutual respect. She hadn't seen an example of it first-hand, but she knew it existed.

She'd even wondered briefly what it would be like to experience such an emotion with William. He'd be the sort of man to treat his wife with respect. She was sure of that. But Avva had seen the look on his face when she'd told him she loved her brothers. He could not have looked more scornful. Then there was the fact that he was a nobleman... No, she must not think of love and William in the same sentence.

Her poor mother had not experienced any love. She had been forced into marrying her merchant stepfather when it became apparent her lover had finished with her, discarding her and her babes as if they were nothing. Their stepfather had treated her mother as if she were something he'd acquired at market. Her mother had been worn down by life for as long as Avva could remember, possibly due to her near-constant pregnancies.

Avva had adored every one of the babies her exhausted mother had pushed out into the world. Now there were only two of them left, Dylan and David. She would do everything she could to protect them. She would risk her own life to help William, but never her brothers'.

Whatever the outcome of this, it would not end well for her if she were involved. Nothing ever did for those who were not noble born. If Caerden or any of his cronies caught her, her life would end in a horrific way and her brothers would probably be punished even if they knew nothing.

Even as her head argued all the reasons she could not help William, her heart ached for the man who was lying beaten in her loft. She shouldn't trust him, or even care whether he lived or died, but for some reason she did. What was wrong with her?

Eirwen nickered and she moved over to his stall. The handsome horse peered over his door. She rubbed his long nose, but he tossed his head, knocking her hand off.

'I can't help him any more than I already have,' she murmured. 'It's too dangerous.' Eirwen snorted. 'You might think I lack courage but it is not just me I need to think about.'

The horse turned his head away. 'He'll be all right, you know. It's only a few bruises, they will heal. It's not as though he actually drowned. I saved him before there was any lasting damage.' Eirwen still didn't look impressed. 'All right. You win. I will go and check on him.'

She made her way to the bottom of the ladder and then stepped away from it. She should get William something to eat. He was a big man and would need feeding more than she did. He'd had hardly anything yesterday, as he'd slept most of the day away. She headed to the kitchens and managed to get hold of some fresh apples and seed cakes. Nobody paid her much attention in the bustling room but that didn't stop hot prickles of awareness running down her back, as if invisible eyes were watching her every move.

She rushed back out into the courtyard and took a few calming breaths. No one knew she had a battered knight lying in her loft. She must not act as if she were guilty of a crime. *That* was the fastest way to a trip to the torture chamber.

She forced herself to walk slowly back to the stable, even stopping to talk to John, chatting about the first signs of spring that were beginning to show themselves. She wasn't sure exactly what she'd said, but after a while she decided that she'd done enough to appear normal. She was just about to walk away when John reached out a weathered arm to stop her.

'Ave.' She turned to him. His normal, smiling eyes were serious and her heart stopped. 'Gawain was here earlier. He wanted to know what you'd picked up for me the evening before yesterday.'

Avva's blood ran cold—why hadn't she thought to warn John and ask him to cover for her? She'd never suspected that Gawain would check up on her, that's why. She was so foolish.

'I told him it was for the benches I'm repairing.'

Avva could only nod jerkily, fear gripping her movements.

'Be careful, Ave.' John's gaze was steady and kind.

'Thank you, John,' she murmured.

He nodded and turned back to his woodwork, appearing to forget about her instantly.

For a moment she could only stand and stare at his bent head, before she slowly turned back towards the stables, the food gripped tightly in her hands.

She climbed up to the top of the ladder without noticing she'd done it. She hauled herself into the space and then froze.

William's blanket had fallen to his waist, leaving his chest uncovered. The skin was covered in large purple-looking bruises and grazed skin, but that wasn't what stole the breath from her lungs or made her heart race.

She'd seen men stripped to the waist before, but seeing their naked bodies had never had an effect on her before. They'd never made every nerve in her body suddenly spring into life, craving only one thing: his touch.

The corded muscles of his stomach twisted as he moved and a strange fluttering sensation began in her stomach. Even as her brain screamed at her to look away, she found herself transfixed. Her gaze dipped lower still, dark hair curled beneath his navel, disappearing beneath the blanket.

Somewhere in the hazy distance someone cleared their throat and Avva started, the sound kicking her out of her trance.

She lifted her gaze and met William's eyes. His brown eyes were almost black, a simmering tension lurking in their depths, but there was laughter there as well. Heat flooded her face as she realised she'd been caught staring at his body. She hadn't even realised he was awake.

'Some food,' she said, thrusting the apples and seed cakes towards him.

He took an apple from her, his fingers brushing her hand as he did so. His touch caused the strange fluttering in her stomach to travel through her whole body. She moved away from him quickly. Everything about this man was dangerous, she must keep reminding herself of that.

'You're looking spooked. Has something happened?' His voice was raspy, almost as it had been when she'd pulled him from the river, but he'd been getting better, hadn't he?

She took a bite from her apple, chewing slowly.

When she was sure she could speak normally, she said, 'One of the guards was questioning my behaviour on the night I pulled you from the river.'

William reached over and touched her arm. 'I'm sorry, Avva. I will get out of your way as soon as I can.'

Even though that was exactly what she wanted, Avva was surprised to feel her stomach sinking. She wanted him to go, didn't she? Suddenly, she wasn't so sure. He was staring at her face, but when she didn't say anything he dropped his gaze and removed his hand.

'How is it you think I can help you?' The words flew out of her mouth before she could stop them. It wasn't at all what she'd meant to say. She'd meant to ask him when he thought he might be able to move out of here, but now she was near him she found she wasn't as keen to abandon him to his fate as she'd been telling herself.

William shook his head. 'No, you are right. It is too dangerous. You cannot help me. It was foolish of me to ask. When darkness falls I shall leave you.'

'Your injuries…' Her gaze dropped to his chest again and then quickly away as her stomach squirmed.

'I'll manage. You've done enough.'

This was what she wanted, so why wasn't she thanking him and climbing back down? After this evening, she never needed to see him again. The thought made her heart hurt. She closed her eyes tightly. What was happening to her?

'I have found your sword,' she said quickly.

Surprise flickered in his eyes. 'You have? Thank you, it was kind of you to risk yourself that way. Where is it?'

'It is stored in some hay to the side of the stables. Tell me how else you think I can help and I will let you know if I think I can do it. There is no harm in that.'

'I thought Edward wasn't your King.'

She turned away from him. Her words earlier had been born out of frustration and fear. King Edward III might be so far removed from her he might as well live on the moon. His father had brought war to Wales and she didn't trust his son not to do the same, but…

'I would not be doing it for the King, but for you.'

Her statement seemed to echo around the stables. Even the horses went quiet.

'Avva.' William's voice was deeper again, the intense look back in his eyes. 'Avva,' he said again, his breath appearing to whisper along the back of her neck, even though he was sitting on the other side of the room.

'Besides, if there is a treasonous plot in Caerden, then I would like to know about it. The more I know, the better I can protect myself and my brothers.' She didn't turn to look at him. She had to make clear to him, and to herself, that this was all there was to her offer to help him. It had nothing to do with the strange squirmy sensation in the pit of her stomach, or the way her body seemed to want to lie down next to his.

That was a physical reaction only. It was a reaction she knew she mustn't act on. She must remember her mother and the misery she had suffered all because she had succumbed to the late Baron's desire for her. Avva would not put herself in the same position, despite her belief that William was a better man than most.

'Right,' he said, still in that deep voice.

'That's all there is to it.'

Again, there was a strange silence. She hoped he would leave it there. If he said anything further, she would lose her nerve and leave the loft, making it clear she wanted him gone.

She heard his gentle exhale, but she still didn't turn to look at him. 'I'd like to know where Caerden and his men have gone.' He took another chunk out of his apple.

'That's easy. Caerden has taken his troops on a training exercise to the coast.'

William shook his head. 'That's not what I've heard.'

'Oh.' She did turn to face him then. He still hadn't covered himself with the blanket and she forced her gaze to stay on his face, away from the muscles that had such a strange effect on her.

His lips twitched—she obviously wasn't as good at

hiding her reaction to his naked body as she'd hoped. For a moment she lost the thread of their conversation. 'Where…?'

Fortunately that seemed to be the right thing to say because William carried on. 'I was told, by Thomas, that a castle to the north of here was experiencing trouble with raiders. According to Thomas, Caerden has taken himself, and most of his best men with him, to support his troubled neighbour. I have also heard contradicting reports that Caerden's men are camped outside Chepstow. I want to know which one of these is correct.'

'Oh, well, sometimes Thomas gets confused. Unless it's something to do with food or women, he can barely get himself dressed.'

'Avva, why are you having such a hard time accepting that the Baron is plotting against the King? It is not as if you have any love for Caerden and his ilk.'

'I…'

'This place is rotten to the core. There is no training at the coast. I don't believe there is trouble in the north either. I believe that Caerden is moving his troops into position for something. You said yourself Caerden is a man who thinks only of himself. Does he seem like a man who would go out of his way to defend a neighbour's castle?'

'No, but…'

'There is only one reason to move troops and it is not for peaceful reasons. I can assure you, neither the King nor any of his men have ordered the movement to defend or protect from an invasion of forces outside England. There is no large training exercise planned. It is suspicious, Avva, surely you can see that?'

'Yes, but…'

'And what about what we heard? Wasn't it obvious Thomas and Barwen were plotting something?'

'What we heard when?'

William cleared his throat. 'We heard them talking about how they wanted me out of the way. Remember? We were...we were behind the arras.'

Avva wished she wasn't looking straight into his eyes. She'd have stood a better chance of hiding her reaction from him. She could not stop the heat flooding her face as she remembered exactly what they had been doing in the hidden alcove, the way his mouth had moved over hers.

It hadn't been her first kiss.

That had been with an apprentice stable boy who'd been taken on at the castle stables at the same time as Aven. She'd believed herself in love with him, but it turned out it was his stories about the horses he worked with that had captured her attention. He'd kissed her a few times, but it had fizzled out and he'd married the baker's daughter.

Avva understood why now.

William's touch had lit something inside her, something she hadn't realised was missing. Something she wanted to feel again. But not now and not with this man, even if his lips were tantalisingly close to hers.

'I'll see what I can find out for you.' She pushed herself away from him, her heels scrabbling across the floor to get her to the edge of the loft faster.

'Avva...'

She paused, her legs dangling over the edge.

'Be careful.'

She nodded, before jumping to the ground.

As she made her way out of the stables, she couldn't help but feel that he'd been about to say something else. She wasn't sure whether she wanted to know what.

Chapter Eleven

William awoke with a jolt, his hand automatically reaching for his sword. He frowned as his weapon wasn't where he expected it to be. It took a moment for him to get his bearings. He was in Avva's loft and he must have fallen asleep again after she'd left. He hoped he had not slept away another day.

Below him came a noise, the heavy clomp of feet on the wooden ground, definitely not Avva's footsteps. Then came the frightened whinny of a horse and some muffled cursing—he'd recognise that distinctive baritone anywhere. Barwen Montford was back. How William loathed that man for his casual cruelty. He was another one on William's growing list who would experience his wrath before this mission was over.

'There you are. Saddle this horse up.'

'Bluebell, sir?' came Avva's softly spoken response.

'That's what I said.'

William didn't hear a response, but he assumed Barwen taking Bluebell was unusual. As quietly as he could, he leaned across to his clothes and pulled his dagger from its sheath. A single sign that Avva was being mistreated and he would gut the man like a pig, the subtle uncovering of a treasonous plot be damned.

He strained to listen, but the only sound he could hear was the creak of leather as a saddle was attached to a horse and the pacing of the heavy boots. Although he couldn't see anything, William assumed Barwen was moving impatiently up and down the length of the stable.

After what felt like an eternity of waiting, he heard a horse being led out of its stall and towards the entrance.

'Bluebell is highly strung, sir.' Avva's voice was strained. It probably cost her dearly to speak out to such a man. William couldn't help but admire her bravery at confronting Barwen. She obviously valued the comfort of her horses over her own safety.

'Don't tell me how to ride a horse, lad.'

'Ah, there you are.' William shuddered as Thomas joined the group. There was something about the man's voice that sent shivers down his spine. It wasn't that he was physically threatening, more like he was a cold, creeping fog that would swallow you whole if you didn't protect yourself. 'What will you tell Caerden about the knight?' Thomas sounded worried, which he should do. After all, William was alive and mostly well. The same could not be said for the men who attacked him.

'I will tell him the truth, Thomas.'

'But no one has seen the knight since I sent the men after him. He has not returned to the tavern or been seen in the town.'

'Neither have the men.'

'They were your men I sent after him, Barwen. Don't forget to tell Caerden that.'

'You should have seen to him yourself. You had plenty of opportunity. I understand the knight spent all afternoon with you. If I had been here, he would not have walked away from that encounter.'

William rolled his eyes. Barwen might be a fighter, but he was no match for William.

Thomas cleared his throat, clearly not pleased with the direction of the conversation. 'I could not have killed him, I do not have the same training as you.'

'That is true.' William could hear the disdain in Barwen's voice.

'Do you think not knowing the knight's whereabouts will change the plan?'

'The plan will need to be changed. I don't think Caerden will thank you for that. The objective is the same.'

Thomas inhaled deeply. 'Good.'

'We will go down in history.'

Thomas laughed. 'Caerden's name will go down in history. You and I will be forgotten, don't think otherwise. We will reap the rewards in his lifetime and that is enough for me.'

Barwen growled. 'You're a fool, who only thinks with his belly. This is a momentous occasion for all of us. Our names will go down in history because of the influence we will hold. The possibilities are endless.' Barwen made another sound of disgust. 'Return to your feasting, Thomas, and let the real men do the work.'

'If that is all you think I do...'

'It is not what I think, it is what is true. I don't profess to understand it, but you are useful to Caerden. Although how he will react to this latest foul up, I don't know.'

There was the sound of shuffling feet and then leather creaking again.

William strained to hear if Barwen or Thomas said

or did anything to Avva. He wouldn't be able to restrain himself if either of the bastards laid their hands on her again. He heard nothing—it was as if the two men had forgotten her presence. It was entirely possible, the stable master would mean nothing to them. No more was said and presently hoofbeats moved away from the stable door. The heavy plod of footsteps suggested Thomas was leaving, too. William waited until he was sure he could no longer hear anyone in the stable below before he pushed himself up onto his knees, the simple movement causing him more pain than he wanted to admit. He shuffled over to the edge of the loft and peered down to the ground.

Avva was standing with her back to him, her hands on her hips, obviously watching the departing rider. William's heart contracted. She looked so vulnerable and alone. He wanted to do something to make sure she was always protected, but he didn't know how he could achieve that.

He could find a position for her in his parents' household, but that would only cause future problems. He wouldn't be unfaithful to his wife and having Avva nearby, when William inherited the barony from his father, would be too much of a temptation. He would also have to see her married to someone else—a beauty like Avva would not remain unwed for long. No, it would not do. The jealousy would consume him. He would have to find a way to walk away from her, knowing that it was someone else's job to keep her safe. He closed his eyes tightly—enough of this.

'Where do you think he's going?'

Avva jumped, clutching a hand to her chest.

'Sorry, I didn't mean to frighten you.'

She turned, stepping into the stables as she did so. William experienced the same punch to the gut as he always did whenever he caught sight of her face.

'I'm coming up. Are you decent?'

William glanced down at his naked body. 'You probably wouldn't think so.'

'Then cover yourself up, before I get up there.'

William smiled and moved back to his corner of the loft, draping the blanket over his midriff.

Avva's head appeared over the lip of the loft, frowning as she caught sight of him. 'I thought you were going to cover up.'

He nodded to the blanket, fighting a smile at her indignant expression. 'I have.'

'Not all of you.' She waved a hand in the general direction of his chest.

He'd be damned if he covered up that part of him. He'd seen the way she looked at him earlier—it had given him a strange sort of hope that this ridiculous infatuation he was experiencing wasn't completely one-sided. Not that he could do anything about it, but it didn't seem fair that only he should be suffering from this overwhelming desire.

'Don't tell me you've never seen a man's chest before.' He shouldn't tease her, but he couldn't help himself. Watching the colour spread across her cheeks as she climbed into the loft gave him more pleasure than he'd care to admit to anyone.

'Of course I have,' she said frostily. 'I've just never seen one so...'

'So?' He was a bastard for teasing her, but this was the most enjoyment he'd had since he'd kissed her.

'You know exactly what I mean.'

He didn't, but he hoped it was complimentary and she wasn't repelled by the heavily bruised skin. Feeling slightly less confident, he pulled the blanket up a little way. She pursed her lips, but didn't say anything further.

'I don't know where he's going.'

'Who?' His muddled mind had no idea what she was talking about.

'Barwen. You asked me where he was going and I don't know.'

Dear God, what was wrong with him? He was so wrapped up in showing Avva his bare torso he wasn't concentrating on his mission. He was letting Theo down and, at the rate he was going, Benedictus, the King's Knights leader, was going to throw him out of the order before he'd even completed his first solo mission. This had to stop. Right now.

He shook his head, trying to clear his mind.

'What is Barwen's role exactly? I was introduced to him as someone who was a key figure, but it was not explained exactly how.'

Avva shrugged. 'Barwen is the head of the guards, but Thomas is lazy, remember. Barwen does a lot of his dirty work so that either Thomas or Caerden don't have to. Barwen delights in torturing people.' She shuddered.

William leaned back against the wall. This was so frustrating. If only there had been the slightest suspicion that something was off in this district before he'd set out on this journey, he'd have brought a team of men with him and not just James. He'd been too hasty in sending his squire away, too. If he hadn't, James could be following Barwen right now and William would never have lost that fight. Instead, he was stuck in a loft, lusting over a

girl who was pretending to be a man and essentially failing at what should be a simple mission.

He needed to get back on the right course. Even if it
killed him, he had to get out of the loft and get moving.

'Did you find out anything?' he asked, deciding that
the best course of action from now on was to look at her
as infrequently as possible. It was the sight of her that
seemed to addle his brain.

'I found out a little.' No, it turned out the sound of
her voice also got to him, damn it. 'There's no training
operation at the coast. Messages are coming and going
to Chepstow, to the east of here.

'Chepstow. Are you sure?'

'Yes.'

'Not from Caernarfon Castle?'

'No, definitely not. John's brother is one of the messengers. He stopped to speak to John before leaving
again.'

'You've mentioned John before. Who is he and can
you trust him?' William tried to ignore the sudden stab
of jealousy. He must remember that he would be leaving
here soon. Who Avva spoke to or married in the future
should be no concern of his. He couldn't, and wouldn't,
marry her, so why did his insides feel so twisted?

'John is the castle carpenter. He is as close to a friend
as I have in this castle. I trust him with this information.'

Relief flooded through William's veins, relaxing muscles he hadn't realised were tense. He remembered the
carpenter from Avva's tour of the castle. He was an old
man, who regarded Avva with an avuncular affection.
Theirs was not a romance.

'Do you trust him completely?'

'I don't trust him with my life, but then there is no-body I trust with that.'

William's heart clenched. For a brief moment he wanted to be the one she depended on, but he knew such wishes were impossible.

'And, no, I don't know what the message was, before you ask.'

He nodded. 'You couldn't ask without drawing suspicion, I don't want you caught up in whatever this is. It's not safe. How far is Chepstow from here?'

'About a day's hard ride, possibly more. Wait…what are you doing?'

'I need to get to Chepstow. I have to know what's going on. The life of the King depends on it.'

'How can you be so sure?'

'You heard him talking about the plan. What do you think that was about? No, I must go.'

'You can't go. You're…well…look at you.' She gestured to his chest again.

William felt heat spread across his face. She hadn't been looking longingly at his chest after all. She'd been disgusted by the bruises that littered his body. He was a hapless fool who deserved to fail at this mission. It would serve him right if he was thrown out of the King's Knights and the King denied him his petition.

'I cannot lie here, doing nothing, because of a few bruises,' he snapped, annoyance with himself coating his words.

He reached across to his shirt. It had dried, but the fabric was stiff and unyielding. He lifted his arms to pull it over his head, but stopped when cool fingers brushed along his biceps.

'Have you seen yourself?'

'Huh?' The soft touch had robbed him of proper words.

'You're battered. You nearly drowned.'

'I've had worse.' But he didn't carry on pulling on his clothes, not while Avva was still touching his skin. He held still, expecting her to move away at any moment, but instead her fingers lightly traced the curve of the muscles in his arm.

'Your skin is torn here.' She lightly pressed down. 'Does it sting?'

It hadn't until she'd prodded it, but he would keep that to himself. Anything to keep her hands on him for as long as possible.

The hairs on the back of his neck tingled as her fingers moved to his shoulder. 'There's not a patch of your skin that is not covered in bruises.' Her voice was soft and husky.

Slowly, so as not to spook her, he turned his head to face hers. She was close to him now, her blue eyes wide and her lips slightly parted. He leaned towards her, lightly brushing his lips to her soft cheek.

Her fingers flexed against his shoulder but she didn't pull away. He moved along her jaw, pressing small kisses against her skin. A soft sigh escaped her, his body tightened in response. He brought his mouth to hers. For a long moment, he hovered above her, feeling her breath flutter over his skin. Then, so softly he was barely moving, he pressed his mouth against hers. He held his breath, holding himself still until her lips moved. Her tentative response sent sparks of lust straight to his groin.

He reached up to touch her face, his fingers trembling as they lightly caressed her cheek. He was completely undone. No other woman had ever made him feel this reverence. He couldn't have pulled away if the King himself had ridden into the stable demanding attention.

His lips met hers again, a flicker of triumph racing through him as her mouth moved in a firmer response. He slid his arm around her waist and drew her nearer.

Her soft curves pressed against his body.

Their first kiss, behind the arras, had been all passion and fire—this one was as soft as a spring breeze, but no less powerful.

His fingers traced the length of her neck and along her collarbone, mapping her body, committing it to memory so that he could recall everything about her when she was no longer in his life.

Her fingers stole into his hair, her fingernails scraping against his scalp, and he groaned. The noise seemed to awaken something in her and she pushed against him more firmly. His ribs protested at the movement, but he ignored the pain and then he forgot about it completely as her mouth opened to him. He swept his tongue inside, the first taste of her so delicious it weakened his knees.

Their breaths were coming in pants now. There was nothing for him but the weight of her in his arms and the way her mouth moved beneath his. He wanted this moment to never end and yet, even as his hand traced the outline of her spine, he knew he should stop.

He could offer her nothing and so he should take nothing from her.

'Avva,' he murmured against her lips.

Her response was an incoherent mumble and he smiled.

Gradually, he slowed the kiss until it was the gentle touch of lips against lips again. His body roared at him to take things further, to lie down next to her and forget the world around them, but he battled to get the urge under control. He gently loosened his grip on her and brought both of his hands to her face, cupping her soft skin in his calloused palms.

'Avva,' he said again, slightly louder this time.

He lifted his head and gazed down at her. Her pupils were huge, her soft lips parted. She blinked. 'Oh,' she said softly.

'Oh,' he agreed, his voice sounding gravelly even to his own ears.

Avva licked her top lip with the tip of her tongue and he couldn't help himself.

He lowered his head and kissed her again. She responded instantly, her tongue dancing with his, her soft moans urging him on.

All reason and logic deserted him. He forgot why they shouldn't do this. His shaking hands grasped the ties of her tunic, tugging it loose. She helped him pull it from her body, seeming as eager as he to be closer. He traced her delicate curves under the thin woollen garments she wore. She was so thin, he could almost count her ribs. A part of his mind cursed Caerden for allowing her to get like this, but then he forgot everything again.

Her fingers, which had stayed on his shoulders until now, began to move. Darts of pleasure shot through him as her hands skimmed over his bare chest. Here and there his damaged skin burned under her touch, but it was exquisite torture.

He slowly lowered her, so that she was lying on the bed of straw and he was braced above her. She was so tiny and he was so huge, he didn't want to squash her, but she pulled him down so that most of his weight was on her delicate curves. Everywhere their bodies touched his skin came to life, demanding more.

Her hands were more confident now, skimming over his back and sides. He tugged her garment off one slender shoulder. She gasped as he kissed his way down the sensitive skin of her neck and along her collarbone.

His fingers found her breasts through the material of her gown, the nipples pebbling at his touch. He pulled the sleeve down until one was exposed to the air. It was small and perfect in his hand. She arched against him.

Raising himself up onto one elbow, he tugged the other sleeve down until both breasts were exposed to him.

He lifted his head. Her eyes were glazed now, her lips so red. Her breasts were the same creamy, pale skin as the rest of her body, her nipples pink and hard. He bent to take one in his mouth and she cried out.

He poured all the days of longing and lust for her into his actions and she writhed beneath him, causing the tightness in his body to harden further. He was moments from spending himself and they had barely begun.

Only her thin clothing and his blanket separated their bodies. He wanted to pull the clothes from her, to have all of her skin against his, but he knew that his tenuous grip on his self-control would disappear completely if he did that.

He wanted more than anything to hear her gasps of pleasure as he took her again and again. But he knew, even as his mouth worshipped her, even as all sense appeared to be deserting him, that it would be wrong. He had no doubt that it would be the most exquisite pleasure he had ever had. The way she responded to him, the way his body responded to hers, the way she made him forget the world around them, suggested that it would be unlike any other joining he'd ever experienced. Guilt would consume him afterwards for taking something only her husband should have. She would hate him and that would kill him.

Summoning all his strength, he lifted his head and gazed down at her.

She was breathing quickly, her chest rising and falling in rapid gasps. Her eyes filled with the desire he was sure was reflected in his. He wanted nothing more than to return his mouth to hers, but he stayed still.

He watched as an awareness of the world came back into her expression. Her gaze cleared and her breathing slowed, her lips forming a perfect circle as she whispered, 'Oh.'

He smiled down at her, but he still didn't move. He knew he should cover her up, but he couldn't bring himself to do it. He had used up all his willpower in stopping, but he didn't want to hide away her perfect body. He would never see it again and he wanted to burn the image of every contour into his brain.

'I...' she whispered.

He nodded, understanding what she could not put into words.

Her hands skimmed over his back as she brought them back to herself, setting off delicious tingles all down his spine. She blinked and it seemed to dawn on her that she was bare to him. Her hands scrabbled at her top, pulling the material up and covering herself.

'I... What...?'

Her confusion was adorable, lovable even.

He wanted to convey to her just what she'd made him feel, but the words were stuck in his throat.

He gazed down at her, waiting for the right thing to say to come into his head.

'Avva.' He cleared his throat. 'Avva,' he said again. A small smile appeared at the corner of her mouth. He touched it lightly with his fingertip. 'Avva, I have no words.'

'I know.'

He leaned down and rested his forehead against hers. 'I've never met anyone, who…' He paused. 'I've never felt…'

'You don't have to say anything.'

'But I want you to understand. This, it's not normal for me. You are special, but I can't…my parents…the barony…' It was as if someone had scrambled his brain. None of the words he wanted to say were coming out. He wanted to tell her how this was the closest he'd ever come to caring for someone, that, if he allowed himself to love, then he would love her, to explain why the emotion was so impossible for him. Before he could get his thoughts in order she spoke.

'I haven't asked.' His head whipped up at her tone.

The desire in her eyes had been replaced with something else entirely. The look she gave him was cold and hard, she pushed against his chest. He pulled himself upright, a strange uncomfortable sensation blooming around his heart.

'You're a nobleman. I am a peasant. I know that you are not going to marry me. You do not need to explain.'

Every word felt like the swipe of a blade. This wasn't what he'd meant at all. Marriage had been the last thing on his mind. That rational transaction had no place in the heat of this moment.

'Avva, I…' But she was pulling away from him,

threading her arms through her tunic. 'Avva, don't leave like this. Talk to me.'

'There is nothing to say. I will see if there is anything else I can find out for you. Good day, Sir William.'

With that, she swung her legs over the edge of the loft and dropped to the ground.

William watched her go, an unfamiliar feeling of helplessness washing over him. He should go after her, but really, what was there to say? There would be no marriage between them. His plan was still to marry into a wealthy family. Nothing had changed, but the pain in his chest was not down to the injuries he had sustained. He leaned back against the wall of the loft, the rough wooden slats biting into his skin. The irritation helped him focus. He was here to complete a mission and he needed to get on with it, not moon over a beautiful woman.

He was torn. At first, riding to Chepstow had seemed like the obvious answer to his current predicament. Once there, he could find out exactly what Caerden was doing with his band of soldiers and then make haste to the King's Knights rendezvous. Now that there was no way to communicate with James, this seemed like the most sensible option. His fellow knights wouldn't hesitate to act once he had told them about everything that had happened since his arrival in Caerden...well, perhaps not everything.

He would not tell anyone about his foolish attraction to someone so entirely unsuitable for him. He would not tell of the joy he had experienced when he had kissed her or the pain he was now feeling as he'd come to his senses and realised he could not have her.

He was not the sort of man who took a wife and a mistress, and a mistress was all Avva could ever be to him. She did not have the wealth he needed to restore the Devereux barony and he couldn't marry without it. He shook his head in exasperation. Why on earth was he thinking of marriage and Avva in the same sentence? His attraction to Avva was unusually intense, but it wasn't as if it would compel him to offer for her. He was not in love with her. This was lust, pure and simple. It would fade. He was not his parents.

William closed his eyes. His thoughts were straying away from his mission once more. He needed to focus. After some reflection, he wasn't sure that the best course of action was haring off to Chepstow. Perhaps it would be better to stay here for another day and see what he could find out before he left for Chepstow. Thomas didn't strike him as a particularly strong man. He would probably break after some forcefully applied pressure.

All of these ponderings were moot if he were unable to move very far. His muscles hadn't objected to movement when he'd been kissing Avva, but he had been quite spectacularly distracted.

It was time to put his body to the test. He pushed himself into a crouch. His chest burned, protesting vigorously at the movement. It was impossible to stand to full height in the cramped loft, but he did his best, stretching his muscles as far as they could go. Everything hurt, but it was manageable. He could get on a horse, if he absolutely had to.

He curled his hand around the handle of his dagger and tightened his grip. Pain burned along the cut on his biceps and his ribs throbbed, but he'd had worse in the past and managed to carry on. He wouldn't be at his fighting best, but he would still be better than most.

Chapter Twelve

Avva leaned against the tower wall. She loved this spot, so far away from the bustle of castle life. It was peaceful even when there were guards up here, too. This high up the cool spring breeze was bitingly cold. She blew into her cupped hands, trying to warm her fingers. She should climb back down and return to the stables. She'd been neglecting her duties for most of the afternoon, but William would still be there and she was not sure she was ready to see him again so soon after what had transpired between them.

She'd known he was a nobleman. She'd known that he would only want to dally with her and not offer her any kind of future. Yet she had still succumbed to his kisses. No, that wasn't quite right. It made it sound as if William had forced himself on her, and he hadn't.

It had been she who had touched him first. She could pretend that it had been to make a point about how badly damaged his skin was, but the truth was she'd ached to know what his body felt like under her caress. The muscles in his arms held an almost overwhelming fascination for her. She'd wanted to know whether they were as hard as they looked to the touch or whether they were soft. The answer was a mixture of both. The smooth skin had given way to a delicious hardness. She'd been unable to stop her fingertips from skimming over the curve of his arm and along the ridge of his shoulders.

She'd brought herself so close to his face. She wanted to lean across and brush her lips to his battered cheekbone, but shyness had frozen her. She couldn't have pulled away for all the wealth in the kingdom. The soft kiss at the corner of her mouth should have been a warning, not an invitation. Yet, even though he had given her plenty of time to think, she still hadn't pulled away, not even when he'd pressed his lips to hers.

In that instant, need had flooded through her, heating her blood and sweeping away all rational thought.

She had wanted his mouth on every part of her body, to explore the newly awakened sensations running through her. In the cool breeze of the afternoon, it shocked her to remember how far they had gone and to know that she would have gone further still. It was only William coming to his senses that reminded her of everything she held dear.

She *was* the result of misspent lust, of a nobleman abandoning her mother once he had finished with her. She wouldn't wish any child of her own growing up knowing that they were unwanted by their father. Even her stepfather, who hadn't cared for her or Aven, had wanted his own children.

All her life, she had sworn not to make the same mistakes as her mother. One touch of William's lips against hers and the promises she had made herself were swept away. She touched her neck—her pulse pounded beneath her fingertips at only the memory of what had passed between them, the way his lips had moved across her body, his beard tickling her sensitive skin, causing exquisite tingles to course through her. And when his mouth had reached her breast, she'd been lost to the sensation. That she would have lain with him at that moment should frighten her. An unwanted babe would be a disaster. And yet…the thought of carrying a piece of him after they had parted didn't seem so terrible after all.

She closed her eyes. She mustn't think like this. This way was wild, uncharted territory. It went against everything she believed in. She pressed a hand to her belly, unable to stop the idea of a baby growing in there, someone for her to love. Someone who would love her… No. She pushed the thought away. A child out of wedlock would only add to her problems, not solve them.

William would make a good father. It just wouldn't be to her children.

She pressed her palms to her face as a lump rose in her throat. Crying never solved anything and she was not about to give in to tears right now. Not now, when there was nothing to cry about. William had defied her expectations of nobility, he'd been honourable, kind and thoughtful. She could see that he was a good man. He cared deeply about his mission and the oaths he had taken. He would not take advantage of his position and hurt those beneath him. He was not like Caerden. That did not mean she should become his lover, no matter how much she might enjoy his caresses. But she could be his friend.

Right now, he needed her help and she could give that to him.

She pushed herself away from the wall. Mind made up, she would return to the stable and help him in what-

ever way, even if it meant aiding him in his journey to
Chepstow. Having seen his bruised and battered body
up close, she didn't believe he was capable of riding anywhere, not without assistance.

She reached the spiral staircase and stopped. Far in
the distance, she could make out two riders heading towards the town at speed.

Her heart in her throat, she watched as the pair came
closer. The riders were distinctive, her fears were confirmed. Caerden and Barwen were returning. She turned
on her heel and ran.

There was still no sound of the approaching horses
by the time she made it to the stables, her lungs burning
with the effort she'd made to arrive quickly. She rushed
over to the ladder and climbed up.

William was in the process of pulling on clothes. He
did not look comfortable.

'What is it?' he asked before she could offer to help.

'Barwen and Caerden are on their way back here.'

His eyes widened. 'Are you sure?'

'Yes, I saw them from the tower. They will be here
very shortly.'

He thrust his arm through the sleeve of his tunic.
'This changes things.'

'I know. I…' but she didn't get any further. The sound
of pounding hooves on cobblestone reached them. Avva
hurried down the ladder and picked up her sweeping
brush, quickly unbolted the door into Pebbles's stall and
managed to lock herself in before Caerden and Barwen
rode in.

Caerden jumped down from his horse and strode towards her. She couldn't help but cower backwards at
his approach, cursing herself for this show of weakness.

'You, lad.' He glowered at her over the door to the stall. 'Where is that knight's horse?' Avva's heart began to pound—she couldn't bear it if Caerden did anything to hurt Eirwen. 'Well, lad?'

Avva was annoyed to see that her hand was shaking as she held it up to point. 'At the end of the stables, my lord.'

She held her breath, her heart pounding painfully as the two men went to the end of the stables to take a look, but, to her relief, they did not open Eirwen's stall.

Caerden strode back to her. 'Has the knight been to check on his horse since he got here?'

'Not for the last two days,' she answered truthfully, holding Caerden's gaze.

'Do you believe the lad?' asked Barwen, coming to stand next to Caerden and glaring across at her. 'It's been reported that Ave here has been seen walking around the castle with Sir William. Perhaps the two of them are friends.'

Avva swallowed, her knees trembling. 'Sir William asked me to show him some of the castle, my lord.'

'That is Steward Thomas's job,' barked Barwen.

Avva nodded quickly, keeping her eyes on Caerden, hoping that some of Aven's kindness resided in her half-brother, although she'd never had reason to believe it before. 'Aye, it is. Sir William thought that Thomas might find it beneath him to show him the kitchens and the scullery and requested I show him. I thought it best to help one of your guests, my lord. Did I do the wrong thing?'

Caerden studied her for a long moment. Avva's pulse pounded. She hoped William would stay where he was and not leap down to her rescue. Caerden and Barwen were only trying to intimidate her at the moment, but if there was even the slightest altercation it was unlikely it would end well for her.

Caerden stepped closer to the door. Avva forced herself to stand still and not skitter backwards. 'Aven, you and I have known each other for a long time.' Avva nodded. 'I like to think that, despite our obvious differences, you are loyal to me.' Avva nodded again. It was unusual for Caerden to acknowledge their shared parentage, but he did now and then to assert his hold on her. She loathed it. Just as she loathed that his dark hair reminded her so forcefully of Aven—the three of them shared their father's distinctive locks.

'I am pleased you agree.' Caerden smiled in a gesture that did nothing to light up his eyes. Avva held herself upright, even as a chill raced down her spine. 'If you see Sir William, I want you to come straight to me. If you cannot find me, report your sighting to Barwen or Thomas. Do you understand?'

'Yes, my lord.'

'Are you sure you can trust him, Caerden?' asked Barwen, his eyes glittering with malevolence.

Caerden stared at her for a long moment. 'Yes. I am sure. Aven is very protective of his brothers, aren't you, Aven?'

Avva's stomach roiled at the unspoken threat to David and Dylan's safety. 'Yes, my lord, I care for my brothers deeply.'

Caerden smiled—this time his eyes did light up. His visage wasn't improved by the emotion. Avva wondered if perhaps Caerden thought she meant him when she referred to her brothers. He was arrogant enough to believe it, despite the fact that it couldn't be further from the truth to say that she cared for him. She despised him.

'See, I told you, Barwen. We can trust Aven to do the right thing. Come, we must plan our next move.'

Caerden moved briskly out of the stables, Aven seemingly already forgotten. Barwen spared her a final glare before following the Baron.

Avva quickly removed the saddles from their horses and led them into empty stalls. She was desperate to see what William had made of Barwen and Caerden's discussion, but if either of the men returned and found that she had not dealt with their mounts, it would raise suspicion.

She quickly saw to the horses' needs, her mind barely on her job, before clambering back up to the loft.

William was white-faced, his lips thin with suppressed emotion.

'Are you all right?' she asked softly.

His gaze snapped to hers and her heart jolted. 'I will kill him for threatening you like that. How dare he?' He dropped his gaze and began to strap his dagger to his body.

Avva's heart expanded, an unfamiliar emotion rushing through her. Other than Aven, no one had ever looked out for her before. It made up her mind.

'I will help you.' That stopped him. He looked across at her, his expression hard and unyielding.

'No, it is too dangerous.'

'You cannot do this alone.'

He smiled grimly. 'I have been trained for this, Avva. You have not. I do not want you in a position where you have to choose between your brothers' safety and helping me. Besides, I thought you didn't care for the King.'

'I...' How to explain to him that it was not the King she was worried about? That over the course of the last few days what happened to him had become important to her? But it wasn't just that. As Caerden had threatened her, she had become resolved. She could no longer live in fear. If there was a way to end this, then she wanted to be involved. She decided to appeal to William's logical side.

'You are badly injured. Whether you like it or not, you are going to need help. At the moment, only I am available.'

'Last time we were in a fight, I almost lost because I was so concerned about your safety.' She rocked back on her heels, hurt by the truth of his words. His eyes flashed and he reached out a hand before dropping it. 'I'm sorry, I didn't mean to upset you. I'm only telling you this because I want you to understand that while I appreciate your offer, I don't think your continued involvement is a good idea.'

She nodded. She didn't particularly want to get hurt either. 'I have a suggestion. I will help you, but at the first sign of violence I will run away. I would prefer not to be involved in a fight.'

He looked at her for a long moment. She held his stare. Eventually he broke away.

'Let me consider your words for a moment.'

She nodded. She knew what it was like to need time to think.

'I'll see to the horses. They still need rubbing down after their journey earlier.'

He nodded absentmindedly. Realising his mind was already elsewhere, Avva said nothing more.

Bluebell was surprisingly calm when Avva entered her stall. She allowed Avva to run a brush over her without any of her normal fussiness. She even seemed to enjoy Avva's gentle mutterings, which relaxed the other horses, but normally seemed to irritate Bluebell. The rhythm soothed Avva, too, and by the time she climbed back up to the loft she was almost contented.

William was fully dressed now, his dagger in place although his sword was still missing. Her heart fluttered as she took in his magnificent form. It was no wonder she had succumbed to kissing him—he was beautiful.

She was so busy admiring him that it took her a moment to take on board what he was doing. In front of him were several small piles of hay. He was pointing to one of them with the tip of his dagger and murmuring under his breath.

'What are you doing?'

'Running through various scenarios.'

'What does the hay represent?'

'The location of our enemies.'

'How do you know where our enemies are?'

'I don't. That's why there are many piles of hay.'

He looked up and grinned and the breath caught in her throat. She couldn't help but smile back at him.

'I need to get inside the castle,' he said, turning back to the hay.

'Now?'

He tapped his chin with the point of his dagger. 'Is it still light?'

'Yes, but not for much longer.'

He nodded. 'I'll wait until dark has fallen until I make my move.'

Avva's stomach twisted. It was happening now, whether she liked it or not. 'What is your plan?'

'Initially, I was going to try to join up with my fellow knights, but now I don't think there is time. The best course of action is to take down Caerden, Thomas and

Barwen either before they leave here and reach Edward, or before Edward reaches here. Either way, the men need to be stopped and soon.'

'You can't take them all down by yourself!'

William frowned slightly. 'Of course I can.'

'You're wounded.'

The corner of his mouth tilted upwards. 'So you keep saying, but I'm not so wounded I cannot take on three untrained men.'

Avva rolled her eyes. 'Thomas, I grant you, will not be difficult for you. To my knowledge, he has never been in a combat situation and is now so fat and so lazy that even I could take him down.' She ignored William's snort of laughter. 'Perhaps even Caerden will not be much of an issue for you if he is by himself. He is a trained knight, but he has become used to others doing his dirty work for him. Barwen…' Avva sucked in a breath. 'I have seen Barwen fight. He will show no mercy and delights in pain—even, I think, his own. He will not be as easy.'

'This is why I need to get into the castle. I—'

'They will be surrounded by their cronies. You cannot charge in there.'

'Avva.' William reached over and rested a warm hand on her arm. The touch sent a wave of tingles through her body. She was surprised she could feel such a thing at a time like this, but obviously her body wasn't aware of the seriousness of the situation because the sensations continued until he, disappointingly, removed his hand. 'I am not some untrained novice. I do know what I am doing. I will watch and wait for the right opportunity.'

Avva nodded. Of course, she was worrying about nothing. William was not like her and Aven. He'd had training. He could survive by himself. He would not die of an infection because he would not allow himself to be badly cut. And, even if he did, it would not be her responsibility to look after him. Either he would die, or his family would come and claim him. There was no reason for the sick, swirling sensation in her stomach.

'Avva.' She looked up at him. He smiled and brushed a strand of hair away from her forehead. 'It will be fine.'

'Of course. I should…' She gestured down to the stable below. He nodded.

'Please come and get me as soon as the sun has gone down.'

It was her turn to nod before backing away. She'd help him this evening and then she wouldn't see him again.

The serpents writhing in the base of Avva's stomach didn't calm themselves, even though the end of the afternoon passed without incident. She went to collect some food, just before sundown.

She didn't speak to anyone and no one even spared her a second glance despite the huge target she felt had been stuck to her front and back.

Back in her loft, she handed half of the food to William. The groups of hay had become more elaborate in her absence.

'Do these still represent our enemies?' she asked, her heart skittering when he looked up and smiled at her.

'Some of them.'

'Does this work?' She gestured to the piles.

'Yes, it helps me organise my thoughts. It's a trick Theo taught me.'

'Who's Theo? You've mentioned him a few times.'

'Theo is my friend and mentor. I met him when I

started my training as a page. He's a few years older than me.'

'Did he take you under his wing?'

William smiled around a mouthful of bread. 'Not in the beginning. He saw me as an irritant, a bit like a flea he couldn't get rid of and not much bigger than one of those either.'

Avva had a hard time imagining William as small. He was so big, he nearly filled her loft space completely.

'What changed?'

'He used to make me do all the worst jobs. Whatever he didn't want to do he ordered me to take them on. When that failed to keep me away from him, he gave up trying. I wore him down.' William flashed his big warm smile, reminding Avva of the sun coming out during a cloudy day.

'Why did you want to be his companion so badly?'

'Ah.' William broke off another hunk of bread. 'I'll tell you, but if you ever meet him you mustn't repeat a word of what I say.' His lips twitched and Avva resisted the urge to cross the loft and capture the movement with her mouth.

'Of course.' She didn't point out that she was very unlikely to meet this Theo and, if she did, it was unlikely a nobleman would want to engage in conversation with a stable master. She didn't want to remind William that he was different to most men. Not when she was enjoying his company so much.

'I admired him.' There was a glint of affection in William's eyes that caused a sharp pain in the region of her heart. It took her a moment to realise the pain was down to jealousy. She wanted him to have that look on his face when he thought of her, which was foolish. She didn't need William to care for her. Whatever happened, William would be gone from her life within the next day or so, she must remember that.

'Theo was the first person I met when I left my family. He was so calm and ordered, so unlike my parents who were the only people of authority I knew up until then. I wanted to be like him. I have spent my whole life striving to be as accomplished as him.' The light in his eyes died a little. 'And yet here I am. I couldn't defend myself against those untutored lugs.'

Avva straightened. 'That is not true. You were the only man who walked away from that fight.'

William smiled, although the smile didn't reach his eyes. 'I didn't walk away from it. You dragged me and hauled me up the hill in a cart like a bale of sodden hay.'

'You said that if you hadn't had to defend me, that wouldn't have happened and you know it's true.' She was getting angry now. How couldn't he see that he was a hero? She didn't know this Theo person, but she doubted his soul was as warm-hearted as William's.

'You were not to blame for my failure. Protecting people is my role. I should have done it better. No, there is no need to defend me again. I appreciate that you are trying to make me feel better and that is very sweet. But I know what I should be able to do and I fell short. It will not happen again.'

Avva shuddered at the steel in his voice. She believed that he would do everything in his power to protect those weaker than himself or that he would die trying.

'Tell me more about your parents.' She wanted to draw him away from his melancholy thoughts to something far away from here. There was a long pause where she thought he wasn't going to answer. Now that she'd asked the question, she was seized with the desperate urge to find out more about where William came from and what made him into the person he was now. 'I think you said they were always getting into foolish scrapes. What did you mean by that?'

William sighed, not looking a great deal happier to talk about his family than he'd been talking about his failings.

'My parents adore each other to the exclusion of other people, including me. It's isolating, that kind of love. There is no room for anyone else. I will never love like that.' Avva's heart constricted painfully, but she forced herself not to visibly react. 'They are…silly seems to be the kindest word to describe them. Foolish is another.'

'In what way are they silly?'

'They never think through their actions. They run from one thing to the next.'

'Do you love them?'

He frowned. 'Of course I do. They are my family. I am obliged to love them and they are endearing in their own way. It's just…growing up with my parents there was no order. I did not enjoy the uncertainty.'

There was more, she could tell. But he had stopped talking and was staring at a spot just behind her shoulder.

'I think you said you had sisters,' she prompted.

He shook his head, as if coming round. 'Yes, I do now. Lots of younger sisters. They seemed to keep coming for years, although they've stopped now. There were others, but they did not live long. That's what I remember from my younger years. My mother desperate for more children and them dying. The pain both of my parents suffered.' He shuddered. 'I never want to experience that soul-shattering love. That was the root cause of their monetary problems. My father would indulge my mother's every whim to make her feel better and people would take advantage of that generosity. They got through a lot of the Devereux fortune preparing a suite for King Edward II's visit.'

'Did he come?'

William snorted. 'No. I don't think he ever had any firm intention of visiting. Some merchants took advantage of a rumour.' He smiled without humour. 'The merchants weren't so thrilled when I paid them a visit not long afterwards, but by then it was too late. The money was gone and there was no way to get it back. Although get it back I must. My sisters must marry well and for that I need dowries, which is why...'

He looked away from her, a muscle twitching in his jaw.

Avva blinked back tears, telling herself not to be so foolish. She had known there was no chance of a union between them, their stations were so far apart, but a part of her must have hoped just a little bit. But now William had reminded her he needed a union that provided him with money and Avva had none at all.

That William desired her was obvious, but he had never said that he cared for her any more than the next woman. He had told her, more than once, that he didn't want to love, that love made people foolish.

She turned away, so that William wouldn't see her ridiculous reaction. 'This Theo is like a brother to you, then?'

'Yes, an older brother. The other knights are like my kin, too, although I am not as close to all of them.'

'Tell me about them.'

William finished the last of his food. 'Other than

Theo, there is Benedictus, our leader, and his brother Alewyn, a gentle giant, but it is Theo I am closest to as I've known him the longest.' He glanced towards the stable door. 'Is it dark yet?'

Glad for a reason to get away from William while she still had tears in her eyes, Avva dropped down into the stable and peered outside. 'It's dark and all is quiet,' she called up softly. 'Do you need some help getting down?'

William's face appeared over the edge of the loft. 'I'll be fine, thank you.' His head disappeared to be replaced with his feet. He took longer than he should have done to make it to the floor, but she didn't hear any grunts of pain. He turned to face her. His skin was pale and there was a sheen of sweat across his brow.

She didn't comment. From dealing with her brothers she knew that men didn't enjoy any weakness being pointed out to them. She suspected William would take it even worse. If there had been any doubt that she could leave him to investigate inside the castle himself, then the look of pain on his face completely extinguished it.

She would not leave him until the very end, even if it meant risking her own life.

Chapter Thirteen

Avva peered back into the courtyard. Everything was still and quiet. 'Stay there a moment, I will fetch your sword.'

The weapon was heavier than she remembered and impossible to conceal about her person. She hurried back to William's side.

'Thank you,' he murmured as he took it from her.

'Where do you want to go?'

'Can you direct me to a side entrance so that I can get into Caerden's inner sanctum without being seen?'

'I'll take you there.'

'No, Avva. I can't put you…'

'You have no choice.'

He took a step towards her. Lying down, filling her loft space, he'd seemed huge. Looming over her and glowering down at her, he appeared even bigger. She should be scared. Experience had taught her that big men were not to be trusted, yet instead of terror another sensation was building in her stomach.

She wanted to pull his mouth down to hers, for those

firm lips to press against hers, to run her fingers over the breadth of his shoulders.

'You can be as scary as you want,' she said mildly. 'I'm still going to insist on coming with you.'

He growled and the sound reverberated through her body.

She hid a smile—his domineering stance was having the opposite effect on her than he intended. Instead of being afraid, she was in danger of dragging him back up to the loft. Now was not the time to be having those sorts of thoughts. In fact, she should stop having those thoughts about William, even though her body kept insisting otherwise.

She moved away from him. 'Now is a good time to move. Caerden's meal begins at sundown. He should be eating for a while before retiring to his private room. I don't think even an impending revolt will stop him from lording it over everyone in the Great Hall.'

She slipped out of the stables into the evening air, leaving William with no choice but to follow her. She was used to hiding in shadows and the cluttered courtyard threw up many obstacles. She paused every now and again, listening for any unexplained sounds, but all was quiet. Most workers would be eating in the Great Hall now or visiting their families. Behind her came William's quiet footsteps, his steady breathing close to her ear.

They hurried around to the side of the keep, passing quickly by the main entrance. The babble of many voices talking at once reached them as they skirted the corner.

'Do you ever eat in there?' murmured William as they moved further into the darkness.

'Never. It's too risky. I don't want anyone paying too

close attention to me. Besides, Caerden is responsible for my brother's death. I cannot stand to look at him.'

She heard William's footsteps falter behind her before he caught up with her again. Perhaps she should not have told him that. It was something she kept to herself—not even her younger brothers knew the full circumstances of Aven's death.

William would have more questions, he always did.

'You never did tell me what the Baron did to your brother. Will you tell me now?'

Down this side of the keep, the darkness was so complete Avva could not see what was directly in front of her. She ran her fingers along the rough stone wall, searching for the side entrance.

'Avva.'

Her fingers touched wood and she stopped to grope for a handle. William reached out and grasped hold of her hand, stopping her movements. His hand was warm and dry around hers.

'You cannot leave it there, Avva, I want to know what Caerden is capable of. Please tell me.'

Avva took a deep shuddery breath. She could do this. She could talk about her darkest days—perhaps her heart would be lighter for telling the whole story. Lord knew it could not feel worse.

'Caerden and Barwen like to hunt.' She swallowed. Telling this story was harder than she'd anticipated. The terror she always experienced whenever she thought about this dreaded event, the fright experienced by all of the townsfolk, gripped her even though it wasn't happening right now. William's thumb brushed the underside of her wrist, giving her the courage to carry on. 'Sometimes, when there are not enough animals around, they send some of the villeins into the woods and tell them to run. They made…well, Aven was quite often one of them. Aven was fast and agile and always eluded Caerden and the other nobles until the time he didn't.' William's hand tightened on hers, pulling her towards him. She leaned her head against his chest, drawing comfort from the warmth of him. 'Most of the time those captured only receive a pummelling. Nobody wants to be beaten up, but mostly young men are chosen for the hunt and they are fit and healthy enough to recover eventually. On this particular hunt Caerden and Barwen caught Aven. Barwen said something to Caerden, something to taunt him. Caerden didn't like that. He took his anger out on Aven, lashing out with a knife and cutting him in several places. They left him there and it took me a while to find him. By then, it was too late and an infection had already set in. Aven was unlucky.'

A long moment passed, Avva concentrated on the rise and fall of William's chest. That was what mattered now, the living man in front of her. She had cried enough for Aven.

'What did Barwen say?' asked William eventually.

Avva pulled away from him—it turned out she wasn't ready to tell William everything yet. She wasn't sure she would be able to bear the look of disgust on his face when he realised Caerden was her half-brother. Once he knew, he couldn't unknow it. Could she really trust him with her deepest secret? Her heart told her that she could, even that she should, but her head argued that this was too much. Why share something so personal with someone who didn't, and couldn't, love her? 'Look, we don't have all evening to get you into position. You need to let go of me so that we can move on.'

William said nothing and he didn't let go of her hand. Avva tugged herself free. 'We need to go.'

This time she found the handle with no trouble and the wooden door swung open easily. She heard William inhale as if he was about to speak again so she stepped into the dark interior of the castle. Any more confessions could wait. A drop of icy water landed on her forehead and she shuddered. 'This passage is only used by the scullery boys and they'll be busy with the evening repast.'

'Why is this corridor unlit?' William's voice was gravelly, a tone Avva hadn't heard before running through it.

'Caerden wouldn't want to waste candles on the boys.'

'Don't they come to harm this way?'

'Of course they do. That's not something Caerden bothers himself with. I thought that would be obvious to you by now.'

William followed Avva silently, but she was sure she could hear a low rumble as if he were growling. As they got deeper into the keep the clanging and shouting of the busy kitchen at work grew louder.

'Is there a way to avoid going through the kitchen?'

Avva stopped in her tracks, bristling at his words. 'I've kept you hidden for days and brought you into the castle through a side door, but, yes, I'm now going to make you walk through the kitchen where everyone can see you.'

Behind her, William chuckled. The sound nestled close to her heart. He took a step closer to her, his breath brushed along the sensitive skin of her neck. She resisted the urge to lean back into him.

'Sorry,' he murmured into her hair. 'I didn't mean to make it sound as though you don't know what you are doing. I'm not used to depending on another person.'

His apology melted her irritation. She turned slightly towards him. 'There is a way around the kitchen. We will need to be quick and quiet.'

'I trust you.'

She was glad of the dark as her cheeks warmed under his praise. Without another word she set off down the remainder of the dark corridor. As they turned a corner, light from the kitchen spilled out on to the corridor ahead. She came to a pause just before the first pool of light. 'This is where it gets dangerous. Normally, I would walk into the kitchen now and take some food. I don't often meet anyone, but that's not to say it can't happen.'

'Then we'll be quick and quiet.'

She nodded, taking in a deep breath. 'Let's go.'

They walked quickly without speaking. A loud crash from the kitchen had Avva throwing herself against the wall. William's hand flattened against her lower back, urging her on. Her heart pounding, she forced her legs to move. 'That's it,' whispered William. 'Keep going.'

She barely breathed until they rounded another corner and were once more plunged into darkness.

'Are you all right?'

Avva's whole body began to tremble. 'I…'

William pulled her into his arms. 'You're shaking.' He held her tighter. 'This is too much for you. I should never have involved you. Please go back to the stables. I can manage from here.'

She shook her head against his chest. 'I'm fine. I'm staying with you.'

'Avva…'

'Don't argue or I won't tell you which way to go.'

'I could work it out from here.'

'I'd still follow you.'

He laughed and she realised he'd known exactly what to say to calm her down. She was no longer trembling, his words had taken her mind off her fear. Something strange shifted inside her as she realised just how well he had come to know her. She knew she should get moving, but she was reluctant to pull herself out of his arms. One large hand smoothed the length of her spine and she arched into him. He grunted as her body connected with his and she stepped back quickly. 'I'm sorry, I forgot you were hurt.'

He let out a sound halfway between a laugh and a groan. 'That's not why I… I'm fine. Let's get moving again.'

She turned back, her cheeks warm even though she wasn't sure why.

'His room isn't far now. Just up this staircase and a little bit along. What's the plan when we get there?'

'The plan is for you to leave me there and return to the stables.'

'We've been through this. I'm not leaving you unless there is some danger to my life. Now tell me, what are we going to do?'

She heard his deep sigh, but he didn't say anything more about her leaving. 'I plan to wait in Caerden's room until he turns up. When he does I shall make him reveal his plan to me and then…'

'And then?'

'And then, we shall see.'

'Are you going to kill him?'

There was a long pause, so long that Avva didn't think he was going to answer. 'I might have to. Is that a problem for you?'

Avva reached the top of the flight of stairs and stopped outside a wooden door. 'Only if you make me leave.'

William gently moved her out of the way. 'Understood. But please let me enter this room first. We don't know if he's decided not to attend the meal in the Great Hall this evening. If we find him waiting in there, I'd far rather it was me he saw first than you.'

Avva allowed herself to be gently pushed to one side. She wanted to see this through to the end, but she'd prefer to come out of it alive. She wanted the opportunity to live in a world where Caerden wasn't a constant threat.

Now that this series of events was set in motion it was possible, even probable, that Caerden would meet his death. With his ending Avva would finally have justice for Aven's death. Perhaps this wasn't the most Christian thought to be having about her half-brother, but Caerden had caused so much pain and suffering for so many families, including her own, that she doubted anyone would be saddened by his passing.

The sound of the handle turning reverberated around the corridor. William glanced down at her and shrugged. If Caerden was inside, they had just lost the element of surprise. William pushed the door open fully and entered the room before Avva had truly realised what was happening. She scurried after him. Apart from William, the chamber was blessedly empty. William was standing a few steps into the room, a thick frown crossing his brow.

'This room makes me incandescent with rage.' William's fists were tightly clenched and he was staring at a thick rug as if it had done him a great wrong.

Avva stared down at it, but she couldn't see what was making William so angry.

'Caerden has so much wealth and yet those who depend on him are starving. It's not right.'

A strange sensation began to unfurl around Avva's heart. It was as if her heart was expanding, filling up her chest until there was no room left for anything else. This strange new emotion was directed at William—his protectiveness was making her experience something she had never felt before.

He turned to her. 'Is everything all right?'

Her throat felt tight, she didn't trust herself to speak. She nodded wordlessly and moved further into the chamber. A large table took up a big portion of the room and she ran her fingers over the golden spine of the bible resting on its top. She wondered if Caerden had ever opened the book—he certainly had never shown any sign of having any Christian spirit.

She swallowed a few times. The blockage in her throat appeared to have passed, but she knew herself to be irrevocably changed somehow.

'Will you wait for Caerden in plain sight or will you hide?' she asked to fill the strange silence that was building between them.

William tapped a long finger against his chin. 'I think it would be best to hide from him to start with. I always find information obtained under threat of torture to be less reliable than information freely given. He may talk to his cronies and reveal more of his plan.'

Avva pressed a hand to her stomach. She'd known William's world was a violent one, but hearing him talk so calmly of torture made her stomach turn.

'Avva.' She looked up at him. He was smiling gently at her. 'There's no need to look so stricken. I do not torture people as a general rule. Now, I think the best place to wait is behind this arras in the large window seat. It's unlikely he'll head straight over here so it should buy us some time. Besides…' William pulled the arras back, revealing a deep alcove '…it will be more comfortable than crouching behind the chair.'

He smiled at her again and her heart fluttered. She had no idea what that meant, but she didn't think the sensation was a good one. Oh, it felt lovely right now. It was as if her heart was taking flight and the world was a much brighter place just for his smile. She had a horrible feeling, though, that these strange new emotions settling on her were something much deeper. That it wasn't just an appreciation for the way he made her body react when he touched her.

She brushed past him and moved into the alcove. The space was lined with cushions and soft rugs. She settled herself close to the window and looked out of the milky glass. She could just make out the faint outline of the crescent moon. She touched her fingers against one of the panes, her fingertips resting lightly against it. 'I've always wanted to know what glass feels like. It's colder than I imagined.'

William dropped the arras back into position, making sure the material hung low beneath the edge of the alcove opening, as it had before they had entered the room.

The space seemed a lot smaller now that his bulk filled it up. This close she could smell him, that delicious mixture of outdoors and male. She kept her gaze on the window, not trusting herself to be so near him and not reveal the new emotions and sensations that were swirling about inside her.

'Avva.' A small thrill shot through her at the sound of her name on his lips.

'Yes.'

'Will you look at me, please?'

She turned her head. He was so close, his large brown eyes looking directly into hers. She only had to lean forward and their lips would be touching. She tucked her fingers under her thighs to stop herself from doing anything foolish.

'Avva.' He glanced down at her mouth and she knew he was thinking along the same lines as her. She had to stop him before they both succumbed to the madness that had gripped them earlier. It would be blissful, but she knew that was all they could ever share. A man in William's position would never marry her. And an unwanted baby would only make her like her mother, an outcast until some man took her on, a man who wouldn't want to be saddled with another man's bastards and who would not treat her kindly. If she kept that thought to the forefront of her mind, she should be able to resist the temptation of him.

William moved towards her, his lips slightly parted, her heart hammered in her throat. She had to stop this before it began.

'Baron Caerden is my brother.'

William froze. 'What?'

'Not my full brother. Only Aven was that. Caerden is my half-brother. We have the same father.'

William rocked back as if punched. 'I don't understand.'

Avva laughed, although she felt no humour. 'It's fairly simple, William. I imagine it happens all over the country. The late Baron took a shine to my mother, a couple of years after his marriage to his wife, the late Baroness. According to my mother, he actually treated her with some level of affection, which was more than can be said for his later mistresses. Anyway, it was not like she had a choice. No one could say no to the Baron and not live to regret it. Aven and I are a product of that relationship. The Baron lost interest in her when she had two squalling babies. He married her off to my stepfather. I don't think either of them were pleased with the arrangement.'

'I see.'

Avva pulled her fingers out from underneath her and twisted them together on her lap. She could see from the look on William's face that she had killed any desire he had for her. She tried to remind herself to be glad, even as her heart ached.

They sat in silence, the quiet almost a living, breathing entity filling the space between them.

William slowly exhaled. 'Does the current Baron acknowledge the kinship?'

'No—well, sometimes he does. It depends on whether he wants to taunt me or not. Aven and I have hair exactly like him. It's quite distinctive and impossible to deny really. That's what Barwen was taunting Caerden about on the day he attacked my brother. That's what caused Caerden to lash out. I think he was aiming for Aven's face, but Aven was able to protect himself and Caerden only cut his arms and chest. I say *only*, but the wound killed him. When I turned up to work in Aven's place, Caerden didn't question it at all. I think he had forgotten the incident.'

William nodded slowly. 'I will enjoy gutting him like a pig.'

Avva watched as a myriad of emotions crossed William's face. He was angry, she could see that in his tensed jawline, but there was something else at play, something she didn't understand.

'I will enjoy watching you do so,' she said eventually.

William moved so fast, she didn't see it. She only felt his fingers as they plunged deliciously into her hair. Where before there had been coaxing, this time there was only heat. She moaned as she opened her mouth and his tongue swept in.

His hands skimmed over her, tracing the length of her spine, her hip, her calf. All her doubts and fears fled as the rough skin of his palm encircled the bare skin of her ankle. She only wanted to feel more, more of him, more of his skin touching hers, more of his beautiful body eliciting exquisite sensations within her.

She wasn't aware of it happening, but somehow she was lying down, half of his delicious weight resting on her. Her fingers traced the nape of his neck, but it wasn't enough. She wanted to touch the corded muscles of his back, to imprint the memory of what they felt like against her skin.

His hand skimmed over her knee and across her thigh. The ache that had been building at her centre since they'd kissed earlier came rushing back. She pushed against him, silently pleading with him to ease it.

He grunted and raised himself on to his forearms. She tried to tug him back down. His absence was not what she wanted. He smiled against her mouth as she realised his intent. He pulled her tunic from her, the rest of her garments followed quickly.

Her bare skin was so sensitive, the slight press of his leather belt against her hip had her moaning in pleasure.

'So beautiful,' he murmured as he traced his lips along her jaw. 'So perfect.'

Avva had never felt beautiful or perfect before, but, right now with his mouth on her, she believed him.

His mouth moved down her body, his stubble scratching against her soft skin, sending tingles sweeping through her in its wake. Her breath began to come in breathy, little moans. She had to pray that Caerden didn't choose this moment to enter his private room because she could not keep quiet, not when this need was building inside her, becoming deeper with every heartbeat.

And then she forgot about Caerden completely as William's mouth settled between her thighs. Right at the place she needed him most.

The first sweep of his tongue had her body bucking off the cushions beneath her.

'William,' she gasped, shocked at how something so strange could be so wonderful.

She felt his answering smile against the curve of her thigh. Never had she imagined a sensation so pleasant, so overwhelming. She wanted it to go on for ever, and yet it was building towards something, something that was shaping and changing her. Her whole world was his tongue moving over her. Everything else ceased to exist as William worshipped her body. Her fingers stole into his hair, pinning him in place. Awareness was building within her, becoming tighter and centring at her very core. It was glorious. And then it shattered, snapping out to every corner of her body. She cried out, unable to keep silent in the moment.

William stayed with her as the sensation slowly faded from her body, leaving her limp and bone-tired in an immensely pleasing way.

He seemed to realise when her body had gained some semblance of normality. He gently kissed her hip and then the soft flesh beneath her ribs, slowly moving back up her body until his face was level with hers again.

He kissed her lightly on her lips and then pulled back to look into her eyes. He was smiling at her, softly, as if they had just shared some big secret, which she guessed they had.

No one would ever know what had passed between them today. No one would ever know how much had changed since this morning. Now she could put a name on the sensation that had unfurled around her heart. She loved him. No one else would know that, too, not even him.

He was a knight, who would go off and work for the King for many years. He would marry his wealthy heiress and provide dowries for his many sisters. He was not fated to belong to her, but she would know that she loved him and that was enough. It was just one more secret she would have to keep to herself.

He would leave her, like everyone did eventually. But she would have the memory of what had happened between them to keep her warm and happy throughout the rest of her life.

He pulled her into his arms and she curled into his chest. She thought about covering herself up, but dismissed the idea as too much effort. His lips ghosted across her forehead and she sighed softly. She was strangely content, despite the unusual surroundings.

Beneath her ear, William's heartbeat slowed from racing to a gentle, soothing thud.

'We should get you dressed.' His voice rumbled in her ear.

'I suppose.'

Neither of them moved.

'It will be hard for you to keep your male disguise if someone sees you now.'

Avva laughed softly.

Reluctantly, she pulled herself away from him, cool air rushing over her as she did so. She shivered.

'Avva, I...'

She touched his chest. 'Don't.'

'But I...'

'There is no need to say anything.'

'But there is much to say. If love was possible in my life, then please know that I would...'

She pressed her hand to his mouth. 'Please don't say anything more. What we have shared has been beautiful for me. Let's leave it as a wonderful interlude. It will be something to remember with happiness, not with regret.'

She pulled her clothes back on, not looking at William while she did so. When she had smoothed the material out, more times than was necessary, she allowed herself to meet his gaze.

His brown eyes were filled with an emotion she didn't recognise. He appeared on the point of saying something more, but the door to the room clicked open and real life came flooding back to them both in the sound of many hurried footfalls.

Chapter Fourteen

'I thought you said you had dealt with the knight.' William wasn't sure, but he thought that voice belonged to Barwen.

'There's been no sighting of him since I sent men to deal with him.' That was definitely Thomas. William would recognise his sycophantic voice anywhere.

'Until tonight.'

Silence greeted that statement as cold fear wrapped itself around William's heart. Not for him. The others would find out he was still alive soon enough, but if he had been seen, then surely so had Avva.

'We don't know for sure…'

'My man was confident.' Damn, William didn't recognise this person's voice. Just how many men were in the room?

'And they think he was with the stable master?' William glanced across at Avva—her eyes were wide but she showed no other sign of fear. She mouthed 'Caerden' at him. William nodded as his heart pounded painfully. They knew about her helping him. She was no longer safe and it was all his fault.

He was trapped in this alcove, unable to do anything as the men beyond the arras threatened Avva's safety. With his aching ribs and battered body, William wasn't completely sure he would be able to fight more than one man at a time. It went against everything he stood for, but he could not risk charging out of his hiding place right now.

He should have left Avva in the stable as he'd planned. He should have stuck with his convictions and not allowed her to come. Instead he had given in to his desire to have her with him at all times. He was a fool. Even more so because he couldn't quite bring himself to regret his decision entirely, not after what had just passed between them. He was beginning to understand a little of what drove his parents' relationship. He wanted to keep Avva safe above everything else, even over the safety of the King. The thought scared him—this couldn't be happening to him right now.

'Yes,' said the unknown man. 'Rowan said he clearly saw the knight with Aven Carpenter, heading towards the side of the keep.'

'I should have killed that whelp when I had the chance,' Caerden growled.

Beside William, Avva went very still. Everything inside William was roaring at him to charge from behind the arras and run Caerden through, but the unknown quantity of men in the room held him in check.

If anything happened to him, then Avva would be unprotected, not a great situation to be in when Caerden had just all but threatened to kill her.

'We must assume that Sir William is within the keep and that he knows something about what we are up to.

We must hunt for him and this time there must be no doubt that he is dead. I want to see his body for myself.'

'Come now, my lord,' said Thomas. 'Sir William cannot know about our plot to kill the King. In all my dealings with him, I gave nothing to suggest that we didn't wholeheartedly support His Majesty.'

Avva flinched as a loud thud followed by a muffled groan sounded. 'Thomas, you're an ignorant fool. You should have overseen the killing of him yourself. Your squeamishness has got us into the situation we find ourselves in now. Sir William will hardly think we are in favour of the King. The very act of trying to kill one of the King's Knights makes it obvious we are not on the same side as Edward. No, I've had enough of your ineptitude, Thomas. Rokas, take him to the dungeon.'

'You can't do that,' protested Thomas. 'I know too much.'

There was a long pause. Beside him, Avva held her breath as they waited for Caerden's next move.

'Good point. Rokas, ensure Thomas is not able to tell anyone of our plans.'

'No, you can't...' William could hear the panic in Thomas's voice. By threatening Caerden he had invited his own death and there was nothing now that would change that. Thomas would not live to see tomorrow. William shrugged—he couldn't bring himself to care about the fate of a man who didn't care about anyone other than himself.

'I think you'll find I can, Thomas. I should have done it years ago. You've become a liability in a game where the stakes are too high to make any mistakes. Come on, we have no time to waste. We need to find this knight and put an end to his stay at my castle. Barwen, you will search the upper levels. Rokas, when you've done with Thomas, begin the search outside. I have some business to attend to. I will join you when I have finished. Let us be quick. This will all be over within the next few days— let's make sure we are on the winning side.'

William gripped his sword, his soul rebelling on letting the men move out of the room, a creeping dread that he was failing at every turn settled over his body.

'I need to get to my brothers.'

William jumped. In the heat of the moment he'd almost forgotten about Avva. He turned to her. Her eyes were blazing with emotion, but not fear or anger like he'd expected. She should be berating him for getting her into danger. Right now, he hated himself for doing it. Instead she looked as if she were about to march into battle. Fear gripped his heart at the thought of her doing just that. She must be kept safe at all costs.

'You can't,' he told her. 'You have to hide. You heard Caerden. He is going to kill you if he catches you.'

'You don't understand. I know how Caerden and Barwen act. When they can't find me at the castle, they will send men to fetch my brothers. It won't matter that Dylan and David don't know where I am and that they have no idea who you are. At best they will be punished by association. I don't even want to contemplate the worst.'

'No, Avva. I forbid it.'

Avva ignored him and began crawling out of the alcove. He grabbed her ankle, the gesture so different from the loving way he'd held her only moments ago. 'Avva, I will not let you put yourself at risk like this.'

She kicked out, trying to shake him off. He gasped as her foot connected with his ribs, but he only held on tighter.

'Oh, I'm sorry. Did I hurt you?' She half turned back to him, her eyes filled with concern.

Her touch had hurt, but that wasn't the point right now. 'It's fine.' He waved away her concern. 'What is not fine is your belief you can help your brothers at this point. The best thing you can do for them is to remove yourself from the situation.'

'No.' She pushed herself away from him and slithered out of the alcove, landing in a heap on the floor below. William followed her, but not quite quickly enough to stop her. She pulled herself up and skirted around the Baron's table, almost reaching the side door before William managed to untangle himself from the arras.

'Avva.' Her hand just brushed the wood of the door before William's hand encircled her upper arm. 'Listen to me for a moment.' She didn't struggle from his grip. He was far stronger than her, but he would die rather than hurt her.

'You must find and deal with Caerden and his men.' Her voice was cool and calm. He might almost think her unaffected if it wasn't for the fine tremble running through her. 'I must protect my brothers. There is nothing to discuss.'

William's heart contracted painfully. He knew what she was saying was right. He had a duty to go after Caerden. He had sworn an oath and his very existence was meant for the protection of the King. He had to leave her and the thought was killing him. 'The moment you leave the safety of my side your life is in danger. I cannot...' He shook his head, words failing him.

She reached up and lightly rested her fingers against his chest. 'My brothers are all I have left in the world. If Caerden and his men go after them to get to me, then

I will never be able to live with myself. I have to go to them and warn them.'

His whole body screamed out that this was wrong, even as his mind worked through the possibilities. He couldn't go after Caerden himself and keep her safe. The ideal would be to keep her hidden, but perhaps the next best thing would be to remove her from the castle.

'Do you promise that you will head straight to your brothers' home? You will not go to the stables to collect anything on the way or stop to talk to any of your friends.'

'I don't have any friends.'

'Avva.' He hoped his voice carried some of the desperation he was experiencing, because this was an intolerable situation and this solution was the only way he could find it in himself to let her go.

Some of what he was feeling must have come across in his voice because she nodded. 'I promise I will head straight there. I will not go anywhere else, no matter what happens.'

'Thank you.' He pulled her tightly towards him and kissed her thoroughly.

And then he let her go.

They might never be alone again.

She would never know what she meant to him and what it cost him to walk away from her. He wasn't entirely sure himself, only that she had become important to him in a way no one else had done before.

But she would be safe and he would do his duty as he'd been trained to do.

Although he said none of these words, something of what he was feeling must have been evident in his face because her gaze became stricken. She dropped her head until she was intently studying his chest.

'Thank you, Avva, for everything you have done for me.'

She nodded. 'I wish you luck, William. Please know that the time we have spent together has meant everything to me.'

Slowly, he released his grip, his fingers trailing over the back of her hand until he finally let go.

'Hurry, Avva.'

She turned and fled.

William ghosted down an empty corridor.

From Thomas's tours of the castle, he knew the basic outline of the keep. On this level were the Great Hall and Caerden's private chambers. Below him were the kitchens and several other rooms of industry and above them was the long chamber, the one Thomas had shown him as suitable for the King's visit.

He paused. Where would Caerden suspect William to hide? He hadn't seemed to believe that William would head to Caerden's private chambers, which was the first place William would check if he had been in the man's position.

William leaned against the wall and listened.

The faint murmur of many people talking could be heard coming from the front hall, along with the scurrying of servants bringing and taking food away. There was no sound that William would associate with the urgent hunt for him. No shouting or running footsteps.

He turned back on himself and made his way to the large chamber. That was cavernously empty, too. He ran softly through the remaining rooms on the upper floor, but they were eerily deserted.

William returned to the large chamber and stopped still. Could Caerden have known he was in the room? If so, everything he'd said while in there could have been a lie. Or not all of it—Thomas's fear had sounded real, but the rest, *that* could all have been said to send William running off in the wrong direction.

Whatever the truth was, Barwen was not up in these rooms and William was wasting time searching through them.

The darkness of the corridor didn't stop Avva from running. She had to get to her brothers, she had to warn them that she had put them in danger by the very fact that they were related to her. She would give her brothers time to hide and then she would go back to William. She would help him, even if it meant death to her. She was too far in this now to back out, she had to see it through to the end.

She burst through the side door and tripped over something. She sailed through the air, her breath leaving her in a whoosh as she hit the ground.

'Do you know, I never had siblings to play with at home and I always wanted to try that one. Thank you, Aven, for falling so spectacularly. It was very enjoyable to watch.'

Avva lay where she'd fallen, unable to catch her breath and unable to believe what she was hearing. Her worst nightmare, Caerden taunting her through the darkness.

'Do you think you've already killed the whelp?' Barwen asked. Bile rose in Avva's throat, at the realisation he was here, too. She would not live to see another day, but if there was anything she could do right now to keep William and her brothers safe, then she would do it. Whatever it took.

'No. I don't think he's dead yet.' A boot connected with her ribs. 'He's still breathing. Tell me, Aven, is Sir William about to come hurtling along after you, or is he searching for us within the keep?'

'Caerden, we don't have time for you to toy with the lad. Two of my best men are hunting for Sir William. We should go before that blasted knight slows us down.'

Caerden ignored Barwen. 'I want to know what the knight knows, Barwen. I want to know whether he has found another way to warn the King. We put a stop to his squire's meddling in our plans, but that doesn't mean William can't have found another way. Aven can tell us that.'

Avva closed her eyes. She had no doubt Barwen and Caerden would torture her to find out the information she had. At least they would not need to bother with Dylan and David—hopefully her brothers would get through this. She had given them the best start she had been able to. She was only sorry she wouldn't have a chance to say goodbye to them.

'I'll take Aven to the dungeon master,' Barwen said. 'He'll get the information we need out of him while we leave. We can have him send a messenger with the information he is able to obtain.'

'No, please.' Avva would rather die here, out in the open, than at the hands of the dungeon master. She had never set foot inside his domain, but she had heard the screams, and sometimes the smell, emanating from the place. It was impossible to ignore when someone was being tortured.

'It speaks.' Caerden's tone was mocking and hard.

'I'll tell you what you want to know. Please don't take me there.'

'So you'll help me now, little brother?' Caerden bent down, so close that his breath whispered through her hair. 'Did the knight send for reinforcements?'

Avva's mind scrambled to keep up, pain radiating down her side.

Caerden crouched down and grabbed hold of a fistful of Avva's hair. Lifting her head, he forced her to look directly at him. 'What does Sir William know?'

'He knows everything,' said Avva breathlessly. She wasn't sure whether this was true or not, but she hoped it would disconcert Caerden. She was right.

'Damn it, Barwen.'

'The lad's lying. Do not doubt that. The King is on his way to Chepstow—he wouldn't do that if he knew of our plans.'

'And you believe that?' demanded Caerden, his fist still in Avva's hair. 'You are sure your spies are not double-crossing us?'

'I am.'

So, spies were working against the King. William's mission had been doomed to failure before it had even begun. Avva wished there was some way she could let him know, but she probably did not have long left on this earth.

'Are you lying to me, Aven?' Caerden had turned his attention back to her.

'I...don't know what you are talking about, my lord.'

Caerden tightened his fist in her hair and shook her head. She bit her lip to stop herself from crying out in pain.

'Where is Sir William?' Caerden asked again.

'I…' It was on the tip of her tongue to say that William was in the castle, but it turned out Avva couldn't do that to him. In that moment she realised she would rather die a horrible, agonising death than betray any of her knowledge about William. 'I don't know,' she said quietly.

Caerden stood. 'I think you are right, Barwen. A little time with the dungeon master will help Aven remember.'

Avva whimpered as Caerden pulled her to her feet, his fingers biting into her flesh. He threw her towards Barwen, who took hold of her arm tightly.

'Meet me by the horses as quickly as possible. We ride tonight.' Caerden disappeared into the darkness, leaving her alone with Barwen. She tried to tug herself from his grip, but he held her with bands of steel.

She would not beg. She would not cry. She would meet her fate with dignity.

Barwen dragged her towards the courtyard, sparing no thought as to how her legs would keep up. She stumbled and he pulled her along on her knees until she found her footing again.

They crossed the courtyard. She caught sight of people she knew before they scurried back into their domain. She didn't blame them for not coming to her rescue. She would not have done so in their position either. Barwen was too powerful.

She smelled the dungeons before she reached them. She gagged at the stench and she heard Barwen's laughter. She swallowed, trying not to show weakness but it was getting harder now as they approached her fate.

Barwen threw her down the steps. Unprepared for the movement, she didn't put her hands out to stop herself as she plummeted to the bottom. Her face landed on dirt, her mouth filling with it. She spat it out as footsteps made their way towards her.

'This is Aven Carpenter. He has information regarding a knight called Sir William. Find out everything that you can.'

'With pleasure,' said the dungeon master, grasping the back of her hair and yanking her to her feet.

'See that a messenger is sent with the information.'

'In what direction?'

'On the road to Chepstow.'

'Very well. I don't think this will take long.'

Barwen laughed. 'I don't think so either.'

Avva's legs turned to water. She had never experienced much physical pain. She did not know how long she would be able to hold out. She only knew a little about William anyway and none of it, other than his whereabouts, would help Caerden. She knew that William was still in the castle. She knew that she loved him and that she would die for him. That was all.

'I don't know anything,' she called out to Barwen's retreating back.

'They all say that,' said the dungeon master as he dragged her further into the chamber. 'But you'd be surprised by how much people reveal when they are put, say, on the rack. In fact, I think that's where we'll start with you. Now some people like to show their prisoners the rack first. It gives them the opportunity to spill their secrets without being tortured. I'm not going to do that with you. I'm going to start with the torture straight away.'

Avva inhaled a shuddery breath. She wanted so badly to be brave, but she feared she might start screaming before anything happened.

She tried to pull herself out of the dungeon master's

iron grip, but although she was strong, she was no match for this man. Silent tears began to course down her face as they reached the instrument of torture. She'd never seen anyone on it, but she knew what it would do to her. She wasn't going to go on it without a fight.

Using all her weight, she pushed against the master. He grunted as he stumbled back.

'The more you struggle, the worse this will be for you.'

'No,' she cried, pushing him harder.

He fell to the ground, but didn't release his grip. She screamed as she fell on him. His knee connected with her stomach and she screamed again.

He grabbed a fistful of her hair and pulled her off him. 'Enough.'

They continued to tussle, but Avva knew it was a losing battle. When a manacle closed over her wrist she began to still. She would need her energy to help her keep her wits once the pain set in.

As the second manacle snapped shut she began to think. The dungeon master would want something from her. She could tell him anything. It didn't have to be the truth. She could tell him that William was really gravely injured after his fight with the five men. That there was no way he could travel after Caerden and Barwen. Caerden and Barwen would relax and then William could take them by surprise.

She closed her eyes as the dungeon master began to prepare the rack. She would have to withstand the pain for a while to make the information seem believable.

The dungeon master was speaking to her while making threats about what he was going to do to her, but she switched off. If she was going to die here, then she would

be damned if her last moments were filled with his vit-
riol. Instead she would remember something good, a moment in her life when she was happiest.

She searched through her memories. She remembered
laughing with her brothers, Aven alive and healthy, but
even in that happy thought she could picture her stepfather in the background, disapproving of their merri-
ment. She had not been fully happy and relaxed. The only
time she had really felt that way was in William's arms.

She pictured his deep brown eyes, laughing at her.
She felt the weight of his body as he pressed down on
her, his lips on hers and the way he had worshipped her
body with his mouth.

A far-off bang sounded, bringing her back to the present. The dungeon master was gazing back towards the
entrance where another bang sounded. He straightened,
then moved towards the sound.

Alone in the dark, sweat began to bead across Avva's
brow. She wasn't in any pain. The manacles were uncomfortable, but nothing worse. It was more the anticipation of what was to come that was causing chills to
race down her spine.

Loud banging came from nearby, but she couldn't dis-
tinguish the noises from her own pounding heartbeat.

There was a sharp crack and then silence.

Avva began to concentrate on her breathing, a steady
in and out through her lips.

Footsteps sounded on the stone floor. And then…

'Avva. Oh, my God, Avva.' She knew that voice. Was
it from her imagination?

Hands moved to her bindings and she whimpered,
bracing herself for the oncoming pain. Instead the manacles were loosened and her arms were pulled free.

'Avva, say something.'

'William?'

'Yes.'

'Caerden and Barwen…they are…'

'I know.'

'Wait, the dungeon master. He could come back. You need to run. Get away from here.' Her heart began to pound frantically. 'He will kill you if he finds you in here.'

William's heart contracted. How like Avva to think of his safety before her own. Even while chained to the rack she wanted him to look after himself. She was wonderful, his Avva. How he'd ever thought he could kiss her and then walk away, he would never know.

The blinding terror that had coursed through him when he'd heard her scream would never leave him.

William pulled her to her feet. He would love to have a moment to hold her, reassuring them both that she was still alive, but there was no time.

'The dungeon master,' she said again, clutching at his arm.

'You don't need to worry about him. He won't be troubling anyone again.'

'Did you kill him?'

'I did.' William grimaced—it hadn't been much of a fight, not nearly enough to satisfy his rage. Next to him Avva staggered. 'Can you walk?'

'I think so. I was only in there briefly.'

'A moment is too long.' She staggered again and he curled his arms around her. She was so fragile against him, her slender body trembling.

'I'm not hurt. I think it's the shock.'

He didn't respond. Instead he swept her up into his arms and lifted her off her feet—she weighed virtually nothing.

'You don't have to carry me. If you give me a moment I'm sure I'll be able to walk.' He didn't respond to that. She might speak bravely, but she clung to him, her arms wrapped tightly around his neck. 'You can put me down.'

'When we're outside.'

She didn't make any further protest and he allowed himself the pure joy of holding her in his arms.

'Why did you come to the dungeons?' she asked as they reached the base of the steps.

'To rescue you.'

She frowned. 'How did you know I was in there?'

'I heard you scream.' He shuddered. 'The sound will haunt me until I die.'

'I'm sorry.'

He snorted. 'You have nothing to be sorry for. I got you into this nightmare. You didn't want to help me from the beginning and you were right not to want that. I have led you and your family into danger.' And he would bear the guilt for the rest of his life.

'I could have walked away before now. I wanted to help.'

'I thought the King was nothing to you.'

He realised he was desperate for Avva to tell him she was doing it for him. It was a foolish hope, especially when he'd given her no indication he felt anything more than desire for her.

They reached the outdoors and Avva took in huge gulps of fresh air. 'Put me down now.' She wriggled in his arms and he gently set her on the ground, missing the contact immediately.

'You didn't answer my question,' he reminded her, more desperate for her to answer than he'd care to admit.

'You didn't ask one.' Her tone was clipped, not inviting further discussion. He pressed on anyway.

'Why are you helping when the King means nothing to you?'

Avva turned away from him, her shoulders rising and falling. 'I don't want the town to be tainted by a treasonous act. The repercussions could be awful. Besides, now that they know I am involved, I need to see this to the end.'

Pain bloomed around his heart. A pain he couldn't really explain to himself. Why did it matter why she wanted to help him? Why was the answer so important? Especially now when he should be riding to the King's aid.

'I see.' He pressed a hand to his chest, trying to ease the ache.

She turned back and gazed up at him. How he wished he could read her mind. He wanted to know what was going on behind those blue eyes. She licked her lips and he held his breath. 'Caerden and Barwen, before they left, they wanted to know if you'd sent for help.'

He let out a long sigh—so she was not about to confess to feelings she obviously didn't have. It was time to get back to the mission.

'I sent my squire, James,...'

'They know about him, but they said they'd managed to stop him meddling.'

William frowned. 'In that case, the worst has happened. I must assume that the King's life is in grave danger.'

'Caerden and Barwen are on their way to Chepstow. They believe the King is heading there, too.'

'I can't allow them to get there.' William turned and headed for the stables. Avva hurried after him.

'What do you suggest we do?'

'You stay here. I'll go after them. You and your brothers should be safe for now.' William strode down the centre of the stable until he reached Eirwen's stall. The horse nickered in greeting, stretching his head over the door to reach William's hand. 'Please could you get me his saddle?'

'Of course.' Avva went to the spot where she'd stored Eirwen's saddles and side-bags. William watched her go. He didn't want this to be it, to be the last time he saw her. He knew it was foolish to want to prolong the half-agony, half-hope of their encounter. He wasn't even sure what he was hoping for exactly. Perhaps some sort of sign that it would hurt her as much as him to be parted.

'Do you know the way to Chepstow?' she asked as she helped him strap the saddle to Eirwen.

'You're not coming with me, Avva.' As much as he wanted her company, he would not risk her life again.

'There's nothing you can do to stop me riding alongside you. I'd probably outstrip you given your current condition.'

He laughed despite himself.

'If you take me with you, it will be quicker and easier.'

'I can possibly see how it might be quicker with you showing me the route, but how exactly will it be easier?' William strapped the last of his saddlebags to Eirwen's flank.

'Your ribs are still damaged. If I guide Eirwen along

the fastest route possible, you can conserve your energy for the fight ahead.'

He could see the sense in what she was saying, but he couldn't work out whether that was because he wanted her with him.

He exhaled slowly. 'Avva, when I heard you scream, it was worse than any physical pain I have ever received. If it wasn't for me, you wouldn't have been in that dungeon. I'll have to live with the knowledge that I put you in danger for the rest of my life. You could have been tortured for days.' William leaned his head against Eirwen's neck. 'You can have no idea...'

'William.' Avva gently placed her fingers against his cheek. He turned into the touch, resting against her palm. She ran a thumb along his cheekbone, his eyelids flickering shut. They stood like that for a long moment. 'I'm going to come with you.'

He smiled. 'You are very stubborn.'

'I know. It's endearing.'

He laughed softly. 'I wouldn't call it that.' His smile dropped and he fixed her with his powerful gaze. 'I would appreciate your help in getting to Chepstow, but I want you to take Eirwen and leave as soon as we arrive.'

This was important. He wouldn't take her if she didn't agree. He knew he couldn't live in a world where she didn't exist.

She nodded. 'I promise.'

Chapter Fifteen

Avva didn't wait for William to change his mind. Vaulting up on to Eirwen's saddle, she waited for him to leap up behind her. His approach was slower, his movements stiff, reminding her that despite the way he had rescued her, he was still in a lot of pain.

When he was seated, she kicked Eirwen into motion. The powerful horse broke into a gallop before they hit the courtyard.

She thundered past the guards stationed at the gate, not stopping even when they called out to her. Then they were flying. She laughed as the wind rushed through her hair. Every day she'd longed to ride like this, to experience the power of some great animal moving beneath her. It was as amazing as she'd imagined.

William's answering laugh sounded in her ear. His large hands slid around her hips, holding on to her loosely.

They cleared the bridge quickly and were out of Caerden before they spoke again.

'Eirwen is magnificent,' she called back to him.

'You are.'

She twisted in the saddle to look at him. His gaze was intense. 'What do you mean?'

'Look at what life has thrown at you and yet here you are, racing towards danger with a smile on your face.'

'The smile is because of Eirwen.' *And you,* she didn't add. She knew her feelings were foolish, but she would enjoy this last bit of time together for the gift that it was.

His large hand reached up and traced the length of her jaw. 'I'm sorry for what happened earlier. I should not have…'

Her heart dropped. He was not talking about the dungeon, but about what had transpired between them in Caerden's private room.

'Don't.' She covered his hand with hers. 'Please don't be sorry. We both have different lives. I don't belong in yours and neither do you fit into mine. We both know this. Don't apologise for what happened between us. I don't regret it—in fact, I rejoice that I got to experience such pleasure. Nothing has ever given me such enjoyment. I would never have believed a nobleman would be thoughtful and generous. Until now I thought you were all bad. Our time together has shown me there is the possibility of a brighter future.'

'Avva…' His fingers moved over her cheek and across her forehead. As if he, too, were mapping her in the way she had done to him. 'You are killing me with your generosity. I do not know what I have done to deserve this time with you.'

She only smiled at his words, unable to express how much they meant to her. Before long, he dropped his hand and they both turned to look at the road. They didn't speak, but William laced his fingers with hers on the reins and that was enough.

* * *

Once they were out of Caerden's lands, Avva brought Eirwen to a slower pace. It was a long ride to Chepstow and she didn't want Eirwen to become too exhausted to get them there. They only stopped briefly to allow Eirwen to rest, before carrying on. Avva dozed in the saddle, her head falling back on to William's shoulder.

She woke to find his arms wrapped tightly around her, shielding her from the cool, early morning breeze.

'How far along are we?' asked William, his voice husky.

Avva licked her lips, her mouth dry after a night in the open air. She took in her surroundings, recognising the shape of the hills, and was able to say quite confidently, 'We're about halfway.'

She felt his nod against the top of her head. 'I thought as much. We should get there well before nightfall then?'

'I think so.'

They lapsed into silence. Avva traced the back of his arm with her fingertips. He tightened his hold around her. She wanted to talk to him, to find out more about the life he would lead after he left her, but another part of her shied away from the questions. She couldn't imagine him carrying on his life without her in it.

The road to Chepstow was quiet. They only passed one man pushing a cart as the afternoon began to drain away.

'Are you sure this is the way they were heading?'

'Yes.'

'It would make sense if this is the direction his troops were stationed and yet we have seen no sign of anyone.'

'The village of Ferwalt is nearby, perhaps we will find out some information there.'

'Perhaps.'

They lapsed into silence once more. Eirwen did not need much direction and the exhilaration of riding had worn off. Avva paid almost no attention to their surroundings, aware only of the press of his chest against her back, the way his long fingers curled around hers and the solid weight of his body moving behind her. She touched the back of his hand lightly and his fingers flexed around her. Something bubbled up within her. It wasn't until a laugh burst out of her that she realised it was pure joy. A strange emotion to be feeling right now.

'What's so funny?'

'It's just…' She waved one of her hands in front of her. She couldn't explain all the emotion swirling inside her, but it seemed William understood.

'I think I see.'

'You do?' She turned slightly to look up at him. His dark brown eyes were fixed on her.

He nodded. 'For us, this could be the end of everything we know. If we get this wrong, we both risk everything we hold dear and perhaps even our lives. It's exhilarating, letting go of the ties that bind us to our normal life.'

'Yes, that's it.' Although it wasn't quite all to Avva— it was also the speed they were moving, the immense power of the beast beneath her thighs and the man behind her. William, who had shown her how to make her body sing, William, whom she loved so deeply but who would never be hers. It was everything combined together that was making her giddy. As if she had drunk too much ale at a feast and had fallen headfirst in love, which she supposed she had.

'Can you smell that?'

Avva snapped upright, pulling away from William's body. The tone of his question suggested he was not experiencing the same overwhelming emotion as her.

'Smell what?'

'Wood smoke.'

Avva sniffed. 'Yes, faintly. Perhaps we are nearing Ferwalt.' She slowed Eirwen to a trot.

The ground beneath them started to slope. They rounded a bend and found a wide valley spread out below them. Nestled between the slopes was a small village.

'Something's not right.'

Avva squinted, the fading light making it difficult to see. 'What's wrong?'

'Something's burning.'

'It couldn't be a normal house fire?'

'We wouldn't be able to smell that from here.'

Sure enough, a thick, grey plume of smoke rose above the trees.

'Ride,' growled William.

Eirwen responded to the tone of his master's voice and began to fly down the steep path into the valley. Avva heard William's grunt of pain as she held on tightly. Wind whipped at her hair, but this time there was no joy in the sensation.

She wasn't afraid. Her whole life had been lived in fear. Now she was choosing to head towards danger. She was seeing whatever this was through to the end. If she died today, then so be it. She'd tasted more joy in the last few days than she had ever expected to experience.

Eirwen's hooves pounded on the dusty path. William's

hands rested against her ribs. She rethreaded her fingers with his.

They rounded a bend in the path and Avva screamed. In front of them a fire raged as a building began to collapse in on itself, the falling wood sending sparks into the sky. But that wasn't what held her attention.

Barwen and Caerden stood on one side of the path, a group of Caerden's soldiers behind them.

There were five other men, covered in soot, facing them. They all had their swords drawn and seemed ready to fight, but they were dangerously outnumbered.

'Avva, you must go now.' William tilted her chin until she was facing him. He pressed a rough kiss to her lips. 'I'm sorry life couldn't be different. Take good care of yourself.'

'What's happening?'

'Caerden and Barwen have found the King.'

William didn't explain any further. He leapt down from Eirwen and slapped the horse on the rump. Without any further commands, Eirwen wheeled around and started galloping away from the scene. Avva twisted in the saddle. William was striding towards the men, drawing his sword as he moved. There was no sign of his injuries now; he looked every inch the warrior she knew him to be.

Eirwen rounded the bend and the scene disappeared from view.

Avva tugged on the reins, willing Eirwen to slow. The horse's training was absolute and he showed no signs of obeying his rider, following instead the command his master had given him.

'Slow, boy, come on now. William's in danger. We need to go back.'

Her heart quickened as over the pounding of hooves she heard the unmistakable clang of metal against metal.

'Please, boy. I cannot leave now.' She tugged harder on the reins and Eirwen dropped to a trot. She patted his sleek neck. 'Good boy.'

Under her gentle coaxing he eventually came to a complete stop. She jumped down and rummaged through the saddlebags. 'There must be a weapon in here somewhere.'

She knew William didn't want her anywhere near the fight, but that wasn't going to stop her. She'd already come to peace with her death, but not with William's. He must live and if there was anything she could do to make that happen then she would. Her hands closed around a dagger. That would have to do.

She found a tree stump and tied Eirwen up. 'I'm not taking you with me. I know you're used to battles, but I can't bear the thought of you getting hurt because of me. William will come back for you. I am sure of that.'

Eirwen tossed his head and Avva took that as he understood.

She moved quickly back down the path, but she didn't run. She needed to formulate a plan. She had the element of surprise on her side, but she wasn't a good fighter and she was tired. The day already felt as if it had gone on for years. If she could only occupy one of Caerden's guards, then that would be one less for William and the men fighting with him.

She paused before the bend in the road. This was it— once she turned the corner there was no going back. She inhaled deeply and then stepped forward.

The fight had progressed since she'd last seen it. William and other knights had formed a cage around the thinnest man of the group. Her heart pounded as she realised this must be the King. They were surrounded on every side by Caerden's men.

No one noticed her arrival.

She moved into the shadows at the side of the path, hoping the fading light and the undergrowth would hide her until she got closer. She realised Caerden was speaking. 'There is no way out for you, Edward. Surrender to us and we will let you live. Continue in this foolish resistance and you will end your life today.'

The men around him jeered in agreement.

'I will never surrender to you, Caerden.' The middle man spoke and Avva's heart missed a beat at the confirmation that this thin young man *was* the fearsome King. He did not look old enough. 'It is you who will die today.'

The men laughed outright at this. Avva couldn't help but agree with their assessment of the situation. She had seen William fight and knew he was good—presumably his fellow knights were, too—but she remembered what had happened at the river and they were outnumbered far more than five to one here.

William and the other knights held steady. Avva crept forward, the palm of her hand slick around the handle of the dagger.

'You leave us no choice, Edward.' Caerden pulled his sword from its scabbard with a flourish. Avva bit back a snort. She had seen Caerden at swordplay and knew that, if it were a fair fight, he would be no contest for William. Caerden was lazy and would not deliver the killer blow himself. He would let others do the work for him.

Barwen on the other hand...what he lacked in technique, he would certainly make up for in sheer insanity. He would not stop until the King and William were dead.

She took a deep breath. She had made her decision. Once the fighting started, she would go after Caerden. She was stronger than him, of that she was sure. It would take everything that she had, but she would keep him away from the main fight. His fate could then be decided by the King.

One of Caerden's men stepped forward, grinning. Others pressed forward, following his lead. William lost no time in countering their blows. She had barely reached the group and already William and his fellow knights had dispatched four men.

The smiles had already left the faces of the attackers. They were serious now that they'd realised William's skill. The other knights equally matched him and, for the first time, Avva thought that the situation was not as impossible as it might seem at first.

Avva had been right. Caerden stayed away from the fight, watching it all with a maniacal grimace. Barwen was directing the fighting, pointing out weaknesses in the knights' defence.

She spared one last look at the man she loved. He still hadn't seen her approach. He was fighting, ducking and wheeling and countering blows as they rained down on him. He looked magnificent. The sight of him gave her strength. She turned away, ready to begin her own battle.

William glanced up from his fallen opponent. Sweat dripped into his eyes. He had never fought so hard with so little chance of success. The fighting was raging on. He knew he, and the King's Knights, would carry on until all their enemies were slain or until their own lives ended.

They weren't winning, but they were holding their

own and their enemies were losing men. If they could move the battle nearer to the village, there might be an opportunity for escape. He ran his sleeve across his forehead, wiping some of the sweat away. Another man was taking his fallen opponent's place. He raised his sword and then...his whole world dropped away from him.

Avva. What was she doing here? Eirwen should have taken her far from this battle, yet here she was, one of his daggers clutched tightly in her hands as she approached Caerden as yet unseen.

The soldier, sensing William's distraction, threw a heavy blow towards him. William only just managed to block it in time.

The fight continued. Swords flashed and men cursed. Through it all William caught glimpses of Avva and Caerden. His heart swelled in his chest as he watched her advance on Caerden, no trace of fear in her posture.

The fighting moved on and William lost sight of her. Then it turned again and he glimpsed her—she was holding her own, fighting against a man who was significantly taller and stronger than she. They appeared to be shouting at each other, but he couldn't make out the words over the clamour of swords. Caerden took a swipe at her, but she dodged it easily.

She was beautiful, his warrior girl, absolutely glorious in her determination.

'We need to spread out,' yelled the King, pulling William's attention away from Avva. It was not the first time the King had issued such a command. His knights had ignored the order previously. There were too many men to risk his liege's life, but now...they had made a serious dent in Caerden's forces. If the King were allowed to fight, too, they might end this battle in their favour.

It was a risk, but it was a calculated one. But also, and most important to him, was that spreading out might give him the option to help Avva.

'I think he's right,' shouted William above the din.

'It's not an opinion, men. It's a demand.'

William ignored the King. His liege he might be, but Edward's safety was the responsibility of his knights. Benedictus was their leader and none of the knights would do anything without his say so.

'I agree,' called Theo.

'Spread out,' yelled Benedictus.

Without any further discussion, the five of them formed a line. Now William had an uninterrupted view of Avva. She was fighting with everything she was worth and Caerden, coward that he was, was backing away. His heart thrilled—she was going to win.

William felt a surge of triumph, which just as instantly vanished as Caerden called for help. Avva stooped to pick up a sword, but she was too late—a soldier was upon her.

Without thinking, William threw himself over the body of a fallen man and cut her attacker down before he had a chance to engage.

He pushed Avva behind his back. 'I told you to stay away from here,' he yelled, as she tried to get around him.

'I never agreed to do that. Let me at Caerden, William. I can finish him.'

'No. You need to leave. I could not bear it if anything happened to you.'

Her hand curled around his biceps. 'I feel the same about you, William. I cannot leave while your life hangs in the balance.'

'We will win.'

'Then there is no danger in me staying. Go and help your King, William. I will not leave.'

Without waiting for his response, Avva moved away from him. Caerden was hiding behind a soldier and so Avva joined the fray, heading towards Caerden's spot and carrying on the fight. There were only a few men left now. The King was a superior fighter and with knights on his side they were more than a match for the remaining soldiers.

Sensing defeat, a few of them ran from the scene and then there was only Barwen and Caerden left.

Avva was leaning on the sword she had taken, breathing heavily. Caerden was a few steps away, glaring at Avva but, coward that he was, not engaging her in a fight.

Theo was wiping his brow, a satisfied smirk covering his face. William hoped his mentor wasn't too complacent. Barwen wasn't a man to take defeat well. He would fight like a caged beast.

'You've lost, Caerden.' Edward's voice was steady and confident. The voice of a king in victory.

'It's not over yet.' It wasn't Caerden who answered, but Barwen, whose wide eyes were fixed on the King.

Barwen turned and nodded at Caerden. Together they sprang towards Edward, but they didn't get far. William caught Barwen in a deadly blow, while Theo tackled Caerden. It was over in moments.

William turned to look at Avva. Sweat and mud coated her face, her hair clung to her head in clumps—even so, she was the most beautiful woman he had ever seen. He couldn't believe that he would have to walk away from her, that he would have to tie his life to some stranger, all to keep the Devereux barony from falling into oblivion. Where would he find the strength to do it?

Avva met his gaze and his heart flipped over. She smiled gently, but he couldn't find the answering emotion within him to return it.

'That was well done, my men.'

William had forgotten about the King. In that moment it was only Avva who held his attention. He tore his gaze away from her and turned to his liege.

Edward was looking very pleased with the turn of events. William could already imagine how the man would weave today's events into a story of his heroics.

'Thank you, young man.' Edward strode towards Avva. 'You played an important role today and your efforts shall not go unrewarded. Let us head to the village and find somewhere to wash up.' The King slapped Avva on the back and carried on walking towards the village, not waiting to see if the rest of them would follow.

'Come on,' said Theo as he caught up with Edward and fell into step beside him. Benedictus and Alewyn followed on behind.

William walked towards Avva and took her hand into his.

'Thank you for everything you did today. You were magnificent. The King will reward you.'

Her lips twisted in a sad smile. 'I didn't do it for the King.'

'You've said that before.' His heart pounded wildly. When he'd asked her before she'd spoken about her relief that the town would be free from Caerden, but he hoped...he hoped that she had done it because she cared for him. That was a selfish wish, he knew that. It didn't stop him wanting to hear her say it.

Instead of answering him, she leaned up and gently

brushed her mouth against his. 'Your King needs you,' she said, her eyes full of sadness.

His heart twisted. Nobody was waiting for him to catch up, but he knew they would expect him to come. 'You will need to come, too. The King would like to thank you properly.' That at least would give them more time together.

She nodded. 'There is nothing he can give me. It is enough to know that Caerden has gone. The town will be relieved. We can begin to live in peace now.'

She tugged her hand from his.

'Don't…'

'I will fetch Eirwen and bring him to you.'

He swallowed, trying to rid himself of the lump that was forming in his throat. 'Where is he? It is not like him to disobey a direct order from me.'

Avva smiled, properly this time. 'I am a good horse-woman. I managed to get him to stop not far from the bend.'

William was impressed. 'Yes, you are good. Eirwen seems to have formed a real bond with you—normally he is completely loyal to me.'

She laughed tiredly. 'Where will you be?'

'The King likes to make a show. He will be triumphant over this victory. We will not be hard to miss.'

She reached up and pressed another kiss to his lips. 'Eirwen will be with you soon.'

He knew he should hurry and catch up with his fellow knights and his liege, but he watched Avva walk away from him until she was out of sight, her beautiful body swaying with fatigue.

He turned and trudged after Edward. For the first time in his life, he regretted making the oath that bound his life to that of the King's. If only he were free to leave, Avva would be in no doubt as to how much she meant to him, about how he was beginning to question his lifelong mission to restore the barony's wealth. Without Avva, what would be the point?

Chapter Sixteen

Avva leaned against Eirwen's bulk. The cosy stables of the inn the King had decided to stay at were a perfect resting place for the noble animal.

Her whole body was heavy with exhaustion. The right thing to do would be to return home. There were horses that relied on her for food and, although they wouldn't die from lack of attention, they wouldn't be so comfortable without her.

Then there was William. They'd said their goodbyes and they knew there was no future for them. She should leave before they saw each other again. It wasn't as if more time together would change their circumstances.

And yet she couldn't force her feet in the direction of the path.

'There you are.' And the decision was made for her. William had found her and she knew she would not be strong enough to leave until he sent her away. 'You look exhausted.'

'I feel it.'

'Come on.' He held out a hand and she slipped hers into it. His skin was warm and dry as he tugged her from the stables and out into the courtyard at the back of the inn.

The sun had set completely while she was dealing with Eirwen. The evening air was cool against her face. The scent of roasting meat and the sound of laughter was coming from the taproom, but, even though the smell was delicious, she wasn't tempted to let go of William in order to find food.

'I've secured you a room,' said William, leading her to the stairs. 'I'll fetch you some food, once you are settled.'

The floorboards creaked beneath their feet as they made their way up to the top of the inn in silence.

'I'm sorry it's so small. The King has requested the best rooms for himself.'

Avva stood in the doorway, almost unable to step into the chamber. It was far larger than any space she had ever had for herself before and there was a bed, a real bed, not a pallet of straw on the floor. A fire crackled happily in the grate, its warmth filling up the room. Two candles burned on a small table. Two! A laugh bubbled up inside her. William turned to her as it escaped, a slight frown across his forehead.

'It's wonderful, William.' She crossed the room and lightly touched the blankets on the bed. This was more luxury than she had ever expected to experience.

He cleared his throat. 'I'll return shortly.'

'Very well,' she said, turning away from him so that he couldn't see the look of yearning she was sure was spreading across her face.

He stood by the door for a moment longer. She held her breath, half expecting him to say something more, but presently she heard his footsteps move away and back down the staircase.

She let out a long breath and sank on to the edge of the bed. The mattress was softer than hay, but not much more—perhaps beds weren't all they were made out to be.

A soft knock on the door brought a chambermaid with a bowl of water. 'Sir William thought you might like to wash, Master Carpenter. He's provided some fresh garments for you, too.'

That brought Avva up with a jolt. She was covered in sweat and grime—of course William would expect her to be clean. She must look awful to him, covered in the evidence of her battle. Suddenly, she couldn't get out of her clothes fast enough. She dumped the soiled garments on the floor and began to wash herself all over.

The water smelled delightful, a mixture of lavender and another herb she couldn't identify. It was another luxury after a lifetime of washing in buckets of cold water.

She had dried herself quickly and was just pulling on the clean clothes when she heard William's heavy footsteps on the stairs once more.

There was a gentle knock on the door. She swallowed. 'Enter. Thank you for organising the water. I hadn't realised how filthy I was until I started to clean myself.' William didn't answer, he merely stood in the chamber entrance, a strange look in his eyes. 'William…?'

'Sorry, Avva. I stopped thinking for a moment there. Here, I've brought you some stew.' He handed her a steaming bowl and a spoon. She took it from him, her fingers brushing the back of his hand as she did so, the brief contact setting off the now familiar tingles along her skin.

'Have you eaten?'

'Yes. The King ordered food as soon as we arrived. When you didn't join us, I thought perhaps you had already returned to Caerden.'

'I wanted Eirwen to be settled. Perhaps it would have been best if I had left, but I...' Her words faded away. How could she tell him she wasn't strong enough to leave him, that it would have to be he who walked away from her?

William walked across the room and took the bowl from her hands. It was empty, but she had no recollection of eating any of it.

He placed the bowl on the floor beside them. 'I shouldn't ask for this, Avva, not when we have already said goodbye, but I would like one more night with you. Please tell me that you want this, too.'

Avva reached up and touched his jaw. He'd removed the stubble which had made his chin rough, but she could still feel the soft prickles of his beard beneath her fingertips. She didn't know what a night with William would entail. So far he had given her pleasure, expecting nothing from her. She wanted to make him feel the way she did, whenever he took her in his arms. 'Yes, William. I want this last night with you, too.'

William swooped towards her, his lips capturing hers in a kiss that flew straight to her soul. She responded with a passion of her own. She wanted to feel everything, to experience all the pleasure William could give her and to make him feel the same way too.

She wanted to map his body with her fingers, so that she would remember what he felt like when he was gone from her life. She ran her hands along the bulge of his muscles, revelling in the way they flexed underneath her touch.

'Take this off.' She pulled at his leather tunic. It was too thick, too in the way for her exploration. Without breaking the kiss, he pulled the garment from his body and flung it across the room. It landed against the wall with a thud. Hers quickly followed.

He pulled her down on to the bed. She laughed against his lips as she half fell on him. She felt, rather than saw, his answering smile.

'This needs to go as well.' She tugged at the rest of his clothes.

'You are very commanding this evening.'

'I want to see you properly.'

'I'm still covered in bruises and...'

'Oh, I'm sorry.' Avva shuffled backwards away from him. 'I completely forgot you are still injured.'

William smiled. 'I can barely feel any pain when you are with me.' He reached up and drew her back down until she was lying on top of him completely, her legs nestled between his. He cupped her cheek in his hand and began to kiss her again, his lips moving against her softly. This was different from any of his previous kisses—it felt reverential. She arched, allowing him access as he began to kiss down the length of her neck, the graze of his stubble exquisite against her sensitive skin.

'You're still dressed,' she whispered, as his lips grazed her collarbone.

'Don't be impatient,' he murmured. 'We have all night.'

Avva squeezed her eyes tightly shut, William's words reminding her that they did not have for ever.

He gently rolled her until she was underneath him. 'You are so beautiful,' he said, brushing her hair away from her eyes. 'From the first moment I saw you, I have been bewitched by your eyes. They are the colour of the sky on a spring morning.'

'That's very poetic of you.' She couldn't help it—she grinned.

'Are you teasing me?' William growled.

'I wouldn't tease a brave knight such as yourself.' She giggled as his fingers dug into her ribs.

'I do believe you will pay for your insolence, Avva Carpenter.'

She laughed out loud as he pulled her clothes from her body, tickling her as he did so.

'That was unfair,' she said as she flopped back on to the mattress.

'How so?'

'You know I can't fight back because I don't want to hurt your ribs.'

He laughed, the sound a little unsteady as one of his large hands settled on her stomach. 'Avva,' he said, leaning down to brush the underside of her breast with his lips, 'you take my breath away.'

'Oh, William.' Her hand stole into his hair and she ran her fingers across his scalp.

'Every time you touch me, it feels so...' His words trailed off as he traced the curves of her breasts with his fingers.

'I know,' she said, as her nipples tightened in response to the light strokes across her skin. 'Please.' Her hand went to the fabric by his neck, her intent obvious. This time he didn't argue. His clothes followed hers on to the floor.

Avva gasped as the warmth of his skin pressed against the length of her.

His mouth settled over hers once more and she was

lost. There was no outside world, only her and William and this room.

Her eyes fluttered shut as his lips moved over her body, but she forced herself to open them. She wanted to commit everything about this night to memory. She watched as the shadows cast by the candlelight danced across his muscled shoulders. He took a nipple into his mouth and she cried out, sensation flooding through her.

This time she knew where her body was heading. She whimpered as his fingers brushed lightly against the sensitive skin at the core of her body and then again, as he pressed harder.

'William…this…oh…'

'Relax, my love.'

His fingers moved again, pushing into her. She couldn't help herself. Her eyes fell shut as sensation built between her legs, his fingers moving over her and in, setting a delicious rhythm.

'William… I…'

'Shush,' he murmured, returning his mouth to hers and silencing anything else she had to say with a searing kiss, his tongue moving in time with his hand.

The pressure mounted as her body tightened in anticipation. She clutched at his shoulder as wave upon wave of pleasure rocked through her, the force of it causing her to arch her back. He groaned into her mouth, the sound prolonging her enjoyment.

Gradually, the decadent ripples flooding through her gentled and William's touch slowed.

Avva had to bite her lip to stop herself from blurting out just how much she loved him.

William lifted his head and smiled down at her. 'Are you all right?'

She nodded wordlessly.

'I've robbed you of the power of speech, I see.'

She smiled. It was true. She couldn't form any words other than those of love and she didn't want to ruin this night by telling him of feelings he didn't reciprocate. Because, although he might desire her and although he might value her friendship, he had never offered her words of love. She would be wise to remember that.

He placed a gentle kiss against her forehead. 'Are you tired? Do you want to sleep?'

'No, I don't want to sleep.' She wanted to ask him about giving him pleasure. She knew there was more. If he was able to give her pleasure without getting a babe in her, then surely she could do the same for him. Shyness held her tongue and stopped her from asking all the questions that were swirling inside her.

William pulled the covers around her. 'I don't want you to get cold.'

She threw them over him, too, and he settled down beside her. Silence surrounded them like a thick blanket. It wasn't how Avva wanted to spend her last night with him.

She searched around to think of something to say that wasn't about her overwhelming feelings. 'How did the King come to be in this little village?'

William's lips turned down at the corners. 'That's a good question.' He turned and stared up at the ceiling. 'We have spies in our camp—they betrayed us.'

Her problems momentarily forgotten, she propped herself up on one elbow. 'Oh, I'm sorry, William. How did it happen?'

William drew one long finger down the length of her jaw, his pupils darkening.

'William.'

'Hmm?'

'Who betrayed you?'

'Oh, yes, sorry.' He dropped his hand and Avva immediately missed his touch.

'I sent a message with my squire, James, not long after I arrived in Caerden, warning my fellow knights that something was very wrong.'

'They didn't get it!'

'They did. James followed my instructions exactly. The only problem was, the knights who met James were in the pay of Caerden. They twisted everything. James didn't stand a chance. Poor lad is devastated.' William's eyebrows drew together, Avva reached out a thumb and smoothed the frown away.

'What happened then?' she asked softly.

William pushed himself upright, until his back was resting against the wall. Avva took a moment to admire his fine torso before he started talking again.

'James was sent off on a spurious mission, while the King was convinced he needed to head straight to Chepstow without delay. Thankfully, James realised what was happening in time to get a message to the rest of the King's Knights. They are the men you saw fighting with the King earlier. If he hadn't got the message to them in time...' William shuddered. 'It could have ended so differently.'

'What was Caerden hoping to gain by the ambush?'

'It wasn't just Caerden, although he seems to have been the major player. It seems some of the King's Barons thought they could usurp him.'

Avva nodded. The early years of a king's reign were always fraught with danger while the new monarch proved himself. It was a dangerous time, but Edward

III already had a reputation as a fierce fighter. The way he had defeated his mother, Isabella, and her lover to take back his throne should have shown his doubters that he was ruthless in getting his own way.

'Who would have ruled the country in this plan?'

'They hoped to put Isabella back on the throne and have her rule as regent once more. Now that her lover, Mortimer, is dead there is an opening to be the person behind the throne. A number of Barons thought that person should be them, Caerden being one of them.'

'Caerden was too weak to rule. He thought only of himself. He wouldn't have lasted long at all.'

'I know, but perhaps with Barwen beside him...'

Avva winced. 'That doesn't bear thinking about.'

'The plan was to ambush Edward as he made his way around the kingdom. Edward changed his plans quite late in the day and decided to visit Caerden. That would have played well into Caerden's plans. If he had been the one to murder the King, then he would have been the most obvious candidate to be the power behind the throne.'

'But he didn't know of the King's plans to visit Caerden until you turned up.'

'Exactly. My message to the King's Knights threw the Chepstow plans into disarray again. In the days I was stuck in your loft, the plan changed many times with them trying to decide whether to risk staying in Chepstow or returning to Caerden to meet the King there. I can't believe that anyone close to the King would betray him like that. He is generous to his followers. Incidentally, the King really is grateful for the role you played today. When he said he would reward you, he meant it.'

'I cannot think of anything I want that the King could grant.'

'Can you not?' William's gaze slanted down to her.

'No. Caerden is free from the Baron and his compatri-ots. We can live in peace. That is all I have ever wanted.' *That and to make you love me,* but she knew the King could not make William feel a way that he had repeatedly said was impossible for him so she kept the words unsaid.

'You are very selfless.'

Avva shrugged away the compliment. 'Not really. It has been difficult always living under the shadow the barony has cast over the town. I will relish the free-dom that comes from my half-brother's death, as will my younger brothers. So, you see, I am selfish after all.'

William leaned down and pressed a kiss to her fore-head. 'We will have to agree to differ on this point. Now, you should get some rest. It has been a long day and we didn't get much sleep last night.'

Avva's heart clenched. She did not want to miss a mo-ment of their last night together, but her head did feel heavy and her eyes were stinging with the effort of keep-ing them open. She lay down, resting her head against William's body.

'Sleep well, Avva.'

'You, too,' she said quietly.

She lay there, listening to William's steady breathing and enjoying the warmth of his body, and gradually her body drifted off to sleep.

William stared down at the woman sleeping next to him. Her body was soft and pliant against his. He wanted to wake her, to watch her face as she talked to him, but that would be unfair. She was clearly exhausted after her long and difficult day.

Tomorrow she would leave here and return to her life.

The thought pierced through him like a dagger in his already damaged ribs. He knew what he had to do, but it had never felt so hard before.

He shifted and Avva murmured in her sleep, a short string of unintelligible words followed by what sounded like his name. She moved, brushing a leg against his. He groaned as his body once more roared into life. He'd never wanted anyone this much, his body had never been so hard and heavy and yet he wouldn't take her, he could not risk getting her with child if he was not going to marry her. He would not allow himself to lose control. She was an innocent and she would remain that way until she married some nameless bastard who would give her everything William could not.

'No.'

William flinched at the sound of anger in Avva's voice. Whatever dream she was experiencing, it had taken an unpleasant turn, hardly surprising after today's events.

'No, I won't.'

'Avva.' William touched her shoulder. She sat up with a gasp.

'It's all right, Avva. You were dreaming. Whatever you saw, it wasn't real.'

She threw herself at him, burying her head against his shoulder. He wrapped his arms tightly around her, barely registering the pain in his ribs, as she sobbed against him. 'Avva, my beautiful girl, it's all over. There is nothing to be sad about.'

He felt her nod against his chest, but she continued to cry.

'Avva, please stop. You are killing me.' That didn't help either. 'Please, Avva, please.' He threaded his fingers through her hair, the silken strands so soft against his rough calluses. 'Avva…'

She looked up at him, her lashes spiky with tears. 'Avva…what is it?'

'It's…sometimes I dream of my brother, the end of his life. I haven't in a while. It's…' Her gaze dropped to his shoulder. 'Everyone leaves,' she concluded quietly.

William's heart contracted. How could he leave her? He was beginning to think it would be impossible.

Her gaze returned to his and he couldn't help himself. He brought his mouth down to hers and kissed her, pouring everything he felt for her into that moment.

She responded instantly, her hands grabbing the back of his head and pulling him down on to her. He was lost. He no longer cared about his duty to his family or his oath to his liege, all he wanted was this woman. The one who made his blood sing with joy.

He ran his hands down the length of her body, marvelling in the delicate shape of her curves. How anyone could believe she was a man confounded him. She was all perfect woman to him.

'William.'

He raised his head and looked down at her. Her pupils were huge, her gaze unfocused, and her lips were plump from his kisses. He couldn't help himself—he lowered his mouth once more. He didn't know how many long glorious moments passed, but he became aware of her hands pressing against his chest. He lifted his head once more. 'What's wrong?'

'Nothing… I…'

'Yes.' He waited, watching her pulse jump wildly in her throat. If she asked him to move away from her, he would. It would be difficult, but he would do it for her. Right now if she asked him for anything, he would agree.

'I want to know how to give you pleasure,' she blurted out, as colour flooded her cheeks.

Everything in his body froze at her words. It had been enough for him to worship her body, to make her cry out in delight. When he was not going to offer her marriage, it would be wrong for him to take anything more from her.

'You don't need to do that. I'm happy...'

Her hand stroked across his manhood. He lost his train of thought, the pleasure was so intense, like nothing he'd ever felt before.

'You like that?'

His response was a jumble of words that didn't even make sense to him. He'd lost all his power of reasoning as her fingers curled around his length. He began to move, her inexperienced touch driving him wild.

She shifted beneath him, bringing him to her entrance.

'Avva.' Her name was a groan on his lips.

'Yes.'

'We shouldn't...'

'I need to...'

'But...'

'Please.'

That *please* was his undoing. He could no longer resist her, not when his body was clamouring to make them one.

'If you want to stop at any...'

'I won't.'

He brushed her lips with his and slowly eased into her, finally making them one.

Chapter Seventeen

Soft lips kissed Avva's forehead, waking her from a dreamless sleep. Her eyelids were so heavy she couldn't open them. There was another caress, this time across her mouth.

She wanted to reach out and touch those lips, but her arms were heavy and she couldn't move.

Soft footsteps crossed the chamber and then came the creak of the door opening and closing.

Sleep claimed her once more.

She awoke much later at a tapping on the chamber door.

She licked her lips. They felt bruised and she smiled when she remembered why. She tugged the covers up to her chin. 'Come in.'

It was the chambermaid again, bringing another bowl of steaming water. 'Good morning, Master Carpenter. Here's some water for you to wash. Is there anything else I can get for you? His Majesty says you are to be given whatever you need.' The chambermaid beamed as she spoke. It had probably never crossed her mind that she would ever meet with the King, let alone receive orders from him. It had never occurred to Avva that it might happen to her either.

'Is there any food?'

'I'll bring some up for you right this instant.' The maid's eyes sparkled with delight at being able to help.

'Thank you.'

Avva waited until she was sure the maid was on the stairs before getting out of bed. The warm water was blissful against her skin. As she spread it over her body, memories from last night slipped into her mind: the delicious scrape of William's stubble against her cheek, the heavy weight of him pressing her into the mattress, the noise he made as he entered her and the waves of sensation he'd produced as he'd moved over her.

She'd known what she was risking. Known that there was a chance he would get her with child, but she had welcomed it. If they were to be apart for the rest of her life, then at least she would have a part of him to keep with her for always. She would have love in her life, just not the romantic kind.

But then there had been the words he'd whispered in the darkness. He might not have said he loved her, but it was in every word he uttered and every gesture. A man could not act like that and not care deeply. It had given her hope, where she'd not had any before.

Perhaps last night wasn't goodbye after all.

She dressed quickly. It was strange shrugging on the male clothing—she had never felt so female in all her life.

Avva was ready and waiting, when the maid returned with some freshly baked bread. She took the loaf, gratefully biting into the crunchy crust. Maybe it was her mood, but she didn't think she had ever tasted anything quite so mouth-wateringly delicious in her whole life.

'His Majesty would like to see you in the taproom when you are ready, Master Carpenter.'

Avva swallowed. 'I'll be there presently.'

Avva didn't taste the rest of her bread. If William was to be believed, the King really did want to thank her for her help during yesterday's fight. But what on earth would she ask for?

There was only one thing she wanted for herself: William. He had to give himself to her willingly, though. She would not ask for him.

That only really left her brothers. She wanted to see them settled in life, perhaps she would ask for that.

She stood, brushing the crumbs from her clothes, and made towards the door.

It was time to meet the King.

The chambermaid was loitering at the bottom of the stairs. 'The King is talking to some giant men at the moment. Would you like to come into the kitchens and wait?'

'Thank you, but I will wait in the corridor until he is ready to see me.'

Avva didn't think she could bear to sit still. If she remained in the passageway, at least she could pace.

The chambermaid didn't press her and, after a moment of looking longingly towards the taproom, she disappeared, presumably to carry on with her tasks.

It wasn't that Avva wanted to eavesdrop on the King's discussion with his men, there was probably some law against doing just that after all, but standing where she was, she couldn't help but hear the conversation. The deep rumble of male voices weren't even trying to keep their voices quiet.

She wanted to know more about what would happen to her town now that the Baron was dead. He didn't have any heirs and so the King would have to grant the land to someone loyal to him, although right now it must be hard to decide who that person might be. She'd always thought life as a royal was easy, but never knowing who to trust was similar to her own life, where nobody knew the real her. Who'd have thought she would have had anything in common with the King?

There was no door between the corridor and the tap-room. She edged forward, trying to get a glimpse of William.

Avva was quite close when she eventually saw him, her heart skipping a beat when she spotted him leaning against a wooden pillar, his back to her. Three other men were dotted around the room, each of them as big as William and as equally covered in fearsome weapons. She recognised them as the men who had fought alongside William yesterday.

The King was sitting by the fire, his legs stretched out in front of him. He looked better than he had yesterday, a lot less dishevelled, but he still didn't look very kingly, or at least not like Avva's idea of how a king should look.

She turned back to William, with his broad shoulders and muscled arms—he was far more her idea of royalty.

She leaned against the wall and allowed herself the luxury of gazing at William while she was unobserved. She didn't pay attention to what they were saying until the King mentioned William by name.

'You fought well yesterday, William Devereux. I will see that you are rewarded for your efforts.'

'Thank you, Your Majesty, it was a pleasure to serve you as always. Believe me, I thought not of any reward, but only of your safety.'

The King preened at William's response. 'Nevertheless, I shall reward you handsomely. I do not even have to think about what you would like. You will be pleased to know that I have decided to grant your petition to marry Lady Ann of Clyde.'

Avva's world spun—for a moment she could not tell what was up or down. She'd begun to trust in him, to believe that he loved her, cared for her, and now...

She held her breath, waiting to hear William's response. Surely he would say that such an arrangement was not possible.

But William didn't speak. The other men in the room moved towards him, smiling and slapping his back, uttering words of congratulation.

She wanted to run, she didn't want to see this, but her feet remained stuck to the floor as the nightmare unfolded in front of her. And then William spoke. 'Thank you, Sire.'

His words managed to galvanise her into action.

She turned away from the scene before her and ran.

Chapter Eighteen

William waited for an eternity. The King discussed the plot on his life at great length—he wanted every Baron who'd dared to dream they could overthrow him hunted down and disposed of. The message he wanted to send to the kingdom was clear: no one would get away with even the whiff of treason.

When that was finally over, it was Benedictus, the King's Knights leader, who took over. He was taking the various betrayals very hard indeed and he made each of the remaining knights go over their interactions with every one of the men identified as spies during the last few months in minute detail.

All the while, William waited for Avva to appear.

It had been so difficult to leave her sleeping, but he'd not wanted to wake her as they'd not had much sleep. His skin heated as he remembered why.

When the conversation turned to William's role in the whole thing, he was embarrassed by how much praise the King heaped on him. In reality, William had done very little. He'd ended up battered and bruised in a loft and had only just arrived in time to help save the King.

If he'd been even several moments later, the result could have been very different.

But it was the King's granting of William's petition in return for the success of the mission that had William reeling. For so long, he had wanted a wealthy marriage. He had not been thinking of the bride, but of her dowry. If he'd given the woman any thought, he'd hoped that they would be comfortable together. He would be a good husband, but not a madly in love one. He was not going to be like his parents.

When the King had told William he could marry Lady Ann, he'd frozen. He didn't know the woman personally, but he knew that Lady Ann was from one of the wealthiest families in the kingdom. To be joined in such a union would alleviate the financial worries that had plagued him for his whole life. It would also be a practical union without love, the very thing he'd thought he wanted for as long as he could remember. But that was before Avva, before he'd realised what being with a woman he loved would be like.

Last night, as she'd lain in his arms, he had realised something. He could never leave her, never marry another when his heart was full for this courageous woman.

He'd not been able to think of anything to say in response to the King's declaration. His body and soul were rebelling against the notion of marrying this stranger. Then he'd seen his liege's face and Theo's not far behind him. The King was expecting William's gratitude—indeed, he was owed it. Theo's glare reminded him that this was not the time to defy the King. The difference in stature between the Devereux family and the Clydes was phenomenal. The King was granting him a great honour. Unable to do anything else, he'd thanked the King for that honour, all the while feeling as if great serpents were writhing in his stomach.

Edward had moved on to the King's Knights' next mission. Once again, William couldn't concentrate, all his thoughts consumed by what he was going to do about Avva. He knew some men would tell him to marry Lady Ann and keep Avva as his mistress. He would have the wealth and the woman he loved, and he did love Avva, he knew that now, knew that life without her would be unbearable, knew that he was exactly like his parents, hopelessly and helplessly in love with one person for the rest of his life. He would never keep Avva as a mistress and marry someone else. It would be dishonourable to both women.

Now, when he was finally faced with a choice, he realised he could not marry a woman who was not Avva.

'Where's that lad, William?'

William frowned at his king. 'What lad?'

'The one who joined in the fight yesterday.'

It was on the tip of William's tongue to say that Avva was a woman, but he remembered that he had sworn an oath not to tell anyone about her disguise. Even though the reason for that duplicity had gone, William would still not break his word. 'I shall fetch him.'

'I sent for him ages ago. I do not like to be kept waiting.'

How strange. It was not like Avva not to do her duty. William was sure she would have come when asked, but then perhaps she was exhausted and was still asleep. Or maybe she was shy—not everyone was used to talking to the King.

'I shall go and find out what has happened to Master Carpenter.'

He strode out of the taproom and took the stairs to Avva's chamber two at a time. He was desperate to see her, even as he dreaded having to tell her about Lady Ann. He would get out of that, though. It would be difficult, but he would find a way to appease the King.

The chamber was empty, a cool bowl of water sitting on the table, but there was nothing else in the room to suggest that Avva had ever been there. Even the bed covers, which had been rumpled when he had left, were pulled tight.

He ran back down the stairs and found the chambermaid who had waited on them before. 'Where is Master Carpenter?'

The maid blinked at him. 'He left, Sir William, not long after the King spoke to him.'

'When did the King speak to him?' William couldn't see how Avva had got past him to speak to the King. The tavern was small with only one corridor and the stairs.

'Early this morning.'

An icy wave swept through William. 'Master Carpenter has been gone since early morning?'

'Yes, Sir William.' The maid's fingers were curled into her apron, her bottom lip wobbling.

William realised he must be scaring her with his abrupt questions. He forced his shoulders to relax. 'Thank you for your help.'

The maid scurried away from him quickly, suggesting he hadn't been as soft as he'd hoped. Not that it mattered. Nothing mattered other than the fact that Avva had left without saying goodbye.

He strode out of the tavern and into the stables. Eirwen was still there, so Avva hadn't taken a horse, but a quick glance up at the sky revealed that midday had long since passed while he'd been listening to the King drone on. Avva would be nearly at Caerden, if she wasn't there already.

She had left him without saying goodbye.

He stumbled blindly back to the taproom, surprised to find it was nearly exactly as he had left it. His whole world had changed, but for everyone else it was exactly the same.

'I'm afraid there was some confusion, Sire. Master Carpenter left some time ago.'

'Oh.' Edward looked down at his hands. 'Well, that's a shame for him because I was going to offer him a substantial sum as a thank you. But...' he shrugged his royal shoulders '...I'm not about to chase a stable lad across the country.'

And that was it. The subject of Avva was over.

William sank down on to a chair as the conversation around him resumed.

He couldn't believe that, for one moment, he had been prepared to risk everything to keep Avva in his life.

He had actually thought about offering to marry her, forgetting his lifelong dream of restoring the barony to the wealth of his forefathers. He had, for a brief instant, imagined a future where he put his own happiness before that of his family's legacy. But she hadn't wanted that future with him.

She had repeatedly told him she expected nothing from him. While he had uttered words of love during the night, she had not reciprocated. Once again, he'd been a fool. While he was falling in love, she wasn't. She'd told him theirs was a momentary pleasure, but he hadn't listened.

When she had said she had no expectations for their

future, he had thought she was protecting herself but it turned out she had been telling the truth. She wanted nothing from him.

He'd been prepared to risk his future and everything he'd planned since he'd been a young boy, all because of her.

She had told him that there was too much of a social divide between them, but he hadn't heard her—as deep in love as he was, he had thought that was surmountable. But she had meant it. The dream, the one he'd only just dared to imagine, had fallen through his fingers like smoke.

Now he stood in the cold, empty chamber, the reality of his situation setting in. Of course he was not going to give up the chance to marry a wealthy heiress. A union of convenience had been what he'd planned his whole life. He'd been on the verge of turning into his parents, of throwing away the potential to restore the barony to its former glory, all because of a woman who didn't even like him enough to say farewell.

No, the union with Lady Ann was a good progression.

It didn't matter that his heart burned with the pain of losing Avva. He was doing the right thing. He had to be, because otherwise the agony of his heartbreak was pointless.

Chapter Nineteen

Northern England—late spring 1331

The sky was a grey blanket of cloud. Spring, which had already started in the south, hadn't made a breakthrough this far north.

William had entered into his family's land early this morning, having ridden through the night. Eirwen was beginning to tire, but William pressed him on. He wanted to get this visit over with as quickly as possible. He would arrive today, inform his parents about his union with Lady Ann, check on the state of the finances and leave tomorrow.

That would give Eirwen plenty of time to recover while allowing William minimum exposure to his parents' chaos.

The castle came into view and William frowned. Even from a distance he could see that some of the stonework needed fixing. His whole jaw tensed. He tried to loosen it. It would do no good to arrive at his parents' home frowning over the state of it. But really...the whole castle probably wouldn't withstand a siege. Not that there was anything worth taking on the inside, just a wide collection of detritus his parents had amassed over the years.

He passed through a gate in the town walls—the streets were bustling with people. He knew they would expect him to stop and talk—his parents knew everyone by name—but he was tired and wanted nothing more than a long, hot soak.

He did not want to talk to anyone. He hadn't for a while now. Not since Avva had walked out of his life four weeks ago without looking back.

'Master William... Master William.'

William tried not to slump in his saddle, but he couldn't help his shoulders drooping a little. He couldn't ignore the baker—the man had never failed to give William a sweet treat whenever he'd passed as a child. And William had passed by a lot.

William drew Eirwen to a stop outside the baker's shop.

The man's smile was so wide it almost reached from ear to ear. William wondered whether he would ever feel that happy again. He sincerely doubted it.

'You're heading up to the castle to see your parents.'

William nodded, although it wasn't really a question. Where else would he be going?

'You take them this bread.' The baker tucked a loaf into the top of one of William's saddlebags. 'And here are some of those treats you like so much.'

William's heart contracted as the old man's gnarled hands tucked more food into the bag. He managed to choke out a thank you and to ask how the old man's family was faring. By the time William managed to pull away, he knew vast amounts about the man's numerous grandchildren—the baker was obviously very proud of his growing brood.

And so he should be.

William succeeded in avoiding a long conversation with anyone else, but that didn't make his journey through the town any quicker. Everyone wanted to stop and smile at him, to pat Eirwen and touch a part of William, almost as if he were a talisman.

Eirwen bore the attention far better than he did. By the time he reached the stables he was desperate for his own company.

His heart clenched painfully as two stable boys rushed out to take care of Eirwen. They were efficient and jovial, but they were not Avva. The interior of the stables was cosy, but it had nothing of the cleanliness of hers. Such comparisons were unhelpful. He needed to forget her and move on with his life.

'William.' He turned—there was only one person who could ever say his name with such unbridled delight.

'Mother.' He stepped forward and she fell into his opened arms.

'Look at you, so big and handsome. So like your father.' William tried not to roll his eyes. Nobody was as perfect as his father, in his mother's eyes. But at least she thought he was like him, that was progress. 'You should have sent word you were coming, we would have prepared a feast.' Which was exactly why he hadn't. His parents didn't need to waste expenditure on him.

'It is fine, Mother. All I need is a good wash.'

'Yes, you do smell a bit. Come on, let's go and visit your father.'

'But I wouldn't want to see him while I smell of the journey.'

'Nonsense, your father will be delighted to see you. He won't mind.'

William allowed himself to be tugged into the keep. It was only until tomorrow. Tomorrow, he would be on his way again. Tomorrow, he would be able to do things properly again.

The Great Hall was a riot of voices, roaring laughter and the crackle of flames in the giant hearth. His father was not sitting upon the dais, but stood in the centre of the room, laughing with two peasants.

'Son,' he boomed as soon as he caught sight of William. 'Come and hear this.'

William was dragged into the conversation, which appeared to be an argument about who had the right to farm on what land. William couldn't keep up with the argument, but it appeared his opinion wasn't needed. By the end of the discussion, William's father had ruled that the men must share the disputed area and sent them on their way.

'Father,' said William, unable to keep his voice from showing the exasperation he felt, 'they will only be back again when they next get on each other's nerves.'

'Oh, undoubtedly, but you see, Son, they are so vastly entertaining. I should miss them dreadfully if they came to some sort of amicable agreement. It would quite ruin my fun. Garth...' William's father turned as he called for his steward. 'Sort the rest of these people out, will you? I am going to spend some time with my son. Did I tell you he's become one of the King's Knights?'

'Several times, my lord,' said Garth, bowing in William's direction.

'Well, I'm very proud.'

'I know, my lord. As are we all.'

William felt heat sweep up his neck. He wasn't fair to his parents. He didn't deserve their pride when he was ashamed of them. At least neither they nor anyone else knew about his feelings. Well, one person did, but Avva didn't count as she would never meet them. His heart twisted.

He'd thought he'd now be free of thoughts of her, but if anything it was getting worse. He thought about her almost constantly, the ache of missing her wrapped around his heart and refusing to let go.

He followed his parents into their private chambers, noting that even now, after nearly thirty years of marriage, and numerous children, they were still holding hands.

Large cushions surrounded the hearth. His father helped his mother lower herself down into one and then settled next to her, recapturing her hand and holding it in his lap.

'Sit, William, and tell us what brings you north.'

'I…' Somehow, the words of the news of Lady Ann became stuck in his throat.

'You have fallen in love and she will not have you.'

William lifted his head sharply at his mother's words. 'Whatever gave you that impression?'

'I can see it in your eyes.'

William's heart rate increased. 'What nonsense.'

'Do not speak to your mother like that. King's Knight or not, I shall have you over my knee.'

William glanced down at his father—the slightly protruding stomach and the soft jowls which hung down from his chin suggested he hadn't done much hand-to-hand combat in a while. Still, the man really did love his wife, so there was the possibility of his anger helping him at least try to carry out his threat.

'Please sit, William.' His mother's eyes twinkled softly in the firelight, her smile telling him she agreed with William's assessment of her husband's physical fitness.

William had always had a soft spot for his mother—he'd missed her desperately when he'd gone away for his knight's training. She was a bit daft, but very loving towards everyone. He could understand why his father was so smitten.

William lowered himself on to one of the cushions opposite his parents. It was surprisingly comfortable. The fire warmed the side of his face and for the first time in days the knots in his back relaxed.

'Tell me about her,' said his mother softly.

William cleared his throat. 'The King has granted me permission to marry Lady Ann of Clyde. I don't know if you are aware of her family, but they own—'

'Tell us of the woman you have fallen in love with, William,' his mother interrupted gently.

'I'm telling you about my future wife.'

'You're telling us about a transaction. I want to know about the woman who has put shadows in your eyes.'

William rubbed a hand across his face. 'There is nothing wrong with my eyes.' His parents, unusually, remained quiet. 'There was a woman, but she was not… it was going to… I'm marrying Lady Ann of Clyde so it doesn't…' To his absolute horror his eyes began to burn. Dear God, he wasn't going to cry, was he?

He was a grown man, he'd not shed a tear since… He couldn't remember ever crying. Perhaps he had when he was a babe, but he'd known ever since he could remember that real men didn't cry.

He stared into the fire, concentrating on his breathing.

'What was wrong with your woman, William? Did she not love you back?'

William blinked some more. 'I don't know.'

'Did she reject you?'

'She left without saying goodbye.'

'Tell us the whole story, Son.' William glanced at his father. For once he wasn't smiling his customary grin. In fact, his parents looked miserable. It was such an unusual expression on their faces that William found himself pouring out the whole story. His parents sat in silence, listening to his every word. 'So you see, she cannot have loved me or she would have stayed.'

'It seems to me that Avva didn't have any incentive to stay.'

William looked at his mother sharply. 'What do you mean by that?'

'Had you not told her, repeatedly, that there was no future for the two of you?'

'Yes, but I would never have…that is to say…' Even having discussed everything with his parents, William still felt heat wash over his face at his attempt to talk about the night he'd spent with Avva.

'She doesn't know that though, does she, William? For all she knows, that is how you treat all your conquests.'

'I don't have conquests!' William wished he had never brought this up. Talking to his parents about such private matters was almost intolerable. Although—he touched his heart—it didn't ache as badly as it had when he'd arrived and before he'd started talking.

'I am sure you are as chivalrous as a lover as you are

as a knight,' said his father, his habitual smile firmly back in place. William groaned and dropped his head into his hands. 'But the truth is, you didn't give young Avva a chance. You should have found out if she loved you back and only then should you have made a decision about your future.'

'I am going to wed Lady Ann.' Even to his own ears, his voice did not sound convincing. Was there really a possible future for him out there that didn't involve a loveless marriage? Could Avva have felt the same for him and he had been too irrational to find out?

'Why do you have to marry this lady you've never met?' asked his mother.

'She is from a wealthy family.'

'Well, that will certainly make your life comfortable. But is that what you really want? Your father and I have love and each other and you cannot buy that.'

'But what of the dowries for my sisters?'

His father blinked. 'We are not so poor we cannot afford dowries for the girls. They will not be large, but they will do well enough. They are going to be great beauties and are related to a member of the King's Knights after all. Love is what matters, William.'

'Yes, but…'

'But what?' His mother's voice was gentle and not accusatory.

William inhaled deeply. 'You are in love and that's great, but it's not right for everyone.'

'Yes, it is,' said his father. 'There is nothing greater.'

'The babies,' William croaked.

His mother frowned. 'I am sorry you were around for our heartbreak over losing our babies. We should have tried to hide that from you. We will always remember every loss, but we are proud and delighted by our living children. They are a result of our love.'

William's beliefs were slipping through his fingers. There was another reason not to follow his heart. He must remember that.

'But it makes you do ridiculous things.' William regretted his outburst immediately. His parents recoiled as if they'd been hit.

'What in God's name are you talking about?' demanded his father.

William couldn't look at his parents, he didn't want to see the hurt he caused them written across their faces. 'All my life, your expenditure has far exceeded the barony's income and then there's the dressing up and parading around. People are laughing at you.'

William had never meant to say such things to his parents. They might be faintly absurd, but they were never cruel. They were worth a thousand Caerdens, probably tens of thousands. At their continued silence, shame began to creep up his spine. He was an awful person, he deserved to be miserable.

'I like to think,' said his father eventually, 'that people are laughing with us and not at us. But, even if they are, why does that matter, William? It is not for others to tell us how to live our lives. Your mother and I have found great joy in one another. Every day we laugh together, even when everything seems quite dark. After thirty years that is something quite remarkable.'

His mother nodded. 'Your Avva certainly doesn't listen to convention, dressing as a man, taking a man's role to ensure the security and well-being of her younger brothers. That is to be admired greatly, I think. She even risked her life for your safety—you don't do that for someone you don't care about deeply.'

William's stomach swooped uncomfortably. It was true that Avva had said she was not a supporter of the King—could she have been there to help William? She'd never said as much, even when pressed, but then he'd not told her his feelings either. His heart squeezed at the thought. But, if it were true that she loved him, it still didn't explain why she had left without saying goodbye. If she cared so much for him, surely she could have waited out the morning before leaving. Had he made a terrible mistake in not finding out for sure?

'As for the expenditure...' William jumped—he had forgotten his parents were still in the room with him. His mother was looking at him kindly, but his father was frowning as he spoke. 'Some years we may spend more than we receive, but others we don't. We have managed to keep ourselves, and the people who depend upon us, in good health for many years. Of course, some of the tapestries in the Great Hall are a little threadbare, but was anyone in there starving?'

'No.' In fact, the room had been filled with laughter. The contrast between Caerden's Great Hall and his father's was extreme.

William's stomach twisted again—it was a sensation he was coming to despise.

'I think you should stay a few days, William,' said his mother, as she stood and straightened out her skirts. 'You should talk to our people, your sisters, too, see how everyone really feels about us. After all, they will be your people soon enough.'

'Not too soon,' said his father, standing, too.

His mother merely laughed and patted her husband

on the cheek. 'If, after you have stayed and really given it some thought, you still want to marry Lady Ann, then we will give you our full support.'

'We will?' questioned his father.

'We will.'

William stayed for a week. It was the longest he had been in his home for many years, possibly since he'd left it to start his knight's training.

The memories he'd had as a child and an adolescent were gradually overlain by new ones. Yes, his father was still madly in love with his mother which was, on occasion, embarrassing. And, yes, they did spend more money than William thought was wise, but there was a happiness in the town that William hadn't seen anywhere else on his travels. He walked the streets, in a way he hadn't done since he was a boy, ducking into shops when he could and talking to the proprietors. The townsfolk were content and always had enough to eat.

His sisters were funny, clever individuals who were flourishing in his parents' loving atmosphere. Not for them the haunted look of having their joy constantly suppressed like the inhabitants of Caerden.

Every step he took, he was haunted by the thought of Avva. It was as if she travelled with him, a constant presence just out of sight. He wanted to know what she thought of everything he saw. Several times he turned to talk to her, only for his heart to drop when he realised she wasn't there.

By the end of the seven days he was sure of only one thing.

He had made a terrible mistake.

Chapter Twenty

Caerden, South Wales—early summer 1331

Summer had come late to Wales, but after a blustery few months the rain had finally disappeared and the warmth of the sun was beginning to dry everything out.

For most of the townsfolk of Caerden, the rain had washed away the remnants of the old Baron. News had reached them, about a week ago, that the King had given the barony to someone he trusted and that he would be arriving at the castle soon. That had given the townsfolk hope.

Avva had been dreaming her way through life until that point, imagining that William would return with vows of love for her, but the news of the new Baron had woken her from that fantasy. It had made her think clearly about what she wanted and with that clarity had come a resolution.

She had come to tell her closest friend what she was planning to do, but she was finding it hard to get the words out.

John continued to chip away at the piece of wood

in his hands. Avva, who normally found watching his wrinkled hands work with wood fascinating, stared into the distance.

'Have you made your decision?'

'I have.'

'You are going to leave before the new Baron arrives?'

'I am.'

'Where will you go?'

'Caernarfon.' It hadn't been until that moment that she'd finally decided. Caernarfon was a big enough town for her to get lost in.

'Will you pose as a man or be your true self?' asked John, kindly.

Avva straightened. She had kept her male disguise even though she knew Caerden was not returning. She'd only told John, who had smiled at her revelation and not made any further comment. 'It's time to bring Avva back to life.'

'I'll miss you.'

'I'll miss you, too, and the boys. But I want a family of my own and I'm not going to get that living as my twin brother.' Avva tried to smile, but her heart hurt. She tried not to think about William, about what it would be like to carry his children in her belly. Most of the time she succeeded. She had concentrated on making sure her brothers would be all right when she left and on getting through every day, but sometimes the pain hit her full force and she would struggle to breathe.

'You could stay here. I don't think people would be too surprised to find you are Avva,' said John quietly.

Avva smiled—that news would have horrified her only a few months ago, but now she was at peace with it. The villagers had probably known all along, but they had protected her and, although they didn't know it, she had played a huge part in protecting them, too. It was time to move on, to create a new future in a place that didn't remind her so forcefully of William.

She wondered if he was already married to his rich bride. Pain shot through her heart and she pushed herself to her feet. Thoughts like that would do her no good.

'I'll miss you, John.'

John grumbled something under his breath, which Avva took to mean he would miss her deeply, too. She grinned, even as her heart hurt a little. John had been a good friend to her over the years. She would come back, but would she see him again? He was getting on in years, so it was unlikely.

'Here. This is for you.' John handed her the figure on which he had been working.

She took hold of it, the wood smooth under her fingertips. She held it up to the light and gasped. John had carved two figures, their arms entwined and their foreheads touching. The likeness was so like her and William, it was impossible to deny.

'John...' But when she turned back, her friend had gone.

She held the figurine to her lips and squeezed her eyes tightly closed. She refused to cry. She was moving towards her future and so was William. She hoped, wherever he was, whomever he was with, he was happy.

'Bye, John.' Without waiting for an answer, she walked towards the stables—she had work to do.

'You've got your work cut out for you here.'

'Thank you, Theo. As always your input is immensely valuable.'

'I'm just saying, my friend, that this time you may have taken on more than you can cope with.'

William resisted the urge to push Theo off his horse. His mentor would only chase after him and try to get his revenge. And that would slow things down.

He was so close now, he didn't want to stop, even to let Eirwen rest. He'd rushed ahead of James, who was at least a day behind, looking after provisions and probably quite grumpy to have been left trailing in their wake.

'It looks like the land hasn't been taken care of properly for years.'

'Try decades.'

They rode in silence for a moment. William was grateful for the quiet, but didn't think it would last.

'What has got you so anxious?'

William bit back a sigh. 'I'm not anxious.' He really wasn't. Caerden was only around the next bend. He was breathless with anticipation, his heart was racing and he felt like at any minute he would leap from the saddle and start running. It was only the thought of making a fool of himself in front of Theo that made him able to hold it together.

He would be seeing Avva so soon.

They rounded the bend in the road and there it was—Caerden. William kicked Eirwen into a brisk canter.

Theo caught up alongside him. 'What's the rush?'

'You've seen the state of the place. I'm keen to get started.'

They rode in silence for a few blissful moments. 'There's a woman.'

'Theo…'

'Ah, yes, there is. You've gone a dull reddish colour. You'll want to get rid of that, it's not very attractive.'

William clenched his fist around his rein. He couldn't remember why he had thought it was a good idea to bring Theo on this trip. He supposed he might be useful if there was any trouble. Not that he was expecting any.

A new steward had been installed at Caerden. He had reported that there was a great sense of relief and a tentative hope for the future among the inhabitants of the town.

William was pleased when a guard stopped him at the gatehouse. It didn't take long for them to get through and it was something William would have to work on improving, but it was much better than his previous visit.

There were definite improvements in the courtyard, too, but William didn't have time to take them all in. As he headed over to the stables, he couldn't stop a broad grin spreading across his face. He didn't even care if Theo saw him and mocked. It was time to see Avva again. Just to talk to her again would be a bliss he'd once not thought possible.

And, if she didn't want him... No, his brain refused to even think that. Besides, he had the time now. He would charm her until she loved him as much as he loved her.

He jumped down from Eirwen and gathered up his reins.

'I simply refuse to believe there is not a woman involved. I have never seen you so enthusiastic about anything.'

Even Theo's mocking tone could not dent William's mood. He ignored his friend in favour of striding into the stables.

Inside the familiar sweet smell of fresh straw greeted him. He smiled as he took in the clean floors and neat stalls. Avva hadn't let her standards slip in the months since he had last seen her.

'Can I help you, sir?'

William turned. A young lad stood behind him, a brush in hand.

'Where is Master Carpenter?'

The lad frowned. 'Ave isn't here, sir.'

'Well, where is she?' He shook his head. 'I mean he.'

'Ave's gone.'

'You mean he's visiting his brothers?'

The lad's frown deepened. 'No, I mean Master Carpenter has left.'

'For the day.'

'No. He has gone from Caerden.' The lad spoke slowly as if he were trying to communicate something to someone who didn't speak English. William wondered if perhaps he didn't. Where on earth would Avva have gone?

He became aware of Theo slapping him on the shoulder. 'I'm sorry, my friend.' William could only swallow. He couldn't have sacrificed so much and worked so hard only to find Avva gone.

The lad, clearly fearing that his two unexpected guests were not of sound mind, backed away from them both before escaping into the courtyard.

Theo cleared his throat. 'I didn't realise… I mean there's nothing wrong… Edward might frown on it, but I will stand by you.'

William slumped against the stable door, exhausted. 'I'm not sure what you are talking about, Theo, but I'm not in the right frame of mind to take your nonsense.'

Theo frowned. 'I'm trying to be supportive. I didn't know that you like men. I mean, you always seemed as keen as the rest of us to be with women. I didn't know…'

William ignored him. He straightened. He hadn't come this far to be defeated.

'I know who might know where she is.'

'Who? What?'

'Avva.'

Without stopping to explain, he pushed past his friend and strode out into the courtyard.

John the carpenter was outside his workshop.

'Where is Avva?' He perhaps should have started with the niceties, but his patience was wearing thin.

John looked up at him—the old man's gaze seemed to see into William's soul. 'What do you want with her?'

'I want to give her everything.'

Chapter Twenty-One

Caernarfon, North Wales—summer 1331

Avva missed the stables, the smell of the straw and the hot breath of the animals as they exhaled into her hair. She missed Caerden and the gentle flow of the river in summer. She missed her brothers. And, even though he had only been there for a few nights, she missed the sight of William in her loft, his broad shoulders resting against the straw of her pallet as he watched her speak.

Caernarfon with its hustle and bustle was a much busier town than Caerden. It was easy for a widow to get lost among its many people. No one had doubted her when she told them her husband had died of an infection, no one was that interested in her past and for that she was grateful. She was able to be a woman for the first time in years, it was freeing and terrifying at the same time.

She'd found work at an alehouse—the women there were friendly and kind. They all had brothers or relatives they wanted Avva to meet, sure that she would find a husband among them. Avva had vowed that she would soon. Not quite yet—she pretended that she was still grieving for her dead husband and the women respected that. But she wanted a family of her own and to do that she had to have a man. That the man would not be William only haunted her at night.

She had bled not long after she'd last seen him, so there had been no babe to love and care for. She knew she should be glad, but there was only sadness at the loss of what could have been.

She tipped the liquid into a barrel and stirred it with a wooden spoon. It would soon be ready. She was concentrating so hard on getting it right that she screamed when she heard a deep voice behind her say, 'You're a hard woman to find.'

Clutching her chest, she turned slowly, unable to believe the voice she was hearing.

William was leaning against the doorjamb of the alehouse, his arms folded, a soft smile on his lips.

Without thinking she dropped her spoon and ran to him, leaping into his arms just as he unfolded them.

She buried her face in his chest, inhaling his scent. 'What are you doing here?'

'I'm looking for you.' He tightened his arms around her, pulling her close.

She lifted her head to look at him and he brought his lips down to hers. His touch was feather-light, but it was as if the simple touch breathed life into her. The invisible bindings that had wrapped around her for months were finally loosened.

She didn't know how long they stood like that, but the clearing of a throat brought her back to reality. She was kissing a man, who was clearly not her husband, in the alehouse. She pushed away from William, who lifted his head, but didn't relinquish his hold on her.

'Mistress Carpenter, what is going on here?' asked the sharp tones of the head alewife.

'Oh, this is an old friend of mine.' She tried to push away from William again, but he held on tight.

The lady frowned down upon her. 'That is a nobleman, Mistress Carpenter. He is no friend of yours.'

Avva felt William's laugh rumble through her, but when he spoke, his voice was steady. 'My good lady, I would like to speak with Avva alone. May I borrow her for a moment?'

The alewife folded her arms across her ample chest and glared at William. 'You may speak with her within sight of me. I will not have any tomfoolery with my women.'

Avva bit back a giggle of her own—it was funny to see the diminutive alewife standing up to a hulking, great knight, but it was also wonderful. She hadn't had anyone care about her welfare for so long.

'Very well,' said William, tugging her out of the ale-house and on to the street.

A cart rumbled by, narrowly missing their feet.

'This isn't the ideal place for this,' muttered William.

'The ideal place for what?'

He turned to her, framing her face with his large hands. 'Avva, why are you not in Caerden? I came looking for you and you were gone.'

Her heart beat painfully in her chest at his words. He had come looking for her, but not straight away. She had been at Caerden for weeks after she had last seen him. He'd had plenty of time to come to her then. She couldn't fathom why he had come to find her now—it had been months since the last time they had kissed. Maybe he had a bride now and wanted a mistress. She loved him, but she wouldn't share him.

'I couldn't stay in Caerden any longer. I wanted to live as a woman again—moving and claiming to be a widow seemed like the best option.'

'I want you to come home.'

She blinked up at him. 'Where is home?' She shook her head, it didn't matter. She couldn't go anywhere with him, not if he was wedded to somebody else. 'William, it is good to see you again, but I cannot go anywhere with you. I must get back, I need to attend to my duties.'

His hands slipped down her shoulders and encircled her arms. 'Avva, there is much for us to talk about. Come away with me now. I will pay the alewives for the work they will lose without you there. Hey, what have I said to make you cry?'

Avva dashed the traitorous tears away with the back of her hand. 'I cannot come away with another woman's husband. I heard the King grant your wish to marry a wealthy heiress. I will not share you. It is not the sort of person I am, no matter how much I might want to be with you.'

'You want to be with me?' William leaned down and brushed his lips to hers.

'Back away from her,' yelled the alewife. 'I'm watching you.'

William lifted his head, his brown eyes sparkling with laughter. 'Very well, I will wait a little longer to speak with you. What I have to say will be better without an audience. When you've finished for the day, I will come and collect you. There is someone who has been pining your absence more than I have. I won't force you into doing anything you don't want to, but promise me you won't run away again.'

Despite her better judgement, Avva nodded. She wanted to see him again even though it might hurt in the long term. 'I promise.'

He gently kissed her forehead before letting go of her arms.

She was almost back at the alehouse when she heard him call her name. She turned—he was still where she had left him.

'Avva, I think you should know something. I don't have a wife.' He smiled at her, lifting a hand in farewell before striding away.

Dusk was setting by the time Avva had finished her chores. Her fingers trembled as she fixed her braid into something she hoped looked presentable. She was about to see William and he didn't have a wife.

She stepped from the building to find him lounging against the wall opposite the alehouse. He pushed himself upright as soon as he saw her. They met in the middle of the road, his long fingers curling around hers.

'I hope you haven't been waiting long,' she said as William began to lead her along the street in the direction of the large castle which dominated the skyline.

He grinned. 'Part of my training requires me to stand around for long periods of time. It was nothing to wait for you.'

'Where are we going?'

'First, we're going to see Eirwen. He has missed you.'

'I have missed him. He is a beautiful horse.'

'And have you missed me, too?'

'With every heartbeat.'

William stopped abruptly and pulled her into his arms. Before she had a chance to take a breath, his lips came down on hers in a searing kiss. Time stopped.

'Avva,' he said, finally lifting his head. 'I have so much to tell you, but I keep getting distracted. I have longed for you for so long and now I have found you.'

'If you longed for me, why did you not come to me? I heard the King tell you he had found you a bride. You didn't say…' Her words trailed off. She found she couldn't put a voice to the hurt she'd experienced when she'd discovered William was going to marry someone else. The sense of betrayal had been absolute.

'I'm sorry you heard that, Avva. I…' He ran a hand through his hair, making it stand on end. 'You know how I told you about my family, about how my parents squandered the wealth of the barony?'

'I remember.'

'I thought the solution was to marry an heiress. I was not going to fall in love like my father, so it didn't matter who I wed. Then I met you and everything changed.'

Avva's heart took flight as they began to walk again. 'But I heard your fellow knights congratulate you and you didn't say that wasn't what you wanted.'

'The King may look like an ordinary man, but he is not someone you can defy easily.'

'So you are still going to marry your heiress.' She tried to tug her fingers from his, but he tightened his grip.

'No, I am not going to marry Lady Ann. Let me finish my story before you condemn me. I know you have been hurt many times and that the noblemen who should have taken care of you, your mother and your half-brother, have treated you abominably but I am not them.'

They came to the castle gates—a heavily armoured

guard let them through. The inside was twice the size of Caerden's castle and for a moment Avva could only stop and stare.

'It's this way to the stables.'

William tried to lead her in one direction, but she held him back. 'As much as I've missed Eirwen, I would like to speak with you in private.'

William gazed down at her, his expression unreadable. 'Very well, we will go to my quarters.'

Neither of them spoke as they crossed the courtyard and entered the keep. A steep, spiral staircase took them up to the third floor and a small but cosy chamber.

William closed the door behind him.

The silence stretched between them.

William made to pull her into his arms, but she moved away. She knew she wouldn't be able to think if they touched and she needed to hear what he had to say.

'Your story,' she prompted when he didn't say anything.

William brushed his hair away from his face. 'Where to start.' He grinned and her heart fluttered. 'I didn't want to fall in love with you, but I never stood a chance. I believe I fell from the first moment I saw you. From then on, I was only fooling myself that I would ever be able to live without you.'

He reached out to take her hand—this time she didn't pull away. 'When the King told me he had arranged a marriage for me, I couldn't say no straight away. You don't defy the King with ease. But I knew that I could not go through with it. I could not marry anyone but you.'

William pulled her close to him. She rested her head on his firm chest, breathing in the familiar smell of him. She knew she couldn't bear to be parted from him again.

'When I found you were gone from our room…it was as if my world had ended. If I couldn't have you, then I might as well marry Lady Ann, because what did it matter?'

'What changed?'

His lips ghosted across her forehead. 'I went to visit my parents. All my life, I have seen their love as a weakness. Now I know it has provided them with solace when they are sad and greater joy in their happiness. Their love is a strength, which they celebrate every day and which enriches those around them. If I had not been sent away on my knight's training, I might have witnessed it for myself. As it was, I got myself all twisted up over a problem that was never really there.

'Avva.' She slowly raised her head to meet his gaze once more. 'I love you. If you will have me, I want you to become my wife. I will do everything to make sure you never doubt how much I love you and want you in my life.'

Tears pricked her eyes—she had never imagined she could be so happy. 'I love you, too, and I would be honoured to be your wife.'

His mouth covered hers and this time there was no angry alewife to put an end to their embrace. All the longing she'd felt for months poured into the kiss. She felt his groan as their tongues met. Their uneven breathing filled the room.

'Avva, before we go any further, there is still more I need to tell you.'

'What is it?'

'After long talks with the King he decided to change my reward for my role in saving his life. Avva, he's made me the new Baron Caerden.'

Avva could only blink up at him.

'Marriage to me will make you the Baroness.'

Avva couldn't help it—she burst out laughing. 'Won't people find it strange that the new Baron has married the stable master?'

'Does it matter what other people think?'

Avva looked into his deep brown eyes. 'No,' she said quietly. 'I don't suppose it does.'

'Being parted from you was the worst pain I have ever experienced. I finally understand what love is all about. We will make our own future. Our people will be happy, they will not live in fear, they will not experience hunger. We shall take care of them. With you standing by my side, we can do anything.'

Avva's heart expanded. 'I love you, William. I want to be part of a new, hopeful Caerden, but I would want to be with you, even if you were a nobody.'

And those were the last words either of them said for a very long time.

* * * * *

*Look out for the next book in
Ella Matthews' The King's Knights duet,
coming soon!*

*And whilst you're waiting for the next book, why not
check out her other miniseries The House of Leofric?*

**The Warrior Knight and the Widow
Under the Warrior's Protection
The Warrior's Innocent Captive**